UNDER ATTACK

His 'Mech staggered as a series of blows knocked it sideways. Austin struggled to keep the MiningMech upright. It took him a second to realize an autocannon had fired on him and the hammering sounds came from rounds hitting his 'Mech. A large section on his left torso had been damaged, but the 'Mech still functioned. He hunched over to present a smaller cross section for the other 'Mech to fire at, then found himself under missile attack. The salvo whined above and around him, but two found his right arm and blew it off.

Austin grunted as he fought to keep the 'Mech upright. If he tumbled over, he knew he was dead. Autocannon fire and more missiles would end his life in a flash. He couldn't even eject. Such safety devices weren't included in a basic MiningMech.

Austin made a quick assessment of his situation and saw it was hopeless. . . .

THE RUINS
OF POWER

A BATTLETECH® NOVEL

Robert E. Vardeman

A ROC BOOK

ROC
Published by New American Library, a division of
Penguin Putnam Inc., 375 Hudson Street,
New York, New York 10014, U.S.A.
Penguin Books Ltd, 80 Strand,
London WC2R 0RL, England
Penguin Books Australia Ltd, 250 Camberwell Road,
Camberwell, Victoria 3124, Australia
Penguin Books Canada Ltd, 10 Alcorn Avenue,
Toronto, Ontario, Canada M4V 3B2
Penguin Books (N.Z.) Ltd, Cnr Rosedale and Airborne Roads,
Albany, Auckland 1310, New Zealand

Penguin Books Ltd, Registered Offices:
Harmondsworth, Middlesex, England

First published by Roc, an imprint of New American Library,
a division of Penguin Putnam Inc.

First Printing, April 2003
10 9 8 7 6 5 4 3 2 1

Cover design by Ray Lundgren

 REGISTERED TRADEMARK—MARCA REGISTRADA

Printed in the United States of America

PUBLISHER'S NOTE
This is a work of fiction. Names, characters, places, and incidents either are
the products of the author's imagination or are used fictitiously, and any
resemblance to actual persons, living or dead, business establishments,
events, or locales is entirely coincidental.

BOOKS ARE AVAILABLE AT QUANTITY DISCOUNTS WHEN USED TO PROMOTE PROD-
UCTS OR SERVICES. FOR INFORMATION PLEASE WRITE TO PREMIUM MARKETING DIVI-
SION, PENGUIN PUTNAM INC., 375 HUDSON STREET, NEW YORK, NEW YORK 10014.

1

Barren plains 200 km north of Cingulum
Musasalah, Mirach
Prefecture IV, The Republic
3 April 3133

Twilight clutched at the hopeless world.

Nothing appeared as it should, and this bothered Austin Ortega. He had been on this range before, but it was different this time. Subtly different. Bloody light leaked from the sky and dribbled across the rocky plains, giving a surreal appearance. Hills in the distance vomited out black tailings as he remembered, but the uneven terrain where he guided his 'Mech showed mining activity at a variance with Mirach's environment. To Austin's rear lay vast chasms where surface mining had ripped the planet's hide until all the tungsten ore had been extracted, with no effort made at mending the scars or closing the entrances to underground shafts. Walking the *Centurion* Battle-Mech over the broken field would be easy enough if he avoided the pits.

Austin had piloted this model before—many times before—and controlled it with expertise unmatched on the planet. But he had no idea what model Battle-Mech he faced. Not yet.

It was time to get to work.

Austin settled his neurohelmet firmly, tipped his head slightly to check balance response in the 'Mech, and felt tiny feedback tingles in his scalp telling him all was well; then he connected the hose from the command couch to his cooling vest. A soft sigh filled the 'Mech cockpit as the liquid coolant began circulating. He went from too hot to too cold in an instant. That would change once he engaged the enemy. A BattleMech generated incredible heat in the cockpit, which heat sinks couldn't entirely radiate away.

He positioned his arms on the couch armrests, gripped the joysticks confidently, reveling in the feel of his fingers curling around to rest lightly on firing buttons, testing systems vital to the BattleMech's operation, making certain that his weapons were ready for action. Austin chewed his lip as he studied the instruments, which relayed data around the periphery of his forward screen. He worried most about the Luxor autocannon in the 'Mech's right arm, although he saw nothing but green lights across the board. The gun had a tendency to jam at the worst possible time.

Austin piloted the fifty-ton *Centurion* with confidence borne of familiarity. It was a medium Battle-Mech with excellent heat efficiency and good speed and maneuverability, especially suitable for this rocky terrain. He had his LRMs and two lasers, one pro-

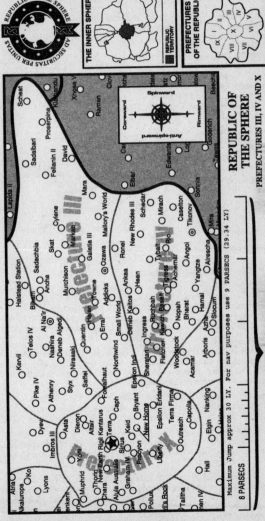

REPUBLIC OF THE SPHERE
AD SECURITAS PER UNITAS
REPUBLIC OF THE SPHERE

THE INNER SPHERE

REPUBLIC TERRITORY

PREFECTURES OF THE REPUBLIC

Spinward

Coreward

Anti-spinward

Rimward

REPUBLIC OF THE SPHERE
PREFECTURES III, IV AND X

Maximum Jump approx 30 LY. For nav purposes use 9 PARSECS (29-34 LY)

40 PARSECS OR 130.4 LIGHT YEARS

8 PARSECS

tecting his vulnerable back, while the forward-aimed Photec laser mounted in his center torso showed only eighty percent charge. Austin worked with growing frustration before he decided he didn't have time to coax the faulty laser. It would either automatically complete the charging cycle or not. His feet worked the pedals as he unconsciously leaned forward, pushing against the restraining straps in his eagerness to get moving. Myomer muscles stretching down the 'Mech's legs contracted as he swung about in a full circle for one last operational check.

All set, Austin thought. He moved the throttle forward a third, and the 'Mech launched into motion, striding over the rugged landscape at twenty kilometers per hour. A quick smile crossed his lips when he saw the forward laser had charged and its indicator registered full.

The *Centurion's* sensors showed infrared, full visual spectrum, and special seismic readouts. With lasers ready and full ranging gear powered up, he sent the *Centurion* at a forty-kilometer-per-hour trot toward an area he thought afforded decent cover for an ambush.

As he crunched along the ragged surface, placing his 'Mech feet securely proved increasingly difficult. The ground between the twenty-meter-high mounds of slag was curiously brittle, and more than once, the fifty-ton *Centurion* broke the surface, its armored feet threatening to plunge into huge tunnels cut to access subterranean veins of ore.

I need to map both surface and hard-rock mining regions, he thought, loading seismic information gathered automatically into his navigation computer so he wouldn't make foolish assumptions about the stability of the ground in the heat of battle. Austin worried more now about how familiar—and yet different—the area looked. He dared not assume he really knew every detail of the slag-littered landscape around him. The terrain was revealing more potential for threat than he had anticipated. Austin took a deep breath and tasted the metallic tang of filtered air. He settled down in the couch, feeling it cradle his every contour, as he studied his forward screen, hunting for the opponent he knew so well. Nothing airborne. Clear sky. Austin knew Dale would want to make this fight real, down and dirty, strategy versus strategy on the ground, for a hands-on feel of victory.

Austin intended to make this *his* victory.

Flipping through the green-glowing displays, hunting for a target in his Heads Up Display, gave him a completely different view of the battlefield. His eyes widened a little when he detected radioactive mounds nearby.

Ore from a pitchblende mine? This was possible but unusual in a tungsten ore field. Austin considered this anomaly for a moment, then cranked up power to his 'Mech's fusion plant and raced forward. The radioactive area provided a sensor-confusing hiding place for his opponent—just the sort of place Dale would use. It was reckless charging forward blindly, but surprise could carry him through to victory.

If Dale even lurked at this patch, using its radiation as a shield.

The *Centurion* surged forward in a heavy-footed gait devouring the landscape at sixty-five kilometers per hour. Austin worked methodically, using seismic sensors to check the ground for tunnels and weak spots that might hamper his advance. As necessary as it was to focus on his surroundings, Austin's attention never wavered from the forward and secondary monitors as he sought any hint that Dale lay ahead.

Austin wasn't certain what caused him to react. None of his screens showed danger. His index finger curled back on the LRM trigger, and ten missiles launched at a small, shadowy zone to the left of the largest radioactive slag hillock. One rocket went whining away as it creased the side of the mound. Seven blew up a patch of ground, sending cinders sailing high into the air to create a glittering fog in the dusk. The dull red light from Mirach's distant sun reflected off the dark slag and produced a mist that both glinted like fresh blood and spun like silver confetti, obscuring visuals.

Austin felt a bit sheepish at wasting the missiles until his sensor alarms blared. Green-glowing, ghost-imaged infrared shimmer on his forward screen revealed heated heavy metal armor. His other two missiles had smashed directly into that spot. Molten metal had joined the slag.

First hit! He wasted no time gloating about his cleverness in detecting Dale before he had revealed himself. The battle had begun.

Got you now, Austin thought, pressing his all-out attack. This wasn't his usual cautious approach, feeling out the situation, gathering intel about his opponent before engaging. Austin wanted this done fast, and changing his trademark tactics would bring him victory.

His forward 806c laser fired, a deadly amber-colored energy spike hitting its target squarely. Shrapnel flashed upward into the waning crimson rays from the sun, showing that a few hundred kilos of aligned-crystal steel exterior armor had been blown away. Austin gunned the *Centurion*'s fusion engine to go in for the kill.

He burst through the shroud of debris kicked up by

his opponent and identified Dale's 'Mech. Dale piloted a fifty-ton *Enforcer III* armed with a BlazeFire ER Large Laser, a ChisComp 2000 ER Small Laser, and an Imperator Automatic Ultra AC/10 Autocannon. No rockets. The *Enforcer* rivaled Austin's 'Mech in class, speed, and maneuverability. They were well matched, but the deciding factor in combat might be the *Enforcer*'s jump jets.

Austin had to hammer away at the other Battle-Mech with his LRMs to keep it from bringing its heavier lasers to bear accurately. Without a stable platform, the inertial guidance and tracking for the lasers degraded. That was the easiest shortcoming to exploit in the Federated Hunter targeting and tracking system.

He fired another barrage of ten LRMs at the chest of the *Enforcer*, hoping the shock would further shake up Dale. Armor shattered off in a cascade that made his IR display useless. Austin changed to visual, brought the targeting reticule to the *Enforcer*, and fired again. He was rewarded with even greater loss of armor. This salvo wouldn't penetrate the StarGuard CIV armor, but Austin wanted to keep Dale from using his McCloud Special Jump Jets. Using them, Dale could dodge and dart through the slag mounds and turn a toe-to-toe fight into hide-and-seek.

Austin fired his forward laser again. His heart skipped a beat when red lights winked on across his control panel and new warning alarms sounded. His forward laser wasn't recharging.

That worried Austin just enough to cause him to hesitate.

This wavering allowed the *Enforcer* to grind about and open up with its BlazeFire laser. Austin involuntarily threw up his arm to protect his face, although the searing blast never reached the cockpit. It did destroy part of his Corean-B Tech targeting and tracking system. He lost fully half his displays in that single attack. A quick status check showed he had also been stripped of a considerable amount of armor on his right leg.

Austin turned the *Centurion* about to bring into play undamaged tracking elements. He saw the *Enforcer* lifting its right arm, saw bright flashes as the autocannon fired, and then staggered when the heavy slugs hammered into his 'Mech. Alarms rang as the depleted-uranium shells ripped away even more of his metallic flesh, leaving part of the metal skeleton exposed on his right leg. He twisted about, lost sight of the *Enforcer*, then kept pivoting to avoid the punishment from the autocannon and to get the other BattleMech in his sights again. As the *Enforcer* swung past on his targeting screen, he launched a salvo of LRMs.

He didn't have to scan his sketchy readouts to know that he had missed.

Austin had no choice now. He cut to his left and kicked the *Centurion* into full speed. Glowing, ionized air all around his 'Mech registered on his instruments, but his outer temperature didn't surge. Dale was firing and missing.

Good, Austin thought. *Let him waste his energy and ammo.*

The mapping he had done earlier aided him now. Mostly blind to the front because of the damage his sensors had sustained, Austin let the navigation computer guide him back through the hillocks and small mountains of dark slag as he kept a lookout to the rear. He had lost contact with the *Enforcer* but knew only too well who was hunter and who was prey now.

Austin had gained a small edge with his preemptive attack and had lost it through damage and the difference in 'Mech characteristics. The *Enforcer*, with its jump jets, could get into the attack faster. Worse than this, Dale was more skilled with long-range weaponry. If Austin wanted to bring down Dale's 'Mech, he had to engage with not only his missiles but also his autocannon and medium laser.

The coolant vest began to sizzle and hiss around him. Austin noticed it only when he slowed the *Centurion* and started a complete damage tally. Whether Dale's laser shot had impaired the cooling system or the *Centurion*'s system had failed on its own hardly mattered. Heat began building in the cockpit. Fast.

If he didn't take out the *Enforcer* soon, he would roast in his own BattleMech.

Austin stopped, then bent slightly at the waist to present as small a target as he could. He swiveled about and took in as much as he could with his undamaged peripheral sensors. Although his tracking readout didn't show it, he knew Dale was on his six. The *Enforcer* stalked him, waiting for the perfect shot that would disable him. Dale wouldn't go for the kill. He would humiliate first by immobilizing the *Centurion* and then coming over to place a heavy metal foot on the toppled carcass while trumpeting his victory on all broadcast frequencies.

Better to be destroyed than to endure such disgrace.

Austin's mind raced. He felt sweat tickling at the edges of his neurohelmet and running down his chest. Panic now and he would lose. Austin had rushed Dale and gained a small advantage earlier. Dale would expect him to go lick his wounds now.

Austin repeated his earlier audacity. Feet working the pedals, he swung the *Centurion* around, watching for the *Enforcer*.

You expected to catch me from behind, Austin thought when he saw the *Enforcer* approaching fast. Teeth clenched with determination, Austin fired another decade of missiles directly into the ground in front of Dale, sending up fresh sprays of debris. The curtain of hot cinders twisted crazily in the dying sunlight and worked to dissipate any laser beam coming his way. He didn't know for certain if Dale was even shooting at him.

Austin's chancy tactic worked. The missiles had ripped open a hole in front of the *Enforcer*, and Dale had blundered into it. Austin checked his earlier mapping and saw that his foe had fallen into a tunnel ten meters underground.

Which way will you run? he wondered. Austin knew Dale wouldn't pop back up into another barrage. He would use the tunnel to shift position and return to the surface some distance away before renewing his attack.

Austin followed the *Enforcer*'s heavy seismic thumping as it moved to his right. Kicking the *Centurion* to a ground-devouring stride, Austin gauged distances and fired another salvo ahead of Dale, hoping to collapse the tunnel roof on the *Enforcer*.

He kept up his relentless advance even after he saw his LRMs had led Dale too much. A new hole to the surface opened where the missiles exploded, but the rest of the tunnel was blocked. Austin readied his weapons. He would get one perfect shot and no more.

Jump jets flaring, the *Enforcer* lifted from the hole. Austin fired with all he had. Missiles crashed into the other 'Mech, but Dale had not been caught unawares. He jumped upward, all weapons blazing.

As if it were his own arm, Austin screamed when a laser slashed through his 'Mech's right arm and took off the autocannon, the detonating rounds in the weapon adding to the fiery hell. Worse, his forward laser winked once with its deadly pure-light lance, but the second shot was delivered with diminished power. The forward laser refused to recharge.

Sensing the weakness in his opponent, Dale came in for the kill. Austin rocked him again with another salvo of rockets, then had even this offense stripped from him by Dale's accurate laser fire. The launcher erupted, rocking him and destroying most of his torso.

No autocannon, forward laser damaged, missiles not responding as he tried to launch them—Austin was a sitting duck. His HUD showed the *Enforcer* advancing, but its lasers fired wildly, most shots going astray. Austin's fierce attack had damaged the *Enforcer*'s targeting system but had done nothing to deny Dale of the lasers' power. It was only a matter of time before one laser blast hit a vulnerable target.

Austin jerked as a laser blast sawed off his 'Mech's left arm. Then more of his right vanished in a mist of molten armor. He tried again to fire his torso-mounted laser but produced only tiny sparks as debris in front of him vaporized, hardly enough for Dale to register on his threat assessment readout.

The *Centurion* was ready for the scrap heap, but Austin refused to surrender. He spun away as if to run, then slowed, bent over to give a smaller targeting cross section, and waited. Time ticked by, a dozen heartbeats for every second, but he did nothing. Austin tracked the *Enforcer*'s approach with his still functional rear sensors. Sweat soaked the front of his vest as the cooling system threatened to die completely, although the persistent, sluggish coolant flow gave him hope. Small, faint hope. Austin made certain his rear laser was fully charged.

By instinct, Austin straightened the *Centurion* to its

full height, no longer trying to present as small a target as possible. In a single huge gulp of information, he took in every detail of the rugged battlefield. Austin fired his rear laser into the *Enforcer*'s torso. Dale had not expected to find a fighting, firing *Centurion* when it appeared that Austin was disabled and trying to escape.

Austin's vision blurred as the heat in the cockpit blasted upward. He felt as if he had been popped into an oven like a loaf of bread. But he saw the firing assessment show that he had speared the *Enforcer* dead in the center of the torso and had killed it. He waited to see if Dale ejected. The other pilot stayed with his 'Mech. Austin's rear laser had destroyed Dale's emergency pod capability along with the rest of the BattleMech.

Then the out-of-control *Enforcer* smashed into the *Centurion*, knocking both to the ground. Austin fired his rearward laser again as he crashed forward. His control panel flared red when his LRM magazine exploded under him. Everything went black.

"Double kill," Dale Ortega said, slapping his brother, Austin, on the shoulder. "You're getting better with that old *Centurion*. You didn't let me beat up on you as much this time."

"Why'd you choose an *Enforcer*?" Austin asked, leaning back in the command couch of the BattleMech simulator. It took him a few minutes to shake free of the virtual experience of piloting a 'Mech and come to the reality of the simulator cockpit. He unfastened the cooling unit and pushed back, swinging his legs off the command couch to get circulation back in them after being tensed for so long.

"I knew you'd go with the *Centurion*, that's why. I

figured an *Enforcer* would end the fight fast. I hadn't counted on the terrain. Is it for real?"

"I don't know," Austin said. "That was a surprise for me, too." He bent over and brought up a debriefing report on the simulator control screen. "It's a real place, all right, and we've practiced on that template once before, which is why it struck me as familiar. But the computer sim added the open pit mines and mounds of slag. We need to study our own geography more."

"You can do the studying, little brother," Dale said airily. "I'll concentrate on the fun."

"Was it more fun when I got first blood?" Austin felt a small glow of triumph at this. He usually played it too conservatively, even in the simulator, and took the first hit.

"You're learning from me," Dale said. His face lit up, gray eyes sparkling and even teeth showing through his broad, cheerful grin. A well-trimmed black mustache twitched just a little. It was impossible for Austin to grow a mustache that looked half as dashing. He had tried. But then, his brother was the one with the good looks and bright, open manner that drew attention.

Both of them had broken their noses in hand-to-hand training a year ago. Dale's had mended perfectly straight while Austin's had kept a small lump to remind him of the encounter. It had always been that way between him and his older brother.

"I wish the sim wouldn't give me so many equipment failures, even before battle. My forward laser went out." Austin regretted the words the instant they left his mouth. He sounded as if he were whining. The simulation computer randomly chose which equipment to damage and fail, just as it sometimes altered the terrain. It only seemed that Dale came out ahead on this score each time. Austin reluctantly admitted to himself Dale won more often because he had better combat instincts.

"Don't pick such a clunker next time," Dale said. "All my armament worked fine, though the computer tried to give me an intermittent power surge. I fiddled with it and got the fusion plant settling down into the black. Easy as . . . taking you down!" Dale's pale gray eyes glowed with amusement, taunting Austin. Austin refused to rise to the fight. "Let's get out of here. We've got places to go and things to do."

With an agile twist, Dale ducked out the hatch at the rear of the simulator and went to stow his gear in a bank of lockers.

Austin powered down the simulator equipment and stretched his long legs. He stood 180 centimeters but was still 15 centimeters shorter than his older brother. Both had close-cropped black hair, but Dale's was thicker, hinting that Austin would eventually end up balding like their father. He left the sim and put his gear into his storage locker.

He and Dale faced off in computer simulators at least once a week, sometimes more, in spite of their father's scorn for such practice. Baron Sergio Ortega was Governor of Mirach and had been since the days of Devlin Stone. Sergio had fought for Stone and had been one of the best MechWarriors in the field. Although he played down his role, Sergio had been granted both his title and the governorship of Mirach because of valor in combat.

Austin wished his father wouldn't dismiss that aspect of his life so much. These days, Sergio concentrated on his philosophical side.

"I want to see it again," Austin said suddenly. He

didn't have to tell his brother what he meant. Dale knew.

"Why? It hasn't moved," Dale replied. Then he grinned condescendingly. "Sure, why not? You deserve a reward for a draw."

"Draw!" cried Austin. "I beat you."

"Double kill is a draw. Those are the sim rules."

Arguing, the brothers threaded their way through the training structure and across the broad lawn outside to a parking lot. In their simulation it had been twilight and the ruddy sun had cast a faint, deceptive glow. In reality, the huge red disk was rising in the east and growing warmer, hinting at a hotter-than-usual spring morning. Two of Mirach's four moons, the smaller Arit and Batn, transited its face.

Austin swung into the car and started the engine. Dale joined him on the passenger side. The sim training facility was at the far north of Governor's Park, the thousand-hectare expanse holding most of what Austin held dearest. Their destination required a drive.

Both he and Dale were officers in the First Cossack Lancers, an elite Republic Militia unit that had been placed under the Baron's command to honor his service with Devlin Stone. Their barracks shone in the morning sun a kilometer away from the training center at the northernmost boundary of the park, but Austin headed elsewhere now. Surging upward through the wooded areas in the center of the park were major governmental office buildings and the Governor's office and residence, the Palace of Facets. Before joining the First Cossack Lancers as a lieutenant, junior grade, Austin had lived there. But his father had usually been occupied with planetary governance, and all too often, Austin had not been included in his older brother's plans.

Austin had come to prefer exploring the vast, well-maintained museum, located at the southwestern corner of the park, near the major roads leading to Mirach's capital city, Cingulum, tèn kilometers away. Austin turned onto the road leading around the perimeter of the park while Dale rattled on and on about the fight, claiming moral victory if not computer-granted triumph. The manicured meadows and carefully cultivated forests rushed past unnoticed, as did traffic on the road. Austin was focused on reaching the museum.

They arrived at the sprawling, glass-and-steel-fronted Museum of Modern Mirach after a twenty-minute drive, left the car in the parking lot, and walked up the broad concrete pathway to the high, polished steel doors. Just inside was the soaring main rotunda, with branching corridors leading deeper into the structure. Each wing was devoted to a distinct epoch of history on Mirach and in The Republic, but Austin stood before the ten-meter-tall *Centurion* BattleMech on display. He could not guess how many times he had stopped at this very spot and stared up at the 'Mech. Each time filled him with awe as new as the dawn.

"Never gets old, does it?" asked Dale. Austin heard the appreciation in his brother's tone, although Dale tried to hide it under his air of nonchalance.

"Hasn't yet," Austin said. The museum rotunda was almost deserted today, save for three young women studying the exhibit plaque at the feet of the *Centurion*.

Austin saw how intently they were taking notes on the *Centurion* and he almost went to ask if he could fill them in on the 'Mech's history. This wasn't just any BattleMech. This was *Sergeant Death*, the one his father had piloted. Austin turned from the three students to keep himself from prattling on about it; nowhere in the history was it recorded that this 'Mech was so named. The 'Mech stood as it had for decades, with shining armor and grim autocannon, yellow stripes on the legs and red hash marks on the arms, lasers and LRMs just like the simulated 'Mech he piloted during simulator training. Because of the distinctive markings on the old 'Mech, Austin had nicknamed it "Sergeant Death," much to Dale's amusement. He had never told his father this, and never would, giving Dale blackmail material since childhood.

"I can't imagine what a battle was like in those days when 'Mechs clashed," Austin said, his voice hushed in respect. "Tanks and battle armor just aren't the same." His heart beat a little faster. Nothing equaled a ready-for-combat BattleMech.

"Let's go up," Dale said. They went around the *Centurion* to the back of the rotunda and took an elevator to a walkway suspended four stories above the white marble museum floor. From this aerial vantage five meters over the 'Mech, they could circle *Sergeant Death* and study it from above. Austin did, but Dale chose to stare out the towering museum windows facing Cingulum.

Austin held down the hollowness threatening to consume him as he stared at the 'Mech. This was the only BattleMech remaining on Mirach, and his father's increasing insistence on pacifist policies made it unlikely any others would be bought or built. The First Cossack Lancers relied on battle armor and armored vehicles. Even the Planetary Legate's force was hardly more heavily armed, save for tank battalions and assorted motorized artillery pieces.

"All we do is play," Austin said harshly, his blue eyes fixed on *Sergeant Death*.

"You mean like we did when we were kids? Yeah," said Dale. "It was fun sneaking into that old pile of bolts and pretending."

"I want to pilot it. For real, not in a computer simulator."

"You think you can do better than Papa?" Dale laughed. "Pick a newer model, one with state-of-the-art armament, and don't try to relive the past. Then all you have to do is find somebody who'll recruit you off-world for a real fight. The Republic is always on the lookout for hotshot 'Mech pilots." Austin saw Dale looking straight down at the women in the rotunda, then draw back, his attention returning to the distant city.

"Are you thinking about Hanna?" Austin asked. He saw the slight twitch at the corner of his brother's lips as he tried to keep from smiling. Over the years Dale had acquired quite a reputation, but since he had met Hanna Leong, he hardly noticed other women.

"She's finishing her broadcast about now."

"She's really something," Austin said. "But don't tell me you didn't notice that blonde down there." He craned his neck as he looked back at the trio of students now taking pictures of *Sergeant Death* for whatever research paper their professor required of them.

"I hadn't," Dale said, and Austin believed him. "She's all yours."

Austin shrugged this off. He worked long hours at training. Being the most junior officer in an elite unit required him to take jobs more senior officers passed along, the so-called George jobs, in addition to his own duties.

"I talked with Papa about resigning my commission," Dale said unexpectedly.

"What? You can't! You're the best in the unit, Dale. Father hasn't convinced you that being an officer is immoral, has he?"

"I'm not the best. You are, Austin. At least, you have the most potential and will be the best when I resign. I've done as much as I can in the FCL." Dale held up his hand to forestall Austin's argument. "I enjoy being an officer but not as much as I thought a few years ago. Papa hasn't talked me into anything. There are other jobs to learn, and he wants to give me a diplomatic post."

"To step into the governorship?" asked Austin.

"Not for quite a few years, I hope," Dale said. "I'm not a quick learner like you, little brother. It might take me until Papa's ready to retire in a couple decades before I'd be half qualified to fill his shoes."

"I'm not as good as you," Austin said, surprised at the unexpected compliment.

"And you missed your chance with the blonde," Dale said, looking back down. "She and her friends just left."

Austin refused to let his brother distract him. He had always known Dale would move from the First Cossack Lancers into a civilian position eventually, but now? The elder son of a Baron needed a wide assortment of skills to rule an entire planet. But now?

"I hope you'll reconsider, especially with so much unrest in the cities," Austin said.

"This might be the best time to see how Papa works. He believes diplomacy always prevails over military settlements."

"He's been insulated from the worst of the rioting. That'd change fast if they leave the city and try to take over the Palace."

"You worry too much, Austin," Dale said. "Come on. I forgot to tell you that we've got an appointment with Papa at eleven."

Austin started to protest. Dale should have told him

earlier about resigning his commission. Then he settled down. Dale *had* told him, in his way.

Dale strutted off to the elevator, whistling. Austin followed more slowly, casting one final look at the *Centurion* before letting the elevator door whisper shut.

=== 2 ===

Palace of Facets, Cingulum
Mirach
3 April 3133

"How do I look?" asked Austin Ortega. He smoothed his uniform.

"What's the difference? It's only Papa we're seeing. You don't think he'd have important people in along with two minor officers in his personal guard, do you?" Dale sounded flip, but Austin saw his brother's expression. A tiny frown marred his otherwise handsome features. Austin saw the beginning of worry lines at the corners of Dale's eyes and wondered what Dale wasn't telling him.

"I need to check in with the watch," Dale said. They saluted the FCL guards at the south entrance to the Palace and turned directly into a large open archway to their left.

"Master Sergeant Borodin," Dale called. The stout man behind the duty desk shot to his feet, at attention.

"Lieutenant Ortega," Borodin barked. "Good to see you, sir. You, also, Lieutenant, JG." Borodin stood rigidly but his dark eyes darted about, taking in every detail. The master sergeant prided himself on being the center of gossip for the FCL, and Austin had to admit that little got past the noncom by the time he posted the duty roster.

"Anything to report, Master Sergeant?" asked Dale.

"Have you seen the new orders, sir?"

Dale went to scan the sheaf of papers Borodin held out. Austin glanced up at the small parabolic mirror mounted high in the archway that permitted Borodin to see everyone entering the Palace. Austin's reflected image was distorted and at this angle reflected him only from the waist up. Short-cropped dark hair covered his head. His broad face with its high cheekbones was handsome, he knew, but not as much as his brother's. He touched the lump where his nose had been broken, then guiltily stepped away to change the reflection in the mirror. Austin liked this view of himself better. Wide shoulders, barrel-like chest, muscled arms showing the results of strenuous physical training required of all FCL soldiers—Austin felt some pride at how he had bulked up since his swearing in six months earlier. Before the FCL—and with the exception of his practice time in the 'Mech simulator—he had spent a lot of time studying and not enough time *doing*.

"Keep up the good work, Master Sergeant," Dale said. "Come on, Austin. We've got to hoof it if we don't want to be late."

"Let's take the shortcut," Austin suggested. Dale

nodded absently, lost in thought. He didn't share what he had learned and Austin didn't ask.

They made their way through the maze of passageways in the Governor's residence, an expanded replica of the Winter Palace in Saint Petersburg on Terra, and finally reached the Great Hall of Saint George leading directly to the Governor's offices. Gold filigree arches opened to expose walls of stained glass showing various scenes of history from both Terra and The Republic. Austin knew where to look to see the spots where entire windows had been replaced, showing the political shift from the Federated Suns to The Republic, but few walking along this splendid corridor would ever take note of such small discrepancies.

Three-meter-tall triptychs served as doors for some corridors leading away to other parts of the Palace, but the exotic inlaid wood, the painted murals, the fine tapestries on the walls, and even the cunningly wrought tables spun from crystalline glass were easily overlooked because of the floor. Every step Austin took caused the wood to compress slightly. The resulting squeak sounded like a bird chirping in protest.

Austin had lived in the Palace of Facets all his life and saw nothing unusual about the expensive furnishings. He and Dale had played in the west wing, amid priceless works of art, tapestries, and furniture ancient two hundred years ago. A favorite pastime had been stacking the antique furniture as high as possible in an attempt to reach the cleverly designed ceilings. Not once had the young carousers fallen nor had they ever reached their lofty goal.

When their games of hide-and-seek turned to more serious military ones, they had haunted the vast libraries, Austin researching battles and equipment and Dale waiting for his younger, more studious brother to give him a précis of what he had unearthed.

In spite of having spent so much time in the Palace, Austin still got a chill when he came down this particular hall, the one giving the name to the entire structure: the Palace of Facets. Overhead, mounted in the ceiling, were hundreds of kilos of precious gems sliced microtome thin. Rubies, emeralds, sapphires, peridots, diamonds, each lending its own peculiar transmitted light to the Great Hall. As he walked, Austin felt he passed through rainbows, multiple colors whirling about him in a vortex of brilliance. And this was only a single hall. He knew of half a hundred other corridors and rooms where the light filtering through the jewels was even more exquisite.

He swallowed hard, remembering the time he had sneaked into his parents' bedchamber. That room had always been off-limits to everyone, staff and family alike, and this had made it all the more magnetic an attraction for him. One afternoon he had sneaked in and stood bathed in the syrupy light cascading down from the ceiling. The aurora surrounding him had been dazzling, hypnotic, almost narcotic. He had barely hidden when his parents had entered unexpectedly. Austin remembered catching a glimpse of his mother bathed in this radiance before he slipped away unnoticed. It had been the last time he had seen her alive before the air transport crash took her life.

Austin walked a little faster, and Dale's stride lengthened as he strained to keep up with his brother. Their steps chirped and echoed down the Great Hall like migrating birds until they came to the tall, carved wooden doors standing open to the antechamber to the Governor's office. The Armorer's Chamber housed not only a full office staff but actual arms on display from worlds throughout The Republic. This was as special and complete an exhibit as any at the museum, even if his father threatened to remove it to some distant part of the Palace. Austin had told his father that anyone not remembering the past was doomed to repeat it. He hoped his argument would make some impression on his father and his increasing distaste for violence and the weapons of warfare. Somehow, he doubted it. He would miss the displays.

"The Baron will see you now," a secretary said, glancing up from his desk when Austin and Dale stopped in front of it. "Go right in."

"Thanks," Dale said mechanically.

Austin glanced at Dale, who appeared more relaxed now, but he had a feeling it was only an act. An image of his brother winding up like a spring flashed through Austin's mind. Dale moved like a jungle cat, sleek and slender and fit. If Austin had bulked up under FCL PT, Dale had gained a long-distance runner's physique. He cut quite a picture, his jet-black uniform impeccable, silver lieutenant's insignia shining in the parti-color light dancing down from above. Two small striped ribbons on his chest showed that Dale had engaged in combat against both the copper miners last year and the attempted invasion of Mirach's other continent, Ventrale, by a company of mercenaries possibly in Jacob Bannson's employ. Bannson was the ambitious head of a huge corporate conglomerate with business interests in two Prefectures. The Republic had put a limit on his activities once accusations of monopoly were leveled at him, and so Bannson had backed off. Now, with the collapse of the HPG net, rumors abounded that Bannson had been employing less businesslike tactics to expand his influence. The Bannson connection to the Ventrale affair had never been proved, although everyone had their own opinion as to who had backed the ill-fated expedition.

Only a unit commendation rode in the same spot on Austin's chest. This was the difference two years made, two years and Republic citizenship. In only a month Austin would also finish his service and qualify as a citizen. Then he could win promotion past lieutenant, JG, and endless scut work details.

They went to the entry where a pair of FCL guards stepped aside smartly and opened the double doors inward on silent hinges, revealing a room even more splendidly arrayed than the Armorer's Chamber and Great Hall beyond. Multihued gemstones from across the planet glittered in the ceiling, sending down an ever-shifting spectrum that cleverly contrived to reunite into a steady white light that illuminated Sergio Ortega's desk. Paneled with video screens, the desk displayed images spanning the entire world, revealing riots as well as the more intimate details of commerce on Mirach.

"Papa," greeted Dale. "You're looking good."

Sergio motioned them into the room. The guards closed the doors behind them as the brothers stood in front of the imposing desk. Despite what Dale had said, their father did not look well. The faint halo of graying hair around Sergio's bald spot betrayed how little brushing had been done of late. Dark circles under his eyes told of long hours working with little sleep. And the small tremor in his normally rock-steady hand as Sergio pointed to chairs convinced Austin of the strain he was under. His father was usually cheerful and upbeat. Now he was distant.

"Your training goes well," Sergio said. It wasn't a question.

"You've seen our latest fitness reports?" asked Dale, almost anxiously. Austin looked at his brother from the corner of his eye, wondering what he might have been up to that would reflect poorly on his service record.

Sergio cleared his throat.

"It's time for you to move out of the FCL and delve into other areas. By the way, Austin, your citizenship has come through."

"Ahead of schedule?" This surprised him. His father was not one to cut corners when it came to family members. Any show of favoritism might cause unwanted disputes.

"You've earned it, son. It comes at a good time, too. You'll have to spend a few weeks learning the ropes around the office. Citizenship frees you of security concerns that might otherwise arise."

It took Austin a second to realize what his father had said.

"Both of us, sir? I knew Dale was being assigned to your staff, but I want to stay with the FCL," Austin protested.

"You surprise me, Austin. Dale enjoys prancing about, showing off his medals to the girls. I didn't think you were the same," Sergio said, dismissing the protest.

"Sir," Austin said, fumbling for the right words to convince his father. "The unrest is growing and Legate Tortorelli seems unwilling to deal with it. You need trained soldiers in your personal guard to—" He cut off his words when he saw the irritation he engendered.

"There's more to life than being able to kill," Sergio said. "Fighting never solved any problem better than diplomacy could. That's why I've ordered the police not to use force against demonstrators unless their lives are in jeopardy. I've also advised the Legate to tread carefully. I had hoped your stint in the FCL would give you some perspective as to the way the citizens think about authority."

"They see us as a Sword of Damocles dangling

above their heads," Dale said. "That's the purpose of the military."

"It is *not*!" snapped Sergio. "The Legate's duty is to protect, not intimidate. The Governor's duty is to make certain that disputes are taken care of before the Legate's power is called upon. We must always seek peaceful solutions. It is far too easy to take a life and ever so hard to build one into a lifetime."

"What steps are you taking to stop the rioting, sir?" asked Austin.

"Calvilena wants to declare martial law in some sections of Cingulum, but I refuse to authorize it. My capital city is not going to be a battleground. I'm doing all I can to ease fears about the HPG net going down, but we've lost a lot of jobs because of it. With off-world contracts being canceled, there has to be a cutback among the miners. It's taking longer than I expected to spur economic growth in other directions, that's all."

Austin didn't doubt that Legate Calvilena Tortorelli wanted martial law for the immense power it would give him. There had always been a give-and-take between the Governor and Legate on Mirach, but Tortorelli had never shown much backbone for a real confrontation. He had excelled in combat when it counted the most for his career. More than one officer in the FCL had said that Tortorelli had been appointed Legate because Prefect Radick saw only the few, rare successes.

Sergio pushed away from the desk and came around it.

"Come along," he said. He opened the office doors. The FCL guards snapped to attention as he left.

"The conference room is ready for you, my lord," the secretary said as Sergio passed his desk.

"Thank you, Gordon." Sergio exited the bustling office, took a private branching corridor, and slowed only enough to allow the FCL guards to open the conference door for him and his sons. A huge oval polished wood table, high-backed chairs around it, dominated the tapestried room. At one end a larger, padded chair waited for the Governor. He settled into it, glanced at monitors set for his viewing, then took a deep breath before pressing a button in the tabletop.

Doors at the side of the conference room opposite where the Baron and his sons had entered swung wide.

"Come in," Sergio boomed heartily, sounding like his old self. "So good of you to come, Legate Tortorelli. And you, too, Minister."

Austin craned his neck about and saw the Legate strutting in, the Minister of Information beside him. Tortorelli was a shortish man gone to seed. His thick middle belied military training, although his uniform bobbed and danced with a dozen medals. Try as he might, Austin had never been able to identify more than three of them. He found it surprisingly easy to dismiss the Legate. While Tortorelli might be Prefect Radick's appointee and able to speak with the full military backing of Prefecture IV, the fall of the HPG net had decreased that authority greatly, forcing Tortorelli to rely on his own meager abilities.

Despite Tortorelli's presence, Austin's eyes went immediately to the Minister of Information, Lady Elora Rimonova. She was not beautiful, and he wasn't sure he would even call her attractive, but there was a quality about her that commanded attention. Whenever she walked into a crowded room, conversation died and all eyes followed her. She was tall, slender to the point of emaciation, with piercing emerald eyes in stark contrast to her bloodless alabaster skin and rust red hair. Elora always looked down her hawklike nose with an air of disdain, her razor-thin lips pulled back in a near sneer. But when she spoke, her voice rang with the power of the Lorelei.

Although he had been at conferences with her over the years, Austin wondered if he had ever really *seen* her before. Her imposing presence had always overwhelmed him, making him happy to scuttle away so she and his father could speak in private. This meeting struck him as different, as if his father wanted him to study her. An anomalous streak of white in Lady Elora's hair just above her right ear seemed out of place, and the varied silver and gold rings on each of her long, bony fingers were even more at odds with the somewhat Spartan Mirach custom and culture. Fashion dictated no more than one or two rings, a practice dating back to the early days of Mirach, when precious metals were needed for more vital uses than personal adornment.

"Governor," Lady Elora said in a voice both silken and seductive. "I am sorry to be so brusque, but if you want to issue a statement for the evening newscast, I must have it soon."

"Yes, I know your schedule," Sergio said, as if speaking to someone in another room, another dimension. "The newscast is more important than ever now that off-world information cannot reach us over the HPG."

"Thank you for understanding. If it weren't for your official promises, unrest would be far worse among the populace." The small sneer grew into what Elora must have considered an ingratiating smile.

Austin listened to official Ministry of Information broadcasts and wondered at the thin veil of truth covering what struck him as a deeper sedition. Lady Elora was entrusted with presenting the Governor's position and headed the government-controlled news agency, but the slant sometimes strayed from what Austin considered the loyalty due his father.

The Minister never came out and said anything directly if she could scurry in the shadows weaving a web of fine words with ambiguous meaning.

Without asking permission, Elora sat in the chair nearest the door where she and the Legate had entered. Tortorelli flopped down next to her.

"My lord, have you given my recommendation further thought? If you have, we can make an official announcement and let Lady Elora advise the people this evening." Tortorelli puffed up with importance as he spoke.

Austin and Dale exchanged glances. Calvilena Tortorelli's fatuous grin suggested he believed his recommendation was something that would enhance the Legate's power. Austin felt his stomach turning into a knot.

"There are elements of the idea I like," Sergio said, tenting his fingers and resting his chin on the steeple. "It would allow me to cut back on military appropriations and divert the money saved into social programs that might ease the tensions."

"An excellent lead for the news, my lord," Lady Elora said. "Legate Tortorelli is a capable military commander. The First Cossack Lancers will fit in nicely with an already established force."

"What?" Austin shot out of his chair. "Father, you're not going to give up your bodyguard? You can't let the Legate control the First Cossack Lancers!"

"Quiet, Austin." Sergio frowned at the outburst.

"Yes, Baronet, you are only a lieutenant, junior

grade. Remember your place," Tortorelli said, looking at him with disdain. The Legate started to say something more, but a look from Elora silenced him.

"From a financial standpoint, as well as a practical one, my lord," Lady Elora said, "such a transfer of power makes sense." She half turned toward Austin. "There would be no added risk to the Governor. If anything, the additional training available to the FCL will enhance an already capable unit."

"Good points, yes, Lady Elora," said Sergio. "I shall certainly consider it. The tax money freed up can be used to qualify for a matching grant from Jacob Bannson." Austin sighed inwardly. His father hadn't believed Bannson had backed the Ventrale incursion. Now, desperate to grow markets on Mirach, the offer that Bannson had relayed via personal courier several weeks earlier still stuck in Sergio's mind. He had discussed it briefly with Austin, but Austin hadn't really believed Sergio would accept it; it would mean too much dependence upon—and give too much power to—a complete outsider. "Bannson?" Lady Elora was taken aback.

"He wants to establish a major trading port on Mirach but is unwilling to do so without significant local financing. With the HPG not working, increased trade to Mirach will benefit us all with new job opportunities."

"Yes, of course," Lady Elora said carefully. "Bannson's trading vessels would bring more off-world news, also. That might soothe the populace, knowing we weren't so completely cut off from the daily workings of other Republic worlds."

Her words sounded sincere, but Austin saw the set to her bony shoulders and the way her hands curled into fists, only to relax immediately. His father's words had taken her by surprise, almost as much as the notion of transferring the First Cossack Lancers to the Legate's command had unsettled him. That pleased Austin. These days, it was a rare circumstance when Elora didn't have information before the Governor did.

"When you have the details, Governor, I'll prepare the news release for your approval." Elora lifted her chin, not quite so haughtily as when she'd first arrived.

"It won't be long before this matter is resolved and ready for your expert touches," Sergio said.

Elora hesitated, then stood and left the conference room. Tortorelli trailed after her as if held by an invisible leash.

"You can't do this, Father!" Austin protested the instant the doors closed behind the Legate and Minister and they were alone in the room.

"He's right, you know, Papa," said Dale. "You need a dedicated bodyguard. You shouldn't have to go through Tortorelli's chain of command. There's no telling who or what he would send—or when. You'd be at the Legate's mercy when you need loyalty the most."

"I told the Legate I'd think about it. I need a final meeting with Leclerc before making a decision."

Captain Manfred Leclerc had commanded the FCL since the unit had been detached from The Republic Militia, and Austin trusted him completely. Arguing with his father wouldn't get him anywhere, but Captain Leclerc would convince the Governor to reject any transfer.

"Let's return to my office. I have your FCL resignation papers ready, effective at the end of the month. It's time for you both to move on." Sergio stood, his colorless eyes daring either Austin or Dale to argue. They didn't.

3

"The crowd is getting unruly," Marta Kinsolving said. Her lips thinned to a line and she brushed back a vagrant strand of auburn hair when she bent forward to study the bank of monitors. Eight cameras showed the main gates to AllWorldComm's main assembly plant. Three screens were filled with chanting, shouting, angry mobs of people who had lost their jobs due to cutbacks. With mining down, a ripple effect had passed through all Mirach's businesses, and AWC had been hit worse than many others. Fully a quarter of AWC workers had been laid off over the past few months, and Marta saw more reductions looming.

"Don't worry so," her security chief said. Inger Ryumin reached past the AllWorldComm CEO and stabbed a finger down onto a red button. "That'll take care of it."

"Public relations," Marta reminded her. "We need to keep some customers."

"This is the way to do it," Ryumin said, an edge in her voice. "I might be out of line, but I think you worry too much about the wrong things. Running the corporation ought to be your primary concern. Security for AWC property is mine. Nobody'll get hurt unless they touch the electrified wires in the fence and gate."

Marta usually kept her sometimes-volatile anger in check but not now.

"You're right about one thing, Chief Ryumin," she flared. "*I* am CEO and you work for me."

"Then get the civil authorities to come out," Ryumin said. "Have them keep our plants from being destroyed and workers beat up. You cut my security force, you didn't approve additional equipment, and I'm not sure I can depend on the funding for the special project you and the other CEOs have cooked up."

Marta appreciated Ryumin's reluctance to mention how the alliance of businesses, the Mirach Business Association, had slowly come together in a pact to refit IndustrialMechs for use in what amounted to a private military force. But funding was scant and the project under wraps. Only if necessary would the 'Mechs be refitted and used, since that would be a slap in the face of both the Governor and the Legate.

"I'm doing what I can to keep AWC solvent. Since the net went down, all our revenue comes from low-margin local communications. The new moon relays take up most of our R and D budget. You know about the labor trouble with the tantalum mines over in Ventrale, the—"

"Marta," Ryumin cut in, "I apologize. I'm just trying to do the best I can with what little I have. Tell me how you want those rioters dealt with and I'll do it."

"You're doing fine, Inger," Marta said, her tone softening a little. They were all under pressure to keep the business running smoothly. The fall of the HPG net made that an almost impossible chore for AllWorldComm, however. Marta fought constantly with her board of directors about the bottom line, and the time she spent performing her duties as president of the Mirach Business Association put her at odds with the directors' wishes. "Keep them out of our assembly plant. Our guards cannot hold them back indefinitely and the fences might be breached."

"Including—?" Ryumin pointed to another monitor.

Marta's brown eyes misted over for a moment. It had come to this. Inger Ryumin had ordered an IndustrialMech positioned inside an assembly building out of sight of the demonstrators. The hulking 'Mech's right arm held a razor-edged, meter-long diamond drill bit. Its left hand sported a twenty-kilogram sledgehammer. If it advanced into the crowd, it could smash and cut unimpeded. The carnage would be terrible. And the MBA spoke of converting even this fearsome mechanism, equipping it with autocannon and rockets.

Marta jumped when alarms sounded and a red light began flashing.

"A hundred or more have broken down the gate," Ryumin said, consulting a data display. "The fence shorted out without stopping them."

"Use the 'Mech," Marta said. She turned to stone inside. She owed it to her employees to keep them safe. Those in the crowd might once have worked here, but they should have accepted their layoffs and not resorted to force against former coworkers. "And get me a secure conference link to Nagursky and Chin."

Marta hated to admit that the other two senior officers in the Mirach Business Association governing troika had been so right so soon. She had to discuss safety issues with the AWC board of directors, but after this violation of her company's property, threatening both production and workers, the AWC directors had to go along with the MBA proposal. The IndustrialMechs would be refitted.

"Will do," Ryumin said, "but that call you placed before the riot started just came through on commlink 703." The security chief pointed to the end of the control console.

"Order the 'Mech driver out," Marta said. "Minimal use of force."

Ryumin picked up the mic to give the command.

All trouble saved up to crash down on Marta at once. She donned a headset and flipped on the secure-line baffle so no one could overhear as she focused her optical pickup. A quick security check showed an untapped link, although Marta knew this report was suspect. Especially considering whom she had called. She turned on the screen.

"Ah, Ms. Kinsolving, so sorry to take this long getting back to you," said Lady Elora. The redhead smiled insincerely, her grin almost a grimace. "Disturbances throughout the city have taken up my time. The Baron wanted pictures and reports from my staff." Elora turned slightly and gestured to someone just beyond the photo pickup perimeter. "You don't mind if Legate Tortorelli listens to what you've got to say, do you, my dear?"

"Go on, make it a party," Marta said sarcastically. She knew her anger was getting the better of her again. Glancing across the room, she saw that Ryumin had unleashed the IndustrialMech against the mob. There was no way to keep this quiet; she had to pass along the confrontation through official channels immediately. And the Ministry of Information provided as immediate a conduit as she could get.

"My dear, you are so kind," Lady Elora said with mock gratitude.

"I want to file a report for the Governor's consideration."

"This sounds serious. Should I put you on record?" Lady Elora lifted a bony finger, pointed it at a control offscreen, and waited. The spotlight fixed on her caused her rings to flash and glitter, distracting Marta for a moment.

"Do as you please. I am registering a formal complaint against the Ministry of Information."

"As CEO of AllWorldComm?"

"The company will issue a comprehensive statement later, but I wanted you to know that AWC protests strenuously the so-called news stories you have aired hinting that the company is responsible for the destruction of the Mirach HPG station and that AWC in some way profits by Mirach's communications blackout. These reports have created unrest at our fabrication plants and necessitated action against rioters attempting to destroy property."

"What action is this?" Elora looked wolfish.

"You're an expert at innuendo and half-truths," Marta continued, a cold rage filling her. Monitors showed men and women being injured by the 'Mech as it herded the mob out of AWC grounds. "You're inciting the people, using AllWorldComm as a scapegoat."

"As Minister, I assure you only the strict truth is

aired on our official newscasts. We are an arm of the government, concerned with informing the public."

"I realize our position is precarious. Never argue with anyone holding the microphone," Marta said. "You might hold it, but AllWorldComm *manufactures* it."

"Are you suggesting that equipment vital to the public's need to know might be withheld from the Ministry of Information unless stories sympathetic to your company are aired? Did something similar happen with the Hyperpulse Generator equipment? Would you comment on AWC's role in the destruction of the HPG station?"

Whatever she said now would be edited, reedited, and twisted into any statement Elora wanted. It would be bad enough when news of the rioters being injured was aired.

"The formal statement will be transmitted by the end of the day."

"I'll be waiting to read it," Elora said. "Oh, one thing before you cut the circuit. What of the disturbance you mentioned? Can you fill me in on that?"

"The pictures are ever so disheartening," Tortorelli cut in. "Are you using a 'Mech to quell the disturbance? Eyewitnesses tell of a powerful fighting machine threatening them."

Marta motioned to Inger Ryumin and opened her side of the conversation. Either Lady Elora or the Legate had a direct visual feed of the carnage outside, and she wanted her security chief to cut it. Ryumin figured out right away what was needed and called up technicians to track down the cameras and destroy them.

"The MBA has a private security force to protect its members' property when necessary," Marta said carefully. Ryumin gave her a thumbs-up. Elora's visuals of the mob scene were scrambled now. But the cat was out of the bag.

"This is a serious matter we need to discuss with Governor Ortega," Tortorelli said. "As Planetary Legate, I insist use of any 'Mech be halted immediately."

"Thank you for your input, Legate Tortorelli," Marta said. She broke the link, ripped off her headset, and threw it across the room in a fit of pique. She stalked out, leaving Ryumin to restore order. Marta had to contact her directors and the senior officers of the MBA to brief them before they saw the distortions Lady Elora was likely to run on an emergency breaking newscast. Old ways of business had to fall by the wayside. This was a different world, one with Lady Elora's bony, beringed fingers strangling the flow of information to the masses.

"My, she seemed so upset," Calvilena Tortorelli said. "Did my suggestion upset her that much?"

"Calvy, does it matter?" Elora sneered as her cameras at the AWC plant went off-line in a rush of static. Marta Kinsolving's security chief was efficient. Elora wondered if Ryumin could be bought off.

"Of course it matters!" Tortorelli pursed his heavy lips and then pouted. "She can't flaunt my authority. I'm Legate!"

"You're right," Elora said, reaching out to place a calming hand on his arm. "Domestic peace must be maintained. That's what we all want, but I'm afraid the Governor isn't doing a very good job with that and—" She abruptly cut off what she was going to say.

"What is it, Elora? You've found out something, haven't you? What is it?"

"It might be nothing," she said slowly, building the

man's anticipation. "It occurred to me that AllWorld-Comm might be forging an alliance with Jacob Bannson."

"Why's that? That pirate can't come onto *my* planet! I was outraged that the Governor was even considering a trading station here!"

"No, he shouldn't be allowed to gain a foothold here, Calvy," she said. "I think my lord Ortega is grasping at straws, but not AWC. Kinsolving might see Bannson as a way of revitalizing her failing company. If not AWC, then the Mirach Business Association might be responsible. Remember those mercenaries and the attack over in Ventrale last year? They might have been a detachment of Bannson's Raiders. I've heard rumors that Bannson's put together a private army. Perhaps that attack was Bannson's heavy-handed way of attempting to set up shop here. After all, where there's money and trade to be had, you'll find Bannson meddling and stealing."

"Never! Not on my world!"

Lady Elora watched as the Legate hurried from her office, face flushed and muttering to himself. He was so easy to manipulate. When she finally contacted Kal Radick and offered him a new world for the Steel Wolves, she could dispense with Tortorelli. And the Baron.

4

**First Cossack Lancers' barracks, Governor's Park
Mirach
12 April 3133**

"**Y**ou'll go blind doing that so much," Dale Ortega
said to his brother. Dale lounged back, the pneumatic
chair sighing softly to conform to his whipcord body,
then hiked his booted feet to the table in the common
room. The other guardsmen were on patrol or doing
maintenance, leaving only Austin and him to stand
duty. And his brother was no fun. Austin ignored attempts at conversation, his nose buried in the stacks
of reports requiring an officer's attention.

Dale felt a glow of pride in how fast his little
brother had gained citizenship. Austin might think
their father had pushed through the paperwork just
for him, but Dale knew it hadn't been that way at all.
Austin's service had been exemplary. He worked hard

every instant he was on duty and even harder when he was off. Dale sighed, remembering his own troubles winning full citizenship. A string of petty problems was to be expected from someone with a bent toward practical jokes, but his father had almost disowned him over painting the huge four-tiered fountain in Chekhov Square a bright red.

"Dale!"

"What?" He swung about and faced his brother.

"Wake up. The newscast. It's starting."

"Who cares?" Dale started to sprawl back and then sat up so quickly the pneumatics hissed like a snake to maintain proper support.

"I thought that would get your attention," Austin said, coming over. He used the IR-beam remote to turn up the sound. "Riots throughout the capital. Ten dead. It's bad enough, but the way Elora's presenting makes it sound worse than it is."

"What's in it for her?" Dale wondered aloud. "She's stirring up the people for no good reason. She's supposed to be Minister of Information and presenting the government's side tactfully in all this trouble. Oil on troubled waters. But listen! Her commentator's making it out that no one's safe and how citizens should take up arms. That's a blatant call to insurrection!"

"Father should crack down. I know he said he had ordered the police to hang back during demonstrations, but his noninterference policy is turning dangerous." Austin was as upset as Dale could remember having seen him. On this, they saw eye to eye.

"Security around the Palace ought to be tightened," Dale said.

"Papa said no when Manfred asked to double the guards and station battle armor around the grounds.

Governor's Park is wide-open and vulnerable without stepped-up patrols. Scout cars, Hoverbikes, and battle armor," Austin said. "The problem is that Father thinks he can talk his way out of anything."

"Maybe he can," said Dale. "After all, can't I talk my way into things?" Dale laughed and then quieted when he saw Austin wasn't going to let go of his rant.

"There's no way to reason with an angry crowd," Austin said. "Father should replace Elora if she won't control on-air content better. I don't care what she says about avoiding censorship and the public's increased hunger for information."

"For once, she might be right," Dale said. "Don't get mad, little brother. Use your head like you usually do. The merest hint of censoring the news would have a terrible impact. We're all blundering around, wondering what's going on everywhere else in The Republic. If the people think they can't find out what's happening in their own backyard, the cork would really pop."

"She's letting her newscasters incite riots," Austin said doggedly.

"Talk about inciting a riot!" Dale exclaimed, pushing out of his chair and hurrying to the door. His long arms engulfed a petite woman.

"You'll crack my bones if you keep squeezing so hard, Dale," complained Hanna Leong.

"You didn't complain last night, my darling," Dale said. He kissed her.

"Hi, Hanna," Austin called. He greeted his brother's sweetheart without looking away from the newscast.

"What're you doing right now?" Hanna asked. Dale held her close when she tried to push away. It felt right to him when she was near. He could rest his chin comfortably on top of her head but refrained since she didn't like it. More than mussing her carefully coiffed black hair, she said it brought back unpleasant memories of her childhood. Dale had wormed the complete story from her about a condescending uncle who patted her on the head at every opportunity, regularly making little of her accomplishments. Part of Hanna's motivation in going for and getting an on-air newscast with the Ministry of Information was her need to gain respect.

Dale found her fascinating, though he had to admit it was her slim beauty and ebony eyes that had drawn him to her in the beginning. Hanna was as competent a reporter as she was a newscaster. Dale wondered if he could use his new position on his father's staff to recommend Hanna for Elora's job. Austin was right on target with criticism about Lady Elora and her performance as Minister of Information. It was time that their father recognize Elora was more of a subversive than a government representative. What better replacement than Hanna Leong?

"He's on duty," Dale explained. "He's *always* on duty. Austin, you'll make yourself crazy watching that." Dale felt Hanna tense when she saw that Austin watched the newscast. "I didn't mean the news would make him crazy, though watching you makes me crazy." Hanna finally pushed out of his grip. "What's wrong?" he asked softly.

"I need to talk to you. Right now. Alone."

"Austin, you mind getting the ready-report from Manfred? He's down at Staging Area 5 doing something to the battle armor. Repairing it or adding armament, I don't know what."

"Routine maintenance," Austin said. "You should check the schedule sometime." He pushed past his brother and Hanna, grumbling about how the unrest in Cingulum spread to other cities.

"He's such a worrier," Dale said, shaking his head. "And it's rubbing off on you. No frowns now. Only smiles when you're with me," he said sternly. Dale bent to kiss Hanna again, but she stepped back.

"It's Lady Elora," Hanna said.

"It's always something," Dale said in disgust. "What about her? If she's giving you a hard time, I'll go over there and mop the floor with her. She's only a Minister. You're my lover."

"This is important, Dale," Hanna said, sitting on the couch. He joined her, giving the mechanism a workout adjusting to two forms.

Dale said, "So tell me what's wrong and how I can fix it."

"There are . . . rumors. How she wants to turn Mirach over to the Steel Wolves. I dismissed them at first, but I think she's sent couriers to Kal Radick."

"Slow down, Hanna. Steel Wolves? What are you talking about?"

Hanna took a deep breath and began again. "There's a lot you don't know. There's a lot the Governor doesn't know. Elora's keeping it all to herself."

"You sound as paranoid as Austin. He thinks she's responsible for the riots."

"She is, Dale. I'm sure of it. Elora's got word that Radick is going out on his own, that he isn't Prefect any longer. He's put together a group of Clan warriors loyal to Clan Wolf. They're calling themselves the Steel Wolves and attacking one world after another. We heard something about an attack on Achernar, but nothing official has come in—"

"I should say not. My father would never keep anything like this quiet. This is huge." Dale knew something about the Clans: fierce warriors, they practiced selective breeding to emphasize intelligence and strength. He'd heard they were enormous people, and some of the most deadly fighters ever known. But they were history to him, not real, and they lived so far away that they were more myth than reality.

"He might not say anything if he wasn't sure, if there are other problems in The Republic."

"The HPG going down has given a life to rumors no one would believe for an instant otherwise." Dale looked into Hanna's eyes and knew she believed what she was saying. He had never known her to jump to conclusions. She was too good a reporter for that. "So why would Radick want Elora to stir up such trouble here on Mirach? What would he gain?"

"What would *she* gain?" Hanna said intensely. "Ever since I got wind of this business, I've been doing some digging. Did you know that there's Clan blood in her veins?"

This was a surprise to Dale.

"Go back to the year that Elora was born, and in the society pages you'll find articles about her mother, a whirlwind romance, and an awfully fast marriage. In civil records—police records—I found something else: the report that Lady Galina Stepanova had been raped by a Clanner. Nine months and that same wedding later . . ."

"A baby girl named Elora, I'll bet," Dale finished for her. "If that's true, why wouldn't Elora hate the Clans?"

"Why should she? She was brought up noble here on Mirach. Between her noble heritage and her Clan paternity, she believes she is just as good as they are. Elora wants to bring down the Baron and then get Tortorelli to quash the rebels. That would leave the planet exposed for the Steel Wolves."

"Take a deep breath," Dale said. "You're tiring me out with all this." What Hanna said about Tortorelli gave him pause. He had seen how Elora swayed the Legate.

"It's more than rumor, Dale. I know it. I can't prove all of it, especially Elora trying to contact Radick, but it makes sense. You don't know her like I do. She resents being a lowly Minister and has built up her status in her own mind—her Clan status."

"They'd never accept her, even if she managed to give them an entire planet," Dale said.

"We know that, but try telling her. She thinks the Wolf blood makes her better than the rest of us. She's ambitious beyond all reason. She has no love for The Republic and figures that if she can prove her worth by delivering Mirach, she'll get a better deal with Mirach under Radick's control."

This was too much for Dale.

"How can you prove she's responsible for the riots? The people are vulnerable because we're cut off from the HPG net and every little rumor of invasion or disaster takes on a life of its own, but to dump that at Elora's door is a big step. Unless she's ordered you to lie on the air."

"She has a select few who will do anything to please her. Elora knows I can't be trusted, not in that way, because of you."

"Me?" scoffed Dale. "If this is true, it's not because of me. She knows you're too honest when it comes to reporting the truth."

"I knew there was a reason I loved you," Hanna said, kissing him lightly.

"Hmm, nice, but not the right time. Do you have concrete proof?"

"Not enough, but it all fits together. If I could present it to the Baron, it might create enough doubt in his mind that he would remove her."

"Papa's got a full schedule these days, but I'll see what I can do. Too bad I haven't transferred to his office staff yet." Dale fell silent for a moment, then smiled and said, "Nobody's around."

"Dale!" Hanna cried. "You're incorrigible. Please get me an appointment. Now, I've got to go. I'm on-air soon."

"Work, work, work," Dale said in mock horror.

Dale's usual buoyant good humor faded as Hanna left. Profound changes were taking place because the HPG net had failed, and he didn't understand them. He needed to talk with Austin.

"Lieutenant Ortega," greeted Manfred Leclerc. "Just in time to help run calibration tests on the battle armor." The FCL commander tossed Austin a test meter. Austin put it down and sat beside the captain. Manfred was about the same age as the Baron, but constant training kept him fit. If he ever felt any strain, in combat or out, Austin had never noticed. Manfred Leclerc had ice water running in his veins, from the tip of his toes to the sharp brain 190 centimeters away. Like the other FCL soldiers, Manfred wore his sandy hair cut short, but bushy eyebrows that wiggled like the ends of a snapping rope when he spoke made him seem hairier than he was. One thing Austin appreciated about Manfred was the captain's prominent nose. It had been broken and so poorly set that Austin was less conscious of his own.

Manfred's strong hands closed over the test meter.

"Worried about leaving the FCL?" the captain asked. "No, not entirely," Manfred went on, answering his own question. "There's something else."

Austin had always felt Manfred could read his mind. He looked around the equipment room and took a deep breath. The usual odors of leather, metal, and burning solder were overrun by a sharp ozone tang from a half dozen guardsmen laser-welding armor. Around the large blacktopped science table Austin saw real precision in their work. Many of the First Cossack Lancers had worked their way up through the ranks, technicians before reaching the prestigious position of protecting the Governor. With the Baron considering reassigning the FCL, it seemed as though all that work, all that loyalty, was about to be thrown away.

The stocky guard captain cracked his knuckles and motioned Austin aside. In a low voice so different from his loud command tone, he asked, "What do you hear about it?"

"The rioting?"

"You know what I mean," Manfred said, impatient. His blue eyes locked with Austin's. "The transfer. Is it for real?"

Austin hesitated. The guard captain wasn't prone to believe scuttlebutt and was as securely grounded in fact as any officer Austin knew, but the rumor carried the ring of truth.

"I don't know, Manfred," he said uncomfortably. "Dale and I were there when my father said he would think about the Legate's request, but he didn't promise." Even if the FCL came under Tortorelli's command, Austin wanted to remain with the unit.

"Friends tell me money is already being shifted around, funds we were supposed to get for new battle armor and a lance of Hoverbikes. That means the Governor is going to send us to hell!"

"Maybe he has something else in mind," said Austin, grasping at straws. Austin's eyes widened at the resignation on Manfred's face.

"What else can there be? Never mind. Putting us in the Legate's command might be better for unit morale, since the Governor's not doing enough to stop the rioting. Call it what it is, Austin: riots. None of this 'civil unrest.' That makes it sound too innocent. People are dying in the streets. Maybe if we were assigned to the Legate we could get out there and put an end to the violence."

Austin started to speak, then clamped his mouth shut. He agreed with Manfred—up to a point. Sergio Ortega needed a bodyguard more than ever, but his father owed it to the people of Mirach and The Republic to restore order however he could, no matter what personal risks he took.

"I'll let you know if I hear anything," he said.

"We're history," Manfred said. "I feel it in my bones. We're going to be under Tortorelli's command, and you're better off on your father's staff. It's been good serving with you." Manfred unexpectedly thrust out his hand. Austin shook it automatically, then stared in wonder at the captain. This had the feeling of a conclusion about it, a parting neither wanted.

"Nothing's definite yet," he said. "Things might work out so the FCL continues to guard the Governor and I can stay as an officer and—"

"No," Manfred Leclerc said firmly. "None of that will happen. It can't."

5

Mirach DropShip Field, Cingulum
Mirach
15 April 3133

"Why isn't he landing? Didn't the field controller give priority authorization?" Sergio Ortega paced back and forth on the glass-enclosed platform looking over the DropShip field west of Cingulum. Afternoon heat shimmered above the expanse of reinforced concrete designed to withstand the mass of even the largest DropShip. In the distance rose multistoried towers filled with controllers and their communications equipment monitoring the JumpShip point above the pole of Mirach's sun and the IR emergence wave.

"The DropShip is coming in now, Baron," said Manfred Leclerc, listening to a report in his earphone. "The honor guard is ready."

"Thank you, Captain," Sergio said, sucking in a

deep breath to calm himself. He hated protocol and pomp and the Lord Governor Sandoval's Envoy came at an inopportune time. Sergio had to speak with the labor leaders and assure them jobs would be forthcoming, to quiet the unemployed and get the rioters off the streets. And commerce? Sergio glanced around the reception platform and ticked off the list of business leaders who had been invited to greet Envoy Parsons.

Marta Kinsolving huddled with the others prominent in the Mirach Business Association. Sergio needed to confer with them all, but had postponed the necessary meetings because of problems dealing with labor organizers intent on disrupting the social fabric for their own gain. Once those rough spots were smoothed over, he could concentrate on the other side of the economic equation.

"He'll land in a few minutes," Lady Elora said. Sergio looked over his shoulder. She wore a stunning purple silk dress with a high collar, clothing befitting such an important visitor. "I've tapped into the commlink from the field controller. The central landing pad has been cleared for immediate arrival."

"Thank you," Sergio said stiffly. He should have expected his Minister to personally attend, although he had instructed his protocol officer to only issue a general memorandum about Jerome Parsons' arrival to the Ministry of Information. "You grace us with your presence, Lady Elora," he said.

Elora bowed slightly in his direction. "The arrival of such an important off-world dignitary, one representing the Lord Governor himself, is the lead story today. My reporters and camera crews are in position to capture every moment, every word, any tidbit of information Envoy Parsons might give about his travels among other worlds of The Republic. I hope you will arrange an interview. It would do much in strengthening public confidence to hear his words."

"Are you giving a speech, Elora?" Sergio asked. It did no good to antagonize her until he learned more about her off-world contacts. She might have been in touch with Parsons already, in spite of the Envoy's refusal to accept anything but guidance communications on his way to Mirach. This comm blackout worried Sergio because he had not been informed of the purpose of Parsons' mission. He knew he would learn the reason for the visit eventually, but Sergio wanted to know *now*. His own plans might need to be changed if Parsons came to forge new alliances across Mirach.

Sergio looked again at Marta Kinsolving and those with her. He noted that Benton Nagursky, the mining magnate, had not seen fit to come, but the aged agrobiologist Dr. Boris Chin had. Two of the three leaders of the MBA troika would get their chance to meet and greet.

Sergio stepped away from Elora and let his protocol officer engage her while he took Leclerc aside.

"There won't be an . . . incident, will there, Captain?"

"Baron, the entire FCL is alert to any threat. Neither exhaust nor bullet can penetrate the ferroglass shields on the reception platform, and Legate Tortorelli has heavier mobile units surrounding the field to keep any protesters away."

"What of my sons?" Sergio asked. "I want them with me, not in battle armor out on the field."

"I anticipated that, Baron," Manfred said. "They're waiting at the base of the reception platform and will join you on the carpet as you go to greet the Envoy. Both are in uniform, however, not diplomatic attire."

"That's all right. They won't be discharged from the FCL for another two weeks," Sergio said, his mind leaping ahead to the meeting with Parsons. He turned and gripped Manfred's arm. "Is everything else all right?"

Manfred hesitated, then nodded. "You can count on me, Baron."

"I know," Sergio said. Before he could say more, the platform began to quiver and the air filled with the deep-throated roar of a descending DropShip. Although they were kilometers distant, the rising shriek of the engines made speech impossible. Sergio let Manfred go about his duties and returned to the center of the platform, surrounded by the most powerful people on Mirach.

Sergio couldn't help reflecting that their power was nothing compared to that of the man who landed in the center of the DropShip field. The Envoy might not command a planetary industry or government but he had the Lord Governor's ear. While Aaron Sandoval made the decisions, those decisions were formed by trusted advisers like Jerome Parsons. Sergio couldn't help wondering why Parsons visited Mirach now. It could not be a coincidence.

He settled himself and waited for the thunderous blast to wash past the impact-proof ferroglass shielding on the platform as the spheroidal Union-class DropShip settled down on its four landing struts. A searing blast dwarfing the existing heat waves radiated off the concrete pad, but the arriving dignitaries immediately left the gleaming silver ship using a specially enclosed transport tube impervious to the elevated temperatures. Sergio's personal armored limousine pulled up at the base of the elevator, heat shielding was brought up automatically to protect those leaving, and then the limousine wheeled about and raced for the reception platform.

Sergio descended the steps and went to the red carpet unrolled to the door of the limo. Both Austin and Dale fell into step behind him, resplendent in their black-and-silver uniforms, but Sergio's attention focused on the man climbing from the limo.

"Papa," said Dale, moving closer to his right elbow. "When you saw Hanna Leong, what did you think? She—"

"This isn't the time or place, Dale." Sergio cut off his son as he stepped forward and greeted, "Your Excellency, welcome to Mirach."

Parsons reached out with his pudgy hand. It looked as if all the bones in it had turned to jelly. He shook Sergio's hand, then hastily drew back, clasping his fingers over the bulge of his considerable belly. His thinning blond hair was long and held in place by small jeweled barrettes, but there was nothing of the dandy in his sharp, clear green eyes. Sergio felt they bored to his soul and missed nothing.

But it would have been easy to overlook this intensity. Vibrant pink-and-cobalt-blue patterns on the vest under Parsons' formal cutaway jacket focused attention on the wrong portions of his anatomy. His trousers were baggy and flared in odd places, emphasizing bandy legs, but Sergio knew a diplomat of Parsons' stature would not dress like this unless it was the height of current fashion. In spite of his own standard diplomatic coal black coat and pants and heavily starched white formal shirt with diamond studs, Sergio felt just a little like an off-world bumpkin in Parsons' sartorially precise presence.

Parsons reared back slightly and tilted his head as he looked down his nose at the Governor.

"My dear Baron Ortega, how nice to meet you after all this time. Lord Governor Sandoval has spoken so highly of you and your delightful planet I feel as if I already know you as a friend and confidant."

"Your visit brings great honor to our humble world, Excellency," Sergio said. "Please come to the reception platform. Everyone is anxious to meet you."

"And I am eager to meet them," Parsons said jovially. He paused, smiled ingratiatingly, and asked, "Are these fine officers your sons, Baron? You must be Baronet Dale," he said, offering his limp handshake to Dale, then turned to Austin and repeated the gesture. "Baronet Austin. A pleasure. Have you attained your citizenship yet?"

Austin's mouth opened in surprise; then he managed to get out, "Yes, Your Excellency. Only last week."

"Stellar! You have sons to be proud of, Baron."

"You honor my family with your greeting, Excellency," Sergio said, hiding his surprise that the Envoy recognized his sons. No dullard served Aaron Sandoval, but Jerome Parsons showed unexpected preparation for the visit to Mirach. Sergio had not thought it was the idle sojourn of a bored diplomat, but now he knew there was far more purpose than he had expected.

"Do let's get on with the introductions," Parsons said. "I need to freshen up afterward. Then perhaps you can find a few moments for private talk, Baron."

"I am at your service, Excellency."

The stout Envoy huffed and puffed as he mounted the few steps to the reception platform, then slowly made his way through the assembled dignitaries. Sergio noted that Parsons greeted most by name and spoke intimately with several, as if they were longtime friends. To the best of his information, Sergio doubted Parsons had ever met any of them before.

"I don't like the time he's spending with Elora, Father," Dale said. "They act like they've known each other for years."

"He is a personable man," Sergio said. He had not missed how long the Envoy spent talking to Lady Elora, either.

"Please, sir, did Hanna—"

"I said we would talk of it later," Sergio said sharply.

Dale stepped back, frustrated. Sergio was glad to see Austin whisper a caution to his brother. This was a public gathering. Not only were Elora's reporters about, but private newscasters strained to pick up morsels of gossip. Since the net went down, off-world arrivals were lead topics. That a diplomat of Parsons' stature had come would furnish Cingulum with news and gossip about his travels throughout The Republic for weeks.

Jerome Parsons moved from Lady Elora and spoke quietly with Marta Kinsolving and Dr. Chin. Sergio wished he had violated diplomatic protocol and installed eavesdropping equipment to monitor every conversation at the reception. He saw the expression on Elora's face and knew the same thought ran through her mind. Sergio had ordered Manfred to oversee construction of the platform only hours before Parsons' arrival, then keep everyone away until the last minute. That might not prevent spy devices from being trained on the gathering, but it kept them from being built into the flooring.

"Austin," Sergio said to his younger son. "When the Envoy moves a bit farther down the reception line, go speak to Marta Kinsolving and arrange a tour of the AWC facilities."

"For you and Parsons?" asked Austin.

"For yourself. Tell her whatever you have to. You'll be a communications protocol officer on my staff."

"A trainee, sir," Austin said.

"You need not be too specific. Just get the tour and keep your eyes open. Envoy Parsons obviously appreciates Ms. Kinsolving's company."

"Is that a pun, sir?"

"Find out," Sergio said. He nodded to Manfred Leclerc as Parsons finished with the last of the assembled dignitaries.

"We can go directly to the Palace, Your Excellency," Sergio said. "Perhaps we can talk en route."

"Excellent idea, Baron, a stellar notion." Parsons paused as he saw Manfred drawing in battle-armored FCL guards to surround the limo. He nodded once, as if approving the arrangement, and huffed and puffed his way down the steps.

Sergio knew he had reached a critical juncture in Parsons' visit. Protocol demanded that the junior enter the limo ahead of the senior. Sergio hesitated at the door, deciding what to do. Did a Planetary Governor outrank an Ambassador-at-large? The matter resolved itself quickly when Parsons hurried inside ahead of Sergio, settling the issue. Even more puzzled at the Envoy's behavior and purpose, Sergio settled down on the seat facing Parsons, who looked exhilarated at having met so many people in such a short time.

"Thank you for inviting so many prominent citizens to the landing field to meet me, Baron. I appreciate the honor you show me."

"Your visit honors us, Excellency." Sergio hesitated, then added, "Whatever the purpose of that visit might be."

"I am so sorry to have kept you in the dark as I have, but these are perilous times. I am sure you agree, Baron."

Parsons reached into an inner pocket of his jacket

and drew forth a small parcel of papers. He held them in the palms of his outstretched hands like an offering, leaned forward slightly, and waited for Sergio to take them.

"From the Lord Governor himself," Sergio said, recognizing the seal. "We don't get many official communiqués since the HPG went down."

"Governor Sandoval wants to bring Mirach more into the mainstream of the Prefecture," Parsons said. He folded his hands on his paunch and leaned back as the limo accelerated smoothly. "Tell me, Baron, do you find serving The Republic to be rewarding?"

"Of course, Your Excellency," Sergio said, trying to fathom the rules of the game being played. The question sounded as if it carried a land mine or two with it. "I am loyal to The Republic."

"And to the Lord Governor?"

"Yes," Sergio said, his mind turning over the small clues. "Aren't you asking the same question? Isn't loyalty to The Republic also loyalty to Governor Sandoval?" Even as he spoke, he saw the flicker in Parsons' emerald eyes suggesting that might not be so. This visit explained a great deal if Sandoval moved on his own, independent of The Republic.

Coupled with what Hanna Leong had told him yesterday, it seemed all the leaders of The Republic might be interested more in furthering their own ambitions than in maintaining unity.

"It is my duty to report if Mirach and its populace are comfortable being aligned with The Republic," Parsons said smoothly.

"I am sure you will find that although the failure of the HPG net has unnerved many on Mirach, our loyalty is unflagging."

"That is good to know, Baron. After all, another

alliance might provide more benefit for a planet with considerable mineral wealth." Parsons made a fluttering motion with his fingers, as if dismissing any such suggestion as being absurd.

Sergio started to open the packet the Envoy had given him, but Parsons reached over and stopped him.

"Those are such dry reports. You'll have time to read them at your leisure and prepare a response for me to carry personally to the Lord Governor."

Sergio inclined his head slightly in Parsons' direction. He would need every possible second to formulate *that* reply.

6

Café Galactica, Cingulum
Mirach
15 April 3133

"Elora fired me," Hanna Leong said in a choked voice. "She put that airhead Bethany into my newscast, told me I wasn't good enough, and then she fired me!"

Dale Ortega saw how hard she tried not to cry. He reached across the small table at the sidewalk café and took her hand. The sounds of the city went away for that moment. Gone were the cars whistling through the twilight not two meters away. Dale barely noticed The Republic Tower, the tallest building on the planet, as he usually did. Something about its cloud-impaling apex, especially at sunset, inspired him and made him believe anything was possible. When he and Austin were youngsters, they had come to loiter at this very café and watch the top stories being laid into place. When his father had dedicated the building to Devlin Stone, Dale and Austin had stood beside him for the first time in an official capacity.

Their mother had died only a week earlier, and Sergio Ortega had wanted to involve his boys more in day-to-day routine to keep their minds off the tragedy. Somehow, Dale never thought of the Tower as being a tribute to Devlin Stone as much as to his mother. Dale struggled to find the words to inspire in Hanna the same comfort it represented for him.

"You can do better," he told her. "You've got talent and you've got more ambition than any other woman I've ever seen." He grinned and added, "You've almost got as much as me."

"Austin's the one with ambition," Hanna said, dabbing at her tears and smiling a little. "You're the one with the boyish charm. Remember?"

"I forget everything when I'm with you. Remember when we met?"

"You spilled a drink on me at a reception I was covering for the Ministry of Information. I thought you were a complete dolt."

"Your beauty dazzled me," Dale said. He surprised himself when he realized he meant every word. Before, with other women, it had been a come-on. Not with Hanna. "That you didn't shout and get all mad that I'd ruined a good dress—"

"It was a gown, thank you," Hanna said.

"You accepted disaster well."

"And I accepted a date with you. You moved fast. Maybe you *are* ambitious," she said. Then Hanna's smile faded. "And Elora fired me. I suppose I should have expected it, but it was still a surprise."

"Did she know you had a meeting with my father?"

Dale asked. "I asked him earlier today about it, but he wouldn't answer. Of course, we were receiving the Envoy at the time." Dale hadn't seen Hanna for a couple days and he had been as caught up in preparations for Jerome Parsons as everyone else. Not only had Manfred Leclerc assigned him to position the FCL guards, but his father had kept him jumping as liaison between the protocol officer and the transportation chief. It had been a relief when his father and the Envoy had driven away. This was the first chance he'd had to learn how Hanna's meeting had gone.

"I don't know," Hanna said. "Maybe Elora knew about our meeting. She tries to know everything." Hanna looked forlornly at him. "She fired me so abruptly, she must know."

"My father will do something," Dale said.

"I can't prove my allegations. Oh, some I can document. She *is* the bastard child of a Clan raider, but that's no crime. I was getting closer to finding out if she had been in touch with Radick. Being fired means I've lost my best contacts in the Ministry."

"Did Papa believe you?" asked Dale. He held her hand tighter.

"He was noncommittal, but I think so. I'm sure Elora intends to use Tortorelli against him and depose him. From things she's said, I believe she's got the crazy idea that delivering Mirach to the Steel Wolves will give her even more power."

Dale motioned her to silence as the waiter came to their table.

"Two coffees. Do you have Terran import?" Dale asked.

"Only domestic," the waiter said, looking up and down the street and avoiding Dale's direct gaze.

"Two coffees. And food always calms me down,"

he said, trying to remember his last meal. He had skipped eating since an early breakfast in the FCL barracks because of preparations for Parsons' arrival. "Kulebiaka and the coffee," Dale said, knowing the meat-and-vegetable-stuffed pastry was always good to tame even his most savage hunger.

The waiter looked down the street again, brushed back his hair, then turned and hurried into the small café. Dale started to call after the waiter, then stopped.

"What's wrong, Dale?" Hanna asked.

"I—nothing, I guess. The waiter seemed more interested in the traffic than he did taking my order." Dale shrugged it off.

Dale took Hanna's hand in both of his and started to tell her he was certain there would be a position on the Baron's staff for her, when he heard the screech of tires and the roar of an engine. A car veered toward them and leaped the curb.

"Hanna!" he cried. He dived across the small round table, arms trying to circle and protect her. The car crashed into Hanna and brushed past Dale. He flew through the air and slammed into the next table. He tried to sit up, but his muscles refused to obey. His thoughts were jumbled and he couldn't concentrate until a mental image of Hanna's frightened face burned away the fog.

Dale crawled toward her on hands and knees and looked down into her face. He felt as if he had fallen down a long, dark shaft. From the way her head canted to one side he knew she was dead.

"Hanna," he grated out, touching her cheek. Sirens blared in the distance, but it didn't matter. The ambulance was already too late.

7

"**Q**uite an impressive organization, Lady Elora," Jerome Parsons said, looking around the broadcast studio. His head bobbed up and down, causing his triple chins to bounce about. "You have done well with a limited technical base. Not that Mirach doesn't have fine minds and decent access to current technology, mind you."

"Please, Envoy, I understand what you mean," Elora said. She moved with deliberate steps that caused her purple silk dress to hiss slightly like an aroused snake. Parsons watched her with some amusement. She knew this focused his attention on her, both visually and aurally. What she seemed not to know was that he had seen such tactics before, on a dozen other worlds. Or perhaps she was vain enough to believe she was more appealing than any other could be. Parsons found such egotism tiring.

"I'm sure you do," Parsons said as he idly brushed the controls with the tips of his pudgy fingers. The roving fingers came to a halt over one section of the control board. He expertly adjusted a control and brought up a view of Cingulum on the monitor screen.

"Such a lovely city in the evening. I am sorry I missed the sunset. With a star decanting such wine red light, it would have been spectacular. But I was trapped in that limousine with its armored-glass tinted windows."

"The Baron has only your safety at heart."

"I am sure," Parsons said, adjusting other dials. "He has a great duty, as do you, Lady Elora."

"What do you mean, Excellency?"

"The Ministry of Information controls more than eighty percent of the newscasts. That is a great burden, I am sure." Parsons saw how she turned cautious.

"The Ministry supports our world's endeavors, however it can. The cost of equipment and the dearth of trained professionals restricts others from joining us in broadcasting the news."

"Being an agency of the government, it helps that you have a direct pipeline to the Baron's office, too," Parsons said.

"Excuse me a moment, Your Excellency," Elora said as a young man motioned impatiently to her from across the room. Parsons watched as she swayed over and spoke with him in hushed tones. Elora returned in less than a minute.

"Business never ends," she said.

"He had the look of a menial about him. In what capacity is he employed at the Ministry of Information?" asked Parsons.

"He doesn't work here," she said smoothly. "He's a waiter at a local café, actually. He came to confirm . . . a reservation I had there." Her face hardened for a moment.

"Such personal service is hard to find," Parsons said, wondering about her look. He shifted the view of the city until he tapped into a news feed at an accident. "How tragic," Parsons said. "A woman seems to have been injured in a hit-and-run downtown."

"Cingulum has become a dangerous city, Excellency," Elora said, reaching over and turning off the camera feed. "You don't really want that signal."

"What signal would you most like to receive, Minister?" Parsons asked. "Perhaps something showing the way to guide Mirach away from a weakening alliance?"

"Is The Republic's grip on the Prefecture weakening?"

"Why, I never said that," Parsons declared, his green eyes widening in mock surprise. He saw that Elora picked up his intent perfectly. She jumped to the conclusion that Sandoval sought new alliances in the wake of the HPG failure. He wondered what else she knew, or suspected.

"You represent Lord Governor Sandoval," she said carefully. "Through my contacts, I've interviewed someone who claims Sandoval is distancing himself from The Republic."

Parsons laughed and made it sound genuine. "That's no more true than, say, Prefect Radick distancing himself from The Republic. It is a shame such rumors abound, but it becomes incumbent upon people like you and me to quell such . . . treason."

"As you say, Envoy," Elora said, bowing slightly.

"If you will excuse me, Minister," Parsons said. "It

is so late and I am woefully drained from today's activities. Worse for my beauty sleep, I must rise before dawn."

"You're leaving Mirach so soon?"

"Oh, no, I'll be here another few days. Tomorrow morning, far too early for my taste, Legate Tortorelli has arranged an inspection of the military. There is nothing quite so tiresome as seeing boxes of equipment or even long lines of soldiers dressed up and standing at attention for no good reason. Why, the last time I endured such an inspection, I got blisters from walking up one line and down the other. No one appreciated it. No one." Parsons heaved a deep sigh of resignation. "Such is an Envoy's fate."

"If you find it too tiresome, perhaps I can arrange something more fascinating for you," Elora said.

"You are such a gracious hostess, looking out for my interests this way," Jerome Parsons said, "but I must attend, no matter how boring I might find it. The Legate was quite insistent about parading his combined forces."

"Was he, now?" Elora frowned.

"Good evening, Lady Elora," Parsons said, bowing slightly. He read people well. Elora had not known the Legate had issued that invitation. So were the seeds of distrust sown.

8

Ministry of Information, Cingulum
Mirach
15 April 3133

"You missed the other one," Lady Elora raged. The man who had worked as a waiter in the café refused to be cowed.

"You said you wanted the woman dead. She is. The man would have cost you more."

"Incompetent," grumbled Elora. She shoved back in her desk chair and glared at the man. He had been useful before. He had to be useful again. Hanna had been rooting out too much information for Elora to be comfortable. What had she done with her data? Undoubtedly she would have told her lover. It would have been far easier if Dale Ortega had died along with her.

But had she told anyone else? Elora continued to

fume. She had ordered that Hanna be watched when it had become apparent the Ministry of Information had a traitor in its ranks, but that observation had failed repeatedly. Hanna might have spoken to any number of people other than the Baronet. Elora frowned when she considered the possibility that Hanna had given what she had discovered to the Baron.

She quickly discarded that idea. The Baron would have fired Elora. Or would he? Was he astute enough to realize how that would appear to the people hanging on every word issued by the Ministry? She had gone out of her way to draw in as large a viewership as possible for the news, always hinting that danger lay around the corner. Removal of a Minister of Information would have been seen as an attempt at censorship.

"I have another job for you," Elora said.

"I can do it."

"You'll have to play at being more than a waiter."

"I can do it."

"Let's see how quickly you can become a soldier. One in charge of supply for the Legate." She smiled as the man looked perplexed. The idea had come to her after learning Tortorelli had scheduled war games.

Let the games begin.

9

Palace of Facets, Cingulum
Mirach
16 April 3133

"**W**ords are hardly enough to convey my sorrow, Dale," Sergio Ortega said. "I know Hanna meant a great deal to you."

Dale Ortega tried to put on a stoic face, but Austin saw the true pain his brother felt. For all his womanizing, Dale had finally found a soul mate in Hanna Leong. To lose her in such a terrible accident had to be painful, perhaps more so than when they had lost their mother in the air transport crash.

Austin tried to decide if it was better to know death was coming, creeping forward inexorably, or to be confronted with the abrupt fact of its finality. Try as he might, he could not decide.

"I'm in contact with the authorities," the Governor

said, "who assure me they'll find the driver and prose-
cute to the full extent of the law. This was a tragedy
that should never have happened."

Dale started to speak, looked at his brother, then
clamped his mouth shut. Austin wondered what Dale
had been going to say but had chosen not to.

"Why don't you take some time off?" suggested
Austin. He wanted to ease his brother through the
grief and knew time away from duties would help
blunt it.

"There's no reason," Dale said. "I only got a few
scratches. I prefer working to sitting and moping."

Austin heard something else in his brother's words.
Dale wanted to be near the resources afforded by the
Governor's office.

Why? Austin wondered. *What's Dale up to?*

"This is a terrible time to speak of political matters,
I know," Sergio said. "Your brother's idea for you to
take a week or two off is a good one. Consider yourself on leave beginning now." Sergio checked his
schedule. "After the Envoy leaves, why don't we go
fishing, the way we did when you were young? You
always enjoyed being out on the sea."

"A small vacation might do you good, too, Father,"
Austin said.

"I prefer to work as much as I can, sir," Dale said,
looking upset at the notion his father would order him
out of the office. "I might not have my mind fully on
business, but any diversion helps."

"Until the Envoy leaves," Sergio said firmly. "Until
then, take it easy. You two are my most trusted advi-
sors. I need you with clear heads and hearts."

"What's the Envoy doing today?" asked Dale.

"Tortorelli is showing off his troops," Sergio said
with some distaste. Austin thought his father was

going to spit. "It's one thing to flaunt a world's achievements, but to ruin it with a show of military might?" He shook his head.

"You should let the Legate control the mobs," Austin said. "That would be a better demonstration of his abilities."

"No!" Sergio settled back down and looked at his son. "I don't want him exercising more force than he has already. That would be counterproductive in restoring peace and would result in even more deaths. I'm going to speak to the people at a series of open forums to offer new aid programs."

"You'd expose yourself to the mobs?" Dale's eyes widened. "They'd lynch you!"

"Oh, come now, Dale. It's not come to that. I am *not* ruling from behind a barricade, surrounded by bodyguards, like Czar Nicholas. I have to go to the people and talk with them, soothe their fears, let them know that the universe is not falling apart because the HPG net has been disrupted."

"Elora plays on their fears with every newscast," Austin said.

"I've spoken with her about overstepping her charter as Minister. She has quite a following among the disadvantaged, and I'm hesitant about removing her. The unemployed might see her firing as an attempt to silence their protests."

"She's trying to gain power by causing more unrest," Austin said. He watched the play of emotions on his father's face and took a shot in the dark. "Hanna spoke to you the day before she died. I saw her name on your schedule. Was it about Lady Elora?"

"It was nothing," Dale cut in. "Don't worry over it, Austin."

"He's right. She and I had a good discussion about many matters." Sergio seemed to close down, and Austin knew it wouldn't do any good trying to learn more, especially since Dale so readily agreed.

"Let's forget about Elora, for the moment," Sergio went on. "I've decided to accelerate the transfer of the First Cossack Lancers to the Legate's authority. Effective immediately."

Austin was too startled to say a word. He stared at his father in disbelief.

"But, Papa, immediately? You don't want Tortorelli using the forces he has. Why give him more? Please reconsider transferring the FCL," said Dale.

"The orders have been issued. Captain Leclerc is readying the unit's transfer to the Blood Hills Barracks. Both of you are now on my staff."

"What will you do for a bodyguard?" asked Austin. "If you plan to go into the city, you'll need guards. Even here in the Palace, you need guards, if only to keep sightseers from wandering in." Austin worried that more than casual tourists would stalk the halls of the Palace. There were too many nooks and crannies in which an assassin could hide. The FCL patrolled constantly and conducted random sweeps to protect the Governor.

"The Legate has agreed to deploy a detachment of honor guard. That's all I really need."

Austin and Dale exchanged looks. Their father placed too much faith in words and not enough in steel when it came to dealing with frightened citizens—and outright scoundrels.

"Send in my protocol officer. We need to discuss the Envoy's itinerary." Sergio's expression softened as he looked squarely at Dale. "Even if you intend to work until we go on our fishing trip, take today off, Dale. A loss such as yours isn't lightly dismissed."

"Yes, sir," Dale said.

Austin and Dale left, but Austin shivered as they passed the two FCL at attention outside the door. They would be replaced soon. Austin wondered if it was true that Tortorelli considered such duty punishment and assigned his least competent soldiers to the task.

Dale spoke quietly to the Governor's secretary, who summoned the protocol officer. Austin watched as Dale sagged, collapsing into himself, this tiny duty accomplished. The emotional toll was beginning to make itself felt.

"Over here," Austin said, pointing to an empty office down the hall from their father's. "The two of us need to figure out what to do."

"I know what I'm going to do," Dale said. He went into the empty office, dropped into a chair, and leaned back. Dale closed his eyes, looking years older.

"What are you up to?" Austin asked. He heard more in his brother's words than the need to come to grips with grief over Hanna's death.

Dale lifted his hands and stared at them, then dropped them.

"I had her blood all over me," he said. Dale looked up at his brother. "It wasn't an accident, Austin. She was murdered. And I would have died, too, except I got lucky."

"Don't be paranoid," Austin said. "Witnesses said the car was going too fast and the driver lost control."

"He signaled. The waiter signaled someone that we were at the table; then he ran just before the car careened up onto the sidewalk. Some assassins use bullets. This one used a car."

"It's hard to think Hanna's death was only fate," Austin said. "I know that it'd be easier for you to believe there was a reason for it. It makes her life more important if she died for some purpose. But it was a hit-and-run. An accident, Dale, only an accident."

" 'Only an accident,' " Dale said bitterly. "I know what I saw. Hanna was murdered, and I intend to find who was responsible."

"What did Hanna talk about with Father?" Austin got the same stonewall response as before.

Dale's jaw set, and he got to his feet.

"Don't interfere, little brother. Don't."

Dale stalked from the office before Austin could stop him. Austin settled down in the vacant chair and thought hard. Unfortunately, the more he tried to analyze the problems facing his brother, his father, and Mirach, the less certain he was there was an answer to any of them.

10

AllWorldComm Laboratory
Mirach
16 April 3133

"I'm so pleased you could fit me into your undoubtedly hectic schedule, Ms. Kinsolving," Jerome Parsons said, smiling benignly. "It must be difficult for you, managing such a huge communications conglomerate and then dealing with me."

"I understand your morning was filled with parades and military demonstrations, Excellency," Marta Kinsolving said carefully. Parsons fished for a response from her, and she wasn't sure what he wanted or why. He had left his entourage behind to be entertained by the AWC office staff. She had told her assistant to ply the junior diplomats with as much food and drink as possible and had left any more subtle interrogation in the capable hands of Inger Ryumin. By the look of

Parsons' rotundity, he appreciated gourmet edibles. His staff would likely also be enticed by food, giving her a chance to speak in private with the Envoy.

"Would you care for something to eat? Drink?" she asked.

"Not at all," Parsons said brusquely. "Your R and D facility is quite impressive, Ms. Kinsolving. I see that AWC is a leader in communications theory as well as cutting-edge technology."

"Since the fall of the HPG, we've worked diligently to find profitable ventures," Marta said cautiously. Something about Parsons made her edgy. Lord Governor Sandoval would not send a dull man, and Marta saw great depths to this one, in spite of the overfed, indolent persona Parsons worked so hard to present to the unwary.

"I appreciate that problem. Other worlds endure similar problems."

"We're putting relays on all four moons. Arit, Kalb, and Batn have small units, and the master remote will be on Kuton. This should allow us to cut costs dramatically and increase message traffic tenfold. As odd as it sounds, we used to beam messages through the HPG to other worlds and then relay them back. That proved cheaper and faster than building, orbiting, and maintaining our own commsats. It also kept Mirach-based personnel at a minimum."

"Now you find that sending a simple signal from one side of the planet to the other is difficult." Parsons nodded. "In light of the effects of your sun's proton storms on commsats, relays on your world's moons are an innovative solution."

Marta suspected that Parsons understood most of the advanced technology she had shown him in this underground laboratory. He was also a master of personal relations. The brief exchange at the landing field with her and Dr. Chin had finalized arrangements for this more protracted meeting in a few seconds.

Why? Marta wondered. *Mirach technology must seem primitive to someone of Parsons' stature in the Prefecture.* She had to play out the charade until he revealed his reasons for coming to the AWC facilities.

"That's right," she said. "The advantage of putting our stations on the moons is that their bulk provides shielding against solar flares. We can use off-the-shelf equipment and don't need to do extensive design work," she said. "Would you like to see some of our bolder research projects?" She half turned and saw Parsons had not budged.

"No, Ms. Kinsolving, I don't think so."

"If you are overtired from the Legate's military demonstrations this morning we can—"

"I've asked other leaders of the MBA to join us," he said flatly, without the flowery language he normally used. "I trust I did not overstep my welcome."

"No, I don't mind. How much time have you allotted us? Are you on a tight schedule?" she asked.

"Very," Parsons said. He pushed back the billowy sleeve of his informal shirt and peered at his watch. "They ought to arrive about now. Will you see that they are escorted here? Or do they have standing clearances?"

"My security chief—" Marta started. She stopped in midsentence when she saw Ryumin ushering Chin and Nagursky into the lab.

"What's this about?" demanded Benton Nagursky in his gruff voice. "I'm no errand boy to be ordered about."

"Your Excellency," said Dr. Chin, bowing slightly. "Please excuse our colleague. Mr. Nagursky deals with constant strife at his facilities and it shortens his temper."

Parsons looked questioningly at Marta.

"No one can eavesdrop on us here," she said, guessing his concern. "My best scientists and technicians certify it once a week and also at random intervals."

"What's your business with us?" Nagursky asked bluntly. He was a gruff, intemperate man who looked as if he labored alongside his miners, but he had the golden touch when it came to finances. Nagursky had built a banking empire, then abandoned it to begin what his advisers told him was financial suicide. His rare-earths mining concern had multiplied his fortune a hundred times over. No electronics device on Mirach—or a half dozen other worlds—could be made without the precious elements dug from the ground by the vertically integrated Nagursky Enterprises.

The company owned everything from the claims themselves to the rugged MiningMechs all the way through the smelters to the sales force responsible for getting the best price possible for the rare earths, both on Mirach and beyond.

Marta saw how amused Parsons was by Nagursky's manner. Considering how his morning must have gone with the Legate, such crustiness might be refreshing. She hoped so. Everything about Parsons spoke of a mission—and not one devoted to woolgathering.

"The Lord Governor strives to learn the concerns of all citizens throughout the Prefecture," Parsons said obliquely. He folded his hands on his paunch and smiled like a Buddha, but there was nothing serene in the man's sharp, bright eyes.

"Marta, I've got no time for this kind of chatter. I got miner strikes in Ventrale threatening to spread back closer to home." Nagursky eyed Envoy Parsons with distaste. Nagursky was everything Parsons was not. Dressed as roughly as any of his mining engineers piloting their 'Mechs underground, Nagursky obviously had little appreciation for the finely tailored clothing Jerome Parsons favored. Where Parsons was stout, Nagursky was heavily muscled. Parsons' green eyes met Nagursky's earth brown ones. Neither man blinked.

"You fear attack? From the crowds of the disaffected? Or some less tangible but still potent force?" asked Parsons.

"Since you let the net go down, we don't know which end's up," Nagursky said with his characteristic lack of diplomacy. "Get to the point. I've got a business to run and so do Ms. Kinsolving and Dr. Chin."

"My time is limited," Parsons said, sounding more like Nagursky than a diplomat now. "My immediate mission is to listen."

"Say again?" demanded Nagursky. "You want me to shout at you?"

"If you wish, if that's the way you can best express your problems and how the Lord Governor might solve them," Parsons said. He settled down in a chair at a large table and leaned back slightly, folding his hands on his belly. His eyelids drooped slightly, and it looked as if he might go to sleep. But Marta thought the reverse was about to occur. Parsons was going to remember every word, every nuance, and every single twitch anyone made in the room as if it had been digitally recorded.

"You want to hear what I got to say about the mining business?" Nagursky asked belligerently. Parsons nodded slightly.

Ben Nagursky launched into a detailed description of trade restrictions between Mirach and other worlds in the Prefecture, all engendered by fear. Other planets erected trade barriers because of the loss of communication. Increased JumpShips meant increased risk from invasion, so every planet restricted travel to the detriment of free trade. He went on to describe the economic woes of Mirach and how Sandoval could alleviate them.

Marta listened to Nagursky's tirade with half an ear. She had heard it all before and agreed. She was more interested in studying Parsons. The man bobbed his head now and then, encouraging the MBA director to continue until he sat breathless. Then Parsons urged Dr. Chin to give an overview of food production on Mirach and the impact of the HPG failure on his research.

"So, Your Excellency," Marta said when Boris Chin had said his piece, "how will the Lord Governor aid us? How will he aid Mirach?"

"I am pleased to hear that you do not consider them one and the same, Ms. Kinsolving," Parsons said. "Too many business leaders think their world's destiny is inextricable from their own. I am especially interested to see that you defend your own corporate interests—"

"Those of the MBA members, too," cut in Nagursky. "We're allied for a reason. One for all, all for one."

"How noble," Parsons said dryly. "I see you will defend your collective corporations but do not seem inclined to seize power from the Governor to further your fortunes."

"Our security guards are no match for the Legate's forces," Nagursky said.

"Don't think me a fool, sir," Parsons said. "Each of your three corporations has an IndustrialMech being refitted. While you are correct that they might not prevail, even one modified 'Mech would wreak massive destruction. You know their capabilities. You've got three in your MBA arsenal."

"Four," Marta said, seeing no reason to lie and wondering how much more he knew.

Parsons hesitated, then reached into a pocket. His eyebrows rose slightly as he studied a small paging device. He tucked it back into his pocket.

Marta's heart leaped into her throat. No signal should have penetrated to this Faraday-caged, comm-protected underground room.

"The Legate has invited me to a war game tomorrow, an exercise pitting his best unit against the Governor's First Cossack Lancers. All in good fun, I am sure," Parsons said in his ironically understated manner. "I will be in a better position to make recommendations after I view this military drill."

Jerome Parsons rose, bowed in turn to Chin, Nagursky, and Marta, then asked her, "Would you be so kind as to escort me to where your security chief pummels my staff with questions?"

"Who're you making your recommendations to?" blurted Nagursky.

Parsons faced him, smiled slightly, then said, "To those in the best position to aid you. Good day, sir."

Marta led the way from the room, Parsons trailing behind like a large overdressed balloon. She walked quickly to stay ahead of him until she could drop an impassive mask that covered her turmoil after listening to the Envoy's questions and comments. Parsons was a time bomb waiting to go off.

Whose bomb was he?

= 11 =

Sardanaplus Highlands, 1255 kilometers east of Cingulum
Mirach
17 April 3133

Lady Elora peered over her director's shoulder. Barnaby, small, ratlike, and annoyed at the interference, muttered constantly to himself until she was forced to comment on his errant behavior.

"Should we cover the war games from some other location?" she asked, but got only a grumble for an answer. They were almost a kilometer from the command HQ, only one reporter and one camera operator allowed to interview the Legate and his staff.

She ran her hand over her slender hip sheathed in a shining metallic yellow skirt. The luminous, colored fabric contrasted with the severely cut, darker blue blouse and made her stand out among the camouflaged uniforms of the Legate's staff bustling about around her. They wore composite helmets, while she had done up her rust-colored hair in a loose mist that floated restlessly on the breeze.

"Is Bethany ready for the remote?"

"She's never ready," Barnaby griped. "Too bad about Hanna."

"Keep your mind on business. The Governor and Legate have entrusted the Ministry of Information with showing the full effectiveness of the armed forces."

"That won't stop the rioting," Barnaby said, distracted. "Did you want to power Bethany's mic so early?" he asked. Barnaby looked up at her. Elora started to rebuke him for his attitude, then realized she had been telling him how to do his job. That wouldn't do. Baron Sergio might get the idea she was manipulating the news.

He was weak because he had not reined in her power sooner. Elora had been careful, slowly building a growing monopoly of news gathering and news broadcasting. Incrementalism was the key. Then it was too difficult to do anything about how she worked.

The Ministry of Information needed her, and the people of Mirach needed her even more now that the HPG had cut off their flow of news from other Republic worlds. She was all that stood between them and utter anarchy, thanks to Sergio Ortega's lackluster leadership in matters both diplomatic and economic.

"Don't worry," Barnaby said. "I got a sound level check, since the wind's picking up. Hear any whistle? Feedback? Think we might get dust out on the battleground? If Bethany's hair is mussed, she'll have a fit."

"Battleground," scoffed Elora, looking over Barnaby's shoulder at their camera feed. "This is as stylized as a No play." She glared at Legate Tortorelli and his advisers as they traced patterns on their computer graphics screen, more for Jerome Parsons' benefit than to lay out a real combat scenario. It was all a sham designed to impress the Lord Governor's Envoy, although it had been announced as a farewell exercise for the First Cossack Lancers, before they were swallowed whole by the Legate's forces.

Lady Elora allowed herself a small smile. The purpose of this exercise would change soon enough.

She looked across the gently rolling wooded hills. Spring had brought fitful growth to the ground cover. She couldn't call it grass. It was a strange combination of succulent and spiny vine that blanketed the terrain, giving it a gray-green appearance that played havoc with the color balance on her cameras. Elora picked up small electronic binoculars and scanned the area to find the opposing forces.

"Why are we here?" grumbled Barnaby. "Bread and circuses? You think this will keep all the demonstrators in check?"

"They might take a few minutes out from pillaging to see how effectively the Legate can end their protests, should he decide to do so."

"You want *that* as the opening statement?" asked her director.

"No." Elora panicked a little. "Bethany's got her script. Let her begin when she's ready."

Elora had got so engrossed in studying the landscape, being certain her cameras were properly positioned to cover every detail of the exercise, that she had been thinking out loud.

"She's on," Barnaby said, switching to a remote camera feed of a svelte blond woman dressed in camouflage. "I hope Bethany can remember where the cameras are. She keeps getting the shot wrong."

"The Governor and Envoy are arriving," Elora said, her heart beating a trifle faster. "After her intro, have Bethany interview them," she told Barnaby. From their expressions, she could tell that the Baron and Parsons were not exchanging pleasantries.

"Cutting to the remote," Barnaby said.

"Good afternoon, gentlemen," the reporter said cheerfully. "What are your thoughts on today's war games?"

Sergio Ortega stiffened. "I feel it's a waste of time, money, and effort."

Such bluntness from a politician startled Bethany.

"She's going to blow it. She didn't expect that from the Baron and doesn't know how to follow up," grumbled Barnaby. He worked to feed the reporter new information over her earphone.

"Is it true that today will be the last unit exercise for the First Cossack Lancers? That you are transferring them to Legate Tortorelli's authority, Governor Ortega?"

"Yes," he said, leaving the inexperienced reporter to fumble with another question.

"Envoy Parsons," she said, turning quickly from Sergio, "whom do you expect to win today?"

"Muscles must be tested to be strengthened," Parsons said. "I look forward to a contest where the best unit will prevail."

"How are you betting, Envoy? On the regular forces or the First Cossack Lancers?"

"Ask me afterward," Parsons said, smiling benignly.

Elora sent Barnaby the signal to cut the feed. He transferred the view to cameras darting about the training field, relieving Bethany of the need to pursue her questioning further.

"Are there cameras on the battlefield that can pick up the units commanded by the Baron's sons?" asked

Elora. Barnaby nodded, busy with the work of finding the proper angles and views for the audience.

Elora went to the end of the director's console, dialed in an access code on a comm-unit, and hesitated, taking a minute to reflect on how this would change the balance of power on Mirach. Then she pressed the SEND button.

"What're you doing?" asked Barnaby.

"Nothing to concern you," Elora said lightly. "Just checking on preparedness."

"I can get a cam out anywhere in a quarter-million-hectare field. You don't have to position them yourself."

Elora smiled. He thought she was stealing his thunder as director. Instead, she was delivering thunder. Soon.

"Barnaby, Barnaby," she chided. "You are so conscientious. Don't worry. The day will be yours. The action is out there, not here." She glanced at the knot of politicians watching soldiers running computer simulations on their command computer screens. Elora knew it was better if she remained here, where her duties might be explained, but she couldn't help herself. She had to be in the middle of the action.

"Get me a car. I want to watch the rest of the exercise with the Legate and his staff."

Barnaby grunted, spent a few seconds relaying the request, then pointed as a camera truck rolled up.

"That'll take you to the Legate's command bunker." His relief at getting rid of her was so obvious Elora had to laugh. She chuckled the entire way to Calvilena Tortorelli's post. When things worked well, it meant her careful planning had paid off. The truck slewed to a halt a dozen meters from a guard point and Elora piled out.

Walking with just a small thrust to her hip, she showed her ID to the guard and hurried to the bunker in time to peer over the Legate's shoulder as he moved 3-D computer-generated miniatures of the actual units across a glowing topographic map. Neither Sergio nor Parsons took notice of her. Elora stepped to one side to better watch the Baron.

"You're not directing your troops personally, are you, Legate?" asked Sergio. "You have a complete layout of both sides."

"In an actual fight, this would be what we'd strive for, Baron," Tortorelli said. "This time, the field units are independent. We only monitor the overall progress here, not direct it. Otherwise, the Envoy might miss some of the action."

"Why, yes, wouldn't want to do that," Parsons said. His attention drifted away from the computer display, but Elora couldn't tell what the man sought—or what he was thinking. "It's always good to get the big picture."

"The exercise will begin in a few minutes," Tortorelli said. "Here are the basics. My Home Guard unit is comprised of four Behemoth II Tanks, four Condors, four JES Tactical Missile Carriers, and infantry in APCs. The company of Hauberk battle armor is arrayed at the edges, while the real firepower is massed in the center of my line. The tank initial barrage will flush out opposition, allowing all the battle-armored soldiers to get a fix on opposition locations and numbers. After the intel is gathered, the battle armor advances under covering missile fire and wipes out the FCL."

"What of the infantry? Do they simply sit and send postcards home to their loved ones?" asked Parsons. Elora looked at the man. The comment carried more than a hint of criticism with it. She had tried to find out something of the Envoy's background and had failed. He might or might not be of noble birth, but what was his training? He knew something of tactics—or did he just guess that Tortorelli didn't?

"Support. If the battle armor finds the going too hard, the tanks move in and support an all-out infantry assault. We attack rather than defend the field HQ." Tortorelli looked pleased with himself.

"And the First Cossack Lancers?" asked Parsons. The Envoy leaned forward, craned his neck, and studied how Captain Leclerc positioned his forces.

"They lack tanks, but have a higher percentage of soldiers in battle armor."

"This is a Mobile Tactical HQ?" asked Parsons, pointing to a glowing white star on the top of a small vehicle.

"Manfred Leclerc demanded that he purchase it," Sergio said. "It's a white elephant, if you ask me. Whenever I travel, it has to be loaded onto a transport. Leclerc insists that it arrive before me, so a protective screen can be in place."

"It's a powerful coordinating center in the field," admitted Tortorelli, "but it cannot compare with my dispersed command. Every unit commander is free to act on his or her own to acquire targets and achieve goals set by my field commandant."

"So you require less coordination once the fight starts?" asked Parsons. "An interesting, no, might I say, novel approach. This is not unlike having a dozen vigilante groups thrown onto the field."

"I—" Tortorelli wasn't sure how to answer because of the way Parsons phrased his comment. He swallowed, then said loudly to cover his confusion, "Give the signal for Operation Kaiser to begin!"

Elora stepped forward, a smile on her lips. Her own offensive had begun much earlier.

"This is ridiculous, Dale," Manfred Leclerc said angrily. "You don't belong here. Take off. I'll send the truce signal and—"

"What would you want me to do, Captain? I'm not going to miss the unit's last official mobilization. After today, the FCL is a footnote in history books."

"I know how you feel about the unit," Manfred said, "but you haven't given yourself time enough to come to grips with Hanna's death." He lowered his voice a little as he looked at Austin. "Austin tells me you're not convinced it was an accident."

"They haven't caught the driver yet, and it was a stolen car. Hanna died because—" Dale bit off his words. "I can do my job, Captain Leclerc," Dale said stiffly. "I don't care what you or my brother say."

"Please, Dale," begged Austin, but he saw his brother wasn't going to budge. He certainly didn't blame him. Their father had given the order for the FCL transfer immediately after this exercise.

"It's not that you're incapable, Lieutenant Ortega," Manfred said. He heaved a sigh of resignation. "Get into the TacCom mobile. We'll need to know where they are, since they outnumber us more than two to one in battle armor."

"I'll keep after their tanks, too," Dale said, a slight smile coming to his lips. "I know my job. In fact, no one's better at it."

"Get out of here," Manfred said gruffly. "As to you," he said to Austin, "get into your battle armor!"

"Right away, Captain!" Austin said, snapping a quick salute. He had scant time to get into his Purifier armor. Already dressed in the tight-fitting bodysuit that was slick on the outside and lined with cooling tubes inside, he felt like he was ready to settle into a BattleMech cockpit. But it was only battle armor.

Only.

Austin knew how effective the armor could be when used by expert fighters. He felt confident in his armor but still wished he had a 'Mech around him.

"You ready, Lieutenant?" asked Jurgen, his technician. The man had brought up the mobile loading unit holding the opened battle armor.

"Ready," Austin said, scrambling up, slipping around, and thrusting his legs down into the armor. It fit like a comfortable pair of pants until Jurgen cranked down the fitting mechanism and it collapsed around him from the waist down. Then he worked his way into the torso unit, letting Jurgen guide the breastplate into place.

"Getting feedback on your bodysuit sensors, sir," reported Jurgen, checking his readouts. "All circuits go."

Austin kept adding segments and Jurgen called out approval each time. They didn't rush, but they maintained a steady pace that soon brought Austin to the point of checking his weapons.

Calibration went well, but he chafed at not having real weapons. The rules of engagement today were to shoot blanks, missiles with paint spatter warheads. No energy weapons. Autocannon with paint bullets. All playacting.

"Want to rip off a salvo to make sure your SRMs work, Lieutenant? It's jury-rigged, since I had to disconnect your lasers for this exercise."

Austin stretched, used his HUD to be sure the targeting matched where the missiles would go, then gave Jurgen the thumbs-up.

"Jumppacks good to go, too, sir," Jurgen said.

Myomer muscles straining, Austin moved about, turning, twisting the one-ton battle armor about, and found movement only slightly more restricted than without. "A perfect fit," he told Jurgen.

"Thanks, sir. Go paint those bastards good, for the glory of the First Cossack Lancers!"

Austin smiled, then walked briskly to take his position. The FCL had limited personnel, but he was pleased to see that Master Sergeant Borodin already had the company assembled and psyched for the mock fight.

"Good to see I drew you, Lieutenant," Borodin said. "I hate these so-called exercises. No real missiles, just marker-equipped projectiles. No lasers or PPC, no Gauss rifles. We just throw dye markers at each other and pretend it matters."

"Those are the rules, Master Sergeant," Austin said. Everyone shared this contempt for the rules Legate Tortorelli had posted. And everyone in the FCL knew this was the last time they were likely to work as a unit. No one thought Tortorelli would keep them together after their transfer to his command.

"Captain Leclerc," Austin reported on a command circuit. "Alpha Company ready!"

"Follow the battle plan and we will win!" came Manfred's encouragement. Then the captain keyed into Austin's private channel. "Don't worry about Dale," Manfred said. "He can keep things humming along in the TacCom. I'm taking a Shandra out and will relay back what I can see. From what I've seen so far, Tortorelli's so-called tactics make me think he fielded the wrong units."

"What have you spotted, Captain?" Austin heard the private circuit click to the officer command channel again. What Manfred said now went to all four of the company commanders.

"No energy weapons," said Manfred, "means their Condor tanks with SRMs are going to give us the most trouble. The Condors are fast. The Behemoths would be better used against defensive positions, and we are staying mobile."

"The Behemoths might stand off and saturate an area with missiles," suggested Lieutenant Newell, commanding Beta Company.

"Get in close enough and they're scrap metal," Manfred said.

"He'll oppose us with his Condors. They have speed on us, but I doubt he can mount a unified attack. And Tortorelli favors putting his Hauberk battle armor company out with his regular infantry. Aim for the support vehicles as we move. Alpha will go straight up the center and draw fire. Beta supports. Delta and Gamma go in from left and right flanks respectively. Updated field maps will be sent to you through the TacCom as we learn Tortorelli's deployment."

"Advance as fast as possible," Austin relayed to Borodin. "Count off. By alternate numbers move forward. No retreat."

"Got it, sir. We're the cannon fodder."

"Where better to be than in the middle of the battle, Master Sergeant? I expect Alpha Company to take out the enemy command and end the fight before Tortorelli's computer screen can refresh!"

Austin heard a cheer go up from Alpha Company. They were psyched; they were ready. He had one last question to ask of Manfred. He keyed his open channel.

"Who's in command of the opposition, sir?" asked Austin. "I tried to pick up some scuttlebutt, but nobody knew."

"I couldn't find out, either, so he might put each unit commander in charge of a specific attack zone. That means he's not going to coordinate well. We'll find out quick enough."

"Crazy command structure," Austin said.

"TacCom, do you read?" asked Manfred. "Close that rear hatch!"

"Loud and clear, Captain," came Dale's voice. "Getting everything squared away. Wait, there it is. We got the word to begin. I'm picking up four Behemoths. Don't know if they'll start a barrage, but if we advance fast, we'll reach them before they can get their Condors into position. Located their HQ immediately behind the Behemoths!"

Austin's HUD blazed with a tiny white star showing their target. Smaller green dots moved about as Dale relayed current tactical information.

"I'm off in the Shandra. Give me an IFF code. Good, TacCom. To victory!" cried Manfred Leclerc.

"All right, you apes," Austin barked on the Alpha channel. "Light those Jumppacks and let's move. We bypass enemy heavies and engage only targets light enough to take out without much fight. We create confusion and diversion, but we go for their HQ! Got it?"

Austin got the response he wanted from his company. They were veterans and had more time in service than he did, but every last soldier knew he was good in the simulator, BattleMech or battle armor, and had practiced enough personally with the entire company in full battle gear to weld them into a single fighting unit. Even better, he had Borodin as company sergeant.

The Jumppack kicked him forward. Austin took to the air, skimming along only a meter above the greasy, spiny grass, his feet kicking hard every time he alighted. Behind came four squads, arrayed in a line, advancing alternately so those behind could cover those in front.

"Double-check weapons as we advance," he ordered. He worried that there might be equipment failure since the Purifier armor had been refitted with the missiles. SRMs were good for much of the First Cossack Lancers' mission. They warded off civilian vehicles, should anyone be foolish enough to try to take out the Governor with a truck or car bomb. But Austin preferred the lasers usually mounted on Purifier battle armor.

The FCL had their plastic warheads loaded with neon-pink dye. A splash on a tank meant little; on a battle-armored soldier a full salvo from an entire squad signified death.

All he had to do was avoid the bright orange dye fired by the Legate's soldiers. Which proved easy as Alpha advanced at a steady ten kilometers per hour.

Already, his unit's furious advance had bypassed the lead units of Hauberk-battle-armor-clad enemy. The Legate's soldiers milled around, confused about what to do as their enemy flashed past them, firing jets at max and not engaging, only shooting on the fly.

"Left, Lieutenant," came Borodin's warning. Austin twisted slightly, keeping his thrust vector on the target, and saw a Hoverbike.

"How many of them are there?"

"Six. I see six of 'em all clumped together."

Austin confirmed it on his map display glowing in front of him.

"Fire!" Even as Austin barked the order, he centered his sights and loosed a barrage of two missiles from his own launcher. The rockets snaked away, leaving behind faint dark exhaust trails. Dozens more joined his as his company followed the order.

Bright pink paint splatted all over the six Hoverbikes, signifying kills. Why Tortorelli's commander had sent them out in a tight formation was beyond Austin's imagining. The Hoverbikes were best used to report on enemy movement. These were worthless now to even radio back a warning about the quickstep advance of a battle-armored company.

"Good shooting," Austin congratulated. He cycled in another rack of SRMs as he hunted for new targets. All the while he pushed forward, one eye on the terrain and the other on his display. A constant flood of intel from scouts reached him, but Austin knew his company was supplying a good deal of it. They met less resistance than anticipated and pushed farther, faster, than the other companies. Even Beta Company following in his wake had a hard time keeping up, and all Lieutenant Newell had to do was to mop up as he came.

"Sir, we're gettin' mighty close to the big tanks," said Borodin.

Austin did a quick range check and relayed it to TacCom.

"All weapons ready," Austin ordered. He couldn't believe they were going to cripple the entire opposing force so easily. A simple, single knife thrust through the center and Tortorelli's battle group would fold.

"Heavy fighting on the perimeter," came Dale's calm voice. "Captain Leclerc's been taken out by a lance of battle armor."

"Hardly any resistance in the belly," Austin reported.

"Rip 'er open," Dale said, eagerness tingeing his words now.

They might have lost their commander, but the battle would be theirs.

"Scouts, check our six," Austin ordered. "I don't want to jet into a trap." This was too easy. Far too easy. "Report!"

"Picking up phantom returns on radar," came the hindmost trooper's report. "Might be a Condor going for the TacCom."

"Anything else?"

Austin watched as his screen filled with indications of the Hauberk escorts on slower moving infantry clustered near APCs.

"We're in range in three, in two, in one—fire, fire, fire!"

Austin hit the ground, braced himself, and revectored so he would sail higher into the air. He saw two Behemoth tanks ahead. His SRMs lashed out, spewing their harmless pink dye over heavy armor, cannon barrels, LRM launchers, and even incautious crews poking heads from turrets.

"Got mine!" came the first report. "Mine, too," came a second.

Austin cut his Jumppack, landed at a run, got his balance, then launched again. The second Behemoth was less than a hundred meters off. Two rockets pounded it. Two more followed and his launcher ran dry of reloads.

As he came down on the far side of the jump parabola, he twisted about and saw a Condor tank jacked into high gear coming back fast. Austin got off a single barrage and missed as he dropped down.

"Condor on the way. Missed it. Someone else in position take it out? Lieutenant Newell?"

"Sorry, Lieutenant," said Borodin. "I think Newell's entire company got caught. One of the Behemoths we didn't target fired into Beta."

"Dale," he called. "Feed me battle assessment update. We're close." He got a faint reply with a considerable amount of dropout.

"We're taking it to them, Austin," he heard. Dale

chuckled. "We sustained losses along our perimeters, but your attack crippled them good. After their first assault, even our perimeter's holding, but most of Beta is gone, survivors trying to regroup. I'll send a demand for surrender. We've lost a quarter of our force, most of them in Beta."

Austin's company had taken out three of the enemy's heavy tanks. As far as he could tell, the Behemoths had lobbed only a few rounds, but they had been devastating.

"Dale, I'm still getting reports of a Condor bearing down on TacCom."

"I'm picking it up. Barkhausen's Delta Company is sweeping across to intercept." Dale's voice faded for a moment and then Austin heard his brother yell, "Get this thing into gear and get us out of range! The tank's going to fire! It—"

Austin staggered as a tremendous explosion filled his earphones and then an instant later rocked the battlefield. Four more detonations followed in rapid succession, as if a tank barrage had gone off—shells with high-explosive warheads.

12

Austin blinked, and for a moment he thought he saw his brother. Before he could force his lips to call out Dale's name, the apparition spoke in an emotion-choked voice.

"Austin, you're all right!"

"Father!" To Austin's ears his cry came out a dull, distant croak, but it was enough for the Governor to understand him.

"Don't exert yourself," Sergio Ortega said.

Austin forced himself to reconstruct what had occurred. He had been leading his company to a quick victory. The enemy HQ was exposed, open after they had taken out the defending Behemoth tanks. He remembered the report of a Condor tank racing for the TacCom where Dale had been. Then an explosion. Austin blinked.

The explosion still rang in his ears. The next thing he remembered was racing back to find the TacCom a smoking ruin. Dale was dead.

The Condor had fired three salvos from Arbalest LRM 15s. The last had been composed of live rounds.

"He's dead, Father. Dale was blown up. They weren't supposed to use live rounds!"

"The instant it was reported, Tortorelli stopped the games," Sergio said, "and I came out in a command car with him." The baron looked even older than he had before. "He's gone, Austin. Dale's dead. There's no question." Sergio turned from him to hide tears.

"Lieutenant," Austin's technician said, "you're still in armor."

Austin let Jurgen help him from his battle armor. He felt a numbness more of mind than of body even after he popped free and stood in his bodysuit beside his father.

"I should never have agreed to this," Sergio said dully, looking toward the plume of smoke from the wreckage. "There *has* to be some other method for solving our problems if even a simple exercise can go so badly wrong. I lost my son to a *game*!"

"Governor, you have my deepest sympathy. I don't know what could have happened. But it's a training misadventure, a terrible mishap. No one's to blame." Legate Tortorelli puffed himself up and tried to look in control. He didn't succeed.

"An accident, Legate, a sad, tragic accident that robbed us of a young officer with a bright future," chimed in Lady Elora. "Lieutenant Ortega will be sorely missed. With your permission, Governor Ortega, the Ministry of Information will produce and air a full hour special in tribute to your gallant son."

Austin moved from them and went to the edge of a cliff. The battlefield was full of such tactical challenges, all the better for training and preparation. Now the challenge had turned deadly. The TacCom had been blown over the edge. If the broadside strike of all fifteen missiles hadn't killed everyone in the Tac-Com instantly, the fall down the fifteen-meter drop would have. Dizziness hit him like a hammer; then, after a moment, he got his bearings again. People moved around him, but he stood in a bubble. Austin felt as if he had stepped into a graveyard. Everyone stood stock-still, silent, staring at him like a bug under a microscope until Lady Elora spoke.

"How does it feel to see your brother killed in such a tragic fashion, Lieutenant Ortega?" She stepped closer and bent slightly. He caught a hint of her gardenia-scented perfume and it caused a new wave of dizziness. How dare she ask such a question? Austin wanted to reach out and throttle her, but with her cameras and microphones trained on him, he simply stared at her, willing her away from him.

"We will interview you later for the tribute," Elora said. Austin walked back to his father's side.

"As of this instant, Legate," Sergio said, "the First Cossack Lancers is assigned your command. The sooner all trace of it is gone from my life, the better."

"Governor Ortega," Tortorelli was saying, bowing slightly. His eyes gleamed with the newfound power. "Rest assured, this unit will hold a place of honor among the others and will always be at your service, whenever you need it."

"I won't need it," Sergio said flatly.

Austin's first thought was that his father needed protection now more than ever, but knew that such an argument would never fly. He tried a different approach.

"Father, Dale wouldn't have wanted the FCL to be transferred," he said. "Keep it in his memory, his honor." Austin saw the set to his father's jaw and knew the answer. There had been little chance before the exercise that he was going to relent. There was none now.

"The sight of their uniforms would remind me of Dale," Sergio said. "I want to return to the Palace. Will you join me, Austin?"

"Soon, Father," he said. "Let me say good-bye." He let his gaze drift in the direction of the wreckage.

"Very well," Sergio said, walking off stiffly.

Austin skirted the area Elora had marked off for her own use. She had pushed aside her newscaster and was doing the report herself. Austin couldn't bear to listen.

With the words "tragic" and "misadventure" ringing in his ears, Austin stumbled away and found the Shandra Manfred Leclerc had ridden during the war games. He quickly swung into the seat, keyed the machine to life, and roared off in the direction of the Condor tank that had destroyed Dale, the TacCom, and its other seven occupants.

The warm air rushing past his face drove away some of the fog of shock and left Austin more determined by the minute. The dull disk of the distant sun caressed him with lukewarm ruby rays and stole away the aches and pains he had accumulated during the exercise. But nothing took away the pain of losing his brother.

Dale was no longer here. Dale's strength, his good humor, his carefree outlook, were all gone. Forever and ever gone.

Shock drained from him, replaced by poison that

burned at his brain and gut. Hanna had been killed. So had Dale. Austin had to find out why. The faster he drove the scout vehicle, the more determined he became. He had been too intent on taking out the tanks during the battle to know what was really going on all around him. This curious tunnel vision, this intensity of purpose, now focused itself on finding the driver who had fired on Dale and killed him.

Austin found it easy to locate the Condor tank. It was parked less than a hundred meters from where the TacCom had crashed. Infantry soldiers milled around the Condor, standing near a woman who had flung away her helmet and shook her head, as if denying the world existed.

"You, you were the tank commander!" he shouted. Austin braked, throwing up a curtain of dirt from the twenty-five-ton vehicle's wheels, and dived from the Shandra. His fists balled and he was ready to hit the woman until she looked up and he saw her haggard, tortured face. He stopped and stared. He had not thought anyone could be more disturbed by Dale's death than he was. Austin slowly relaxed his fists.

The woman—a sergeant from her insignia—was pale and her hands shook as she wiped dirt from her face. Tears welled but did not run down her cheeks. Austin had seen others in this condition. The tanker was in shock.

As he had been.

"You fired the LRMs?"

"I didn't know I had live rounds loaded."

"They said an entire barrage was tipped with high-explosive warheads," Austin said. He stepped closer. She recoiled, then stiffened, standing her ground.

"I didn't know!" She tried to speak in a level voice but strain caused it to break. "I fired what was loaded.

I thought they were marker rounds. Believe me. Please, Lieutenant!"

"What happened? Who loaded your tank?"

The sergeant's shoulders hunched over and she began shaking in reaction. "I don't know. Crew back at the depot. Somebody. There was a last-minute check before the exercise, and a rack was replaced. That's all I know."

"Leave her alone," said an infantry corporal. He interposed himself between the sergeant and Austin.

"Do you know who loaded the live rounds?"

"It was a mistake. A bad one, but there's nothing anyone can do about it now. Go on. Get out of here. Sir."

Austin felt a hot flush rising to his cheeks. He had lost his brother. He wouldn't be ordered about, not by an infantry noncom. Then he saw the sergeant and knew none of them had purposely caused Dale's death. It had been exactly as they said.

A tragic accident.

Austin thought it was more.

13

Palace of Facets, Cingulum
Mirach
25 April 3133

Austin Ortega stood stiffly in the doorway of his father's office, feeling out of place. The past week had gone by in unreal jerks and starts, stretched like it had been a million years long and, confusingly, blinked by in only a few fleeting hours. Dale's full state funeral had been more of a public spectacle than a tribute, but Austin knew it had been necessary. Dale had been heir apparent.

The funeral had been about Dale's status and something more. In a split second *Austin* was in line to become Baron. Only when he was much younger had he considered stepping up to become Baron one day, but with Dale filling his world that had never been more than a childhood game. Now it was likely.

It seemed especially likely to occur soon when he looked at the Baron. Sergio Ortega had aged a dozen years in the past week and looked a shadow of his former self. Austin's father had worked through his shock and had done what rituals were necessary at the funeral at great cost to his physical well-being. Austin didn't know if it was better having Envoy Parsons delay his departure until after the funeral or not. What report about Mirach would he take back to the Lord Governor? In spite of the chance it was entirely negative, Austin found it hard to work up much curiosity about it. Jerome Parsons had come and gone, his mission cloaked in mystery. How it affected Mirach mattered less to Austin than finding who had substituted live rounds during the exercise.

Austin's mind turned over the shards of what he knew. Up and down the line it looked like a mistake. A tragic mistake. But he had assured Dale that Hanna's death was only "a tragic accident." Austin understood why his brother had been so reluctant to believe that. There was logic and there was a gut feeling that refused to yield to mere facts.

Dale's death had to be more. That meant Hanna's was, also.

Austin had tried to get his father to tell him what Hanna Leong had spoken about during their meeting, but the Baron had built a wall around himself and often went off alone. With the FCL under Tortorelli's command now, Austin found himself cut off from yet another source of information. Before, he could have asked the Baron's bodyguard where Sergio went, who he saw, what he did. Such information was always confidential, but he could have eased it out of the guards, being a fellow member of the FCL, as well as Baronet.

Heir apparent. Alone.

It bothered him how Manfred Leclerc had paid his respects at Dale's funeral and then not been seen since. All alone.

The Governor's secretary motioned to him from the Armorer's Chamber.

"They're ready for you, Father," Austin said.

"It's too bad you can't conduct the news conference for me," Sergio said, heaving himself to his feet, "but that wouldn't do. I'm Governor." The way he spoke made Austin feel as though the weight of a world crushing his father down might cause him to relinquish that duty soon.

"I would if I could," Austin said, "but they want *you* to speak to them. Lady Elora has the public more upset than they had been."

"More rioting. I need to speak to the labor leaders. And that Kinsolving woman. You can do that, Austin." Sergio preceded his son from the office and moved like he was pulled by a string to the conference room where the Ministry of Information and other, lesser news companies had set up cameras for the first formal interview since the funeral.

Sergio stepped forward, cleared his throat, and began, assuming the reporters were ready—or perhaps not caring.

"After the sad events of the past week, it is time to forge ahead with solutions to the economic problems facing Mirach. Envoy Parsons has given us hope of aid from The Republic, but it is our responsibility to begin the road to recovery without external assistance."

Austin wasn't sure if he felt at ease with Marta Kinsolving and other members of the Mirach Business Association joining his father in the press conference. After his father's brief introduction, Elora gave Marta and the others far more coverage—Austin could tell by looking past Lady Elora to where her seedy director sat at a console. Small vidscreens monitored each camera in the room before relaying a combined multiphase signal to the broadcast studio at the Ministry of Information. For every minute on-air Elora accorded the Governor, she gave three to the MBA officials, as if they were of equal rank and had more important things to say.

If Sergio said something, Elora cut to Benton Nagursky for a reaction shot. If Marta took the center stage, Elora did not cut away. Austin found himself wishing he could speak with his father's advisers and somehow edge Elora out of her coverage. Her position as Minister made this difficult, but Austin wanted to try. He had suggested her removal to his father and had hit a stone wall, as if nothing could be changed now. But it had.

Heir apparent to the governorship of Mirach, Baronet Austin Ortega. He took a deep breath and knew he had to develop his own staff and governing style.

"As a result of the transfer of my personal guard to Legate Tortorelli's command," Sergio Ortega said, catching Austin's eye and bringing his attention back to the crowded office and the reason for the conference, "money in the Governor's budget has been freed. With Ms. Kinsolving and the cooperation of the Mirach Business Association, we have devised a bold plan to use Mirach's four moons as communications relay points. This will link every point on-planet with any other within seconds. The HPG net might have gone down between planets in The Republic, but we will not be denied rapid, dependable communications.

"Ms. Kinsolving," Sergio said as he turned the mic over to the auburn-haired CEO of AllWorldComm.

"The funding," Marta Kinsolving said forcefully, "will be adequate to establish the first-ever planetary comm net for Mirach." She began to detail the reasons, the costs, and the technology, but Austin found himself interested more in the woman than in her speech. Marta wasn't a beautiful woman, but her energy and determination held his attention. He decided it had to do with the confidence she exuded, as much in herself as in the project. By fully funding AllWorld-Comm to run what Marta called Span-net, the Governor had given her a preeminent position among the members of the MBA.

If she hadn't already been atop that heap. Austin saw how Boris Chin deferred to her and even bellicose Benton Nagursky often yielded the microphone to Marta as questions came from the reporters about MBA participation and the hope for new jobs planetwide.

Austin began to wonder about the MBA and what political aspirations its members had. He knew next to nothing about the ancient, translucent-skinned Dr. Chin other than he was a respected, often brilliant plant genetics researcher, but Ben Nagursky had a reputation for ruthlessness and removing anyone who stood in his way. For Marta Kinsolving to run with these wolves, she had to be equally brilliant—and merciless. This thought set off a chain reaction in his head that led back to Dale's death.

Someone had purposefully mislabeled the deadly missiles, and he doubted it was any of Tortorelli's command. Gaining control of the FCL was quite a coup for Calvilena Tortorelli, but it had been announced and seemed less of a motive than Marta Kinsolving's. She, her company, and the MBA were profiting handsomely. The money to finance her Span-net could have been tied up in legislative session for another year if Sergio had not seen fit to push through the appropriations. She, or AWC, certainly profited both mightily and quickly. But Dale's death had not been linked to this. Austin frowned as he worried over motives.

An angry whisper drew his attention away from Marta to Lady Elora. She chewed out her director for missing some small detail in a camera angle. The Minister of Information had benefited from covering the war games and Dale's subsequent death. The news had become the top-rated show on the air, and along with the growing audience came Elora's new and less subtle jibes about the Governor and his ability to rule—his inability to rule. There had been scattered riots in other cities since Dale died, but Austin knew that it was only a matter of time before the cork popped. He felt tensions mounting whenever he went into Cingulum. Elora urged the people to test the boundaries of the law to find out if The Republic and its rulers were still best for the people of Mirach.

Austin couldn't tell what had sparked Elora's wrath, but the director wilted under it. Barnaby worked frantically to alter settings, to move cameras around, and finally to send the full transmission back to the Ministry of Information.

Final statements were read and the news conference wound down when his father said, "Thank you, Ms. Kinsolving. We look forward to the near future—the very near future—of virtually instantaneous communication." The small crowd of reporters erupted with questions, but Sergio said decisively, "We have no further comments. Thank you all."

Sergio left the impression that Span-net was better than the HPG, although Austin knew that wasn't possible. But he wondered if the AWC project would bypass Lady Elora and the stranglehold she had gained on the dissemination of news.

"Son," Sergio said to him as he started toward the door, "I've got a cabinet meeting. It's always the Ventrale Coalition that gives me headaches and this time is no different. See to the matter we discussed, will you?"

Before Austin could do more than nod, his father rushed off, talking earnestly with his Minister of Mining and Energy. Austin stepped back and let Elora's crew carry their equipment out. They were gone in less than five minutes. Marta remained behind, huddled with Nagursky and Chin.

"My father's going to be in the cabinet meeting for some time," Austin told them, thinking they were waiting to see the Governor.

"We have nothing more to do here. Thank you, Baronet," Dr. Chin said, bowing the barest amount in Austin's direction. Nagursky grunted as if someone had poked him in the belly, jerked his head in the direction of the door, and left with the aging geneticist. Marta leafed through a stack of papers, put them into a folder, and started to leave.

Austin hesitated, then stepped forward. "Is there any way I can help out?" he asked.

Marta's eyebrows arched. Her brown eyes fixed on him.

"I can handle my own paperwork, thank you."

"You promised me a tour of AWC while we waited for Envoy Parsons at the DropShip field." Austin saw her heave a deep sigh of resignation; then she smiled.

"I'm sorry. I didn't mean to appear so reluctant. It's just that my time's being eaten by the Span-net project. Work piles up when I'm not at my desk digging away at it. And of course, there's hardly been time for you, has there? I'm sorry for your loss."

Austin thought she sounded sincere but wasn't sure he should take her at her word. He moved through dangerous minefields and didn't know friend from foe.

"Thank you," he said. "Your earliest convenience would suit me."

"Is your father assigning you as liaison on the Span-net project?"

"I'm doing all I can to take some of the load off his shoulders," Austin answered.

"Come along now if you can get away. I have to check the labs to be certain all the fine gadgets I just promised can be manufactured and delivered on time."

As they walked down the long corridor running the length of the office wing of the Palace of Facets, Austin was aware of eyes on them. Without being too obvious, he caught sight of several soldiers clad in the forest green of Tortorelli's Home Guard trying not to be seen as they spied. Austin wasn't sure if he was pleased that the Legate had assigned guards to the Palace. Why were they acting more like snoops than as guards?

Austin and Marta stepped out the west door into the breezy afternoon. The sun was setting, a huge gravid red blob on the hazy horizon. Clouds had moved in off the ocean and promised rain, but at this time of year Austin knew those clouds probably lied. Cingulum wouldn't see significant rainfall until the monsoon season began in the fall.

"I'll order a car and—" he began.

"You can ride with me. It's a company car," Marta said.

Austin swallowed. The sleekly aerodynamic white

limo looked as if it were a block long with enough room in the rear for everyone in the Palace. A door opened silently and Marta ducked in. Austin followed, to settle down opposite her in a soft leather seat that was almost sinfully comfortable.

"I'm more used to the cockpit of a BattleMech." He saw her sharp reaction. "I meant the BattleMech simulator," Austin hurriedly amended. It's made by AWC, isn't it?"

"Made by one of our units. There's not much call for them anymore." Marta relaxed a little, but Austin saw he had thrown her off stride.

"Tell me about Span-net. Will it really replace the HPG?"

"Of course not," Marta said, still guarded. "We will gain almost instantaneous person-to-person contact, though. All comm now goes through a few choke points at ground-based relays."

Austin almost added, "Monitored by the Ministry of Information," but refrained. He heard this in Marta's description even if she didn't say it straightforwardly.

"Span-net will go around those bottlenecks?" he asked.

"To one of the four moon stations, then back. With a network of relays on-world as well as in orbit, we can handle a millionfold more traffic than the current system, permitting personal video comm as well as commercial content, all in a single handset."

"Will Lady Elora permit this?"

"She might be Minister of Information but she has no say-so over private industry. With your father's blessing—and funding—the Ministry of Information will be relegated to a lesser role than it enjoys now."

Austin leaned back and wiggled a little in the soft leather as he considered this. After the announcement today, AWC would become the target of Lady Elora's propaganda if Marta did not move swiftly to get the necessary equipment in place.

"It will revolutionize communications on Mirach," Marta said.

"But it's not HPG," Austin said.

"No," Marta said, her tone a little more hostile than before. "Since we can't depend on The Republic, we'll rely on our own technology. Span-net will *not* fail the way the HPG did."

After such a bold statement and one reflecting what she thought of The Republic, Marta fell into generalized statements, stolen more from a PR campaign. Austin was glad he had glimpsed, if only for a moment, Marta's true feelings.

She was no supporter of The Republic. Did that mean she would sell out the Governor, given the chance? Where did her allegiance lie? Austin thought Jacob Bannson was a possible candidate. Bannson would approach entrepreneurs, being one himself, and he had asked Sergio to consider a trading post. Perhaps the Governor moved too slowly and Bannson sought another foothold on Mirach, using the MBA.

Austin knew he was only guessing. But he would find that out, for the good of Mirach, just as he'd find out if Marta Kinsolving had anything to do with Dale's death, for his own peace of mind.

═══ **14** ═══

Ministry of Information, Cingulum
Mirach
25 April 3133

Lady Elora's face glowed in phosphorescent green light as she hunched over her desk in the windowless office. Half a dozen monitors winked on and off around her, each responsive to her silent command. There was space on the desktop for writing or spreading out documents, but the rest was a gently banked surface covered with vidscreens and controls that allowed her to tap into any feed from any camera sent out by the Ministry, to observe and edit or spy. Her long, bony fingers danced over the controls, shifting restlessly from one view to the next. Nothing transpired in the Ministry of Information without her approval and overview.

In spite of such tight control, Elora still felt neglected, out of the loop, talked about behind her back by her inferiors. Sitting in her sparse room, she could toil over her spy equipment and compile a list of those who opposed her. And it was such a long list.

She hesitated when a screen showed Legate Tortorelli with three aides—she knew they were bodyguards rather than advisers because Ministry sensors revealed their sheathed weapons as surely as if they were carried in plain sight—bustling along the hallway two levels below her office. The Legate had breezed through security at street level and was on his way to see her, reaching the foot of the restricted-access escalator coming directly to the top floor of the Ministry Tower, where Elora built her electronic nest.

"Let the Legate in," she said, her index finger lightly brushing across a pressure switch. "Keep his guards in the reception area."

She received no response and had expected none. Her staff was capable, except when it came to complex tasks. She still fumed that Hanna Leong had gone missing for the better part of two days before she had been permanently removed. Where *had* she been? Or did it matter, now that Dale Ortega was gone, too?

Such thorny questions stalked her waking moments.

Elora took a deep breath, then let it out slowly. It was time to prepare for the Legate's unannounced visit.

Quick fingers worked over the controls, causing screens to vanish silently into the surface of her desk, leaving behind only faint seams to betray the hidden monitors. A single vidscreen showing the current Ministry newscast remained visible at one side of her desk. Elora leaned back in her chair, pushing aside the feeling of nakedness. So much happened when she wasn't personally monitoring it, guiding it, exploiting it.

This was the price of dealing with Calvilena Tortorelli. He was a bothersome but necessary evil.

Her office door whispered open, and the portly Legate bustled in.

"Calvy!" she greeted with false bonhomie. "So glad you stopped by."

"Elora," the Legate said, sounding frightened. She guessed he was not happy having his bodyguards detained two stories below. "Forgive me for not calling ahead, but matters have been churning about me so. Terrible things, simply terrible!"

"Please, sit down. I—" Lady Elora recoiled when Tortorelli interrupted her.

"Is this room secure?"

"Yes, it is," she said carefully. "What's wrong?"

"No windows?" he asked. "You're on the top floor of a fifty-story building and you don't have any windows?"

"Security risks, Calvy. You know that. A laser shining against a glass pane turns the window into a microphone transmitting for everyone to hear."

"What I wish to discuss is highly sensitive. Highly."

"I live by the credo that walls have ears, Calvy," she said, beginning to wonder what was so important. Whatever it was, it clearly frightened him.

"What I have stumbled across must be kept in the strictest confidence. If anyone else learned what I have uncovered, well, let's say Mirach would be damaged severely."

Elora considered what this might be and decided she had to divert him, if the Legate brought her the information she suspected from his behavior.

"Tell me, Calvy. You know I can keep a secret."

"Baronet Dale's death," he said in a husky whisper. "It wasn't accidental."

"Calvy, *you* assassinated the Baronet?" she said with mock surprise.

"What are you saying, woman? No, no, not me. But I found the man who substituted the live missiles. A security camera recorded him. He wasn't in my service and he certainly was not in the FCL."

Elora said nothing about the haphazard way Tortorelli had planned the war games and how he had spread authority over too many junior commanders. What bothered her was how the assassin had been caught in the act on camera.

"You've arrested him? Turned him over to the Baron? No, he should go to the civil authorities," she said.

"He vanished, Elora. Gone. Like smoke. But the Baron will think I knew about it."

"Who else knows?" she asked. "Of the pictures and the assassin?"

"A handful of technicians. And their commander."

"Scatter them around the planet, Calvy," she said. "Transfer them and keep them separated. Promote the officer; make it a staff position where you can watch him. You dare not let a hint of this get out."

"But I don't know who he is. Was. Oh, Elora, this is a nightmare!"

"One easily handled by an experienced commander such as yourself," Elora said soothingly. She considered how difficult it would be to remove all the witnesses, and decided eliminating one careless employee was better than creating questions over the death of half a squad in the Home Guard.

"I should tell the Baron. I had nothing to do with this, he needs to know, and that other son of his keeps asking questions."

This signed the assassin's death warrant. Elora

didn't know how it would be done, but it had to be done soon. And it would.

"Would Sergio be better off if you went to him? I think there might be more to the Baronet's death than you think, Calvy. See what I've uncovered?"

She touched a spot on the surface of the desk. The small screen at the corner of her desk turned toward the Legate like a radar unit seeking its target. "This was recorded after the Baron's news conference by accident and might shed light on whom the assassin works for. We were doing a feature on industries vital to Mirach. Of course, I had to do a significant portion on AllWorldComm."

"Of course," Tortorelli said, squinting at the screen, trying to figure out what he was seeing.

"Ms. Kinsolving and Austin Ortega earlier today were touring the AWC assembly area when this was recorded."

Her Ministry's best technicians had spent long hours putting this snippet together to garner the maximum effect.

"I'm no expert, mind you," Elora said slowly, "but it sounds as if they are discussing the political stability of Mirach and that Ms. Kinsolving is disparaging your attempts to maintain order."

"Why, I—" Tortorelli sputtered a bit. "It does sound that way. She's almost advocating outright rebellion! And to the Governor's own son!"

"Austin is a bit naive when it comes to sedition," Elora said. "Or perhaps not. After all, who has benefited most from Dale Ortega's death?"

"Baronet Austin is next in line of succession," Tortorelli said, reaching the conclusion Elora wanted. "But that was his own brother!"

"Ambition knows no bounds," Elora said. "He *was*

on the battlefield and could have aided the assassin in getting to the LRMs. And he certainly knew where the TacCom was every instant of the exercise."

"But his own brother!" exclaimed Tortorelli.

"This discussion might be innocent. As I said, this is only a tiny portion of their long conversation."

"The Governor must be told of this immediately. Send a copy to—"

"Please, Calvy," Elora said, motioning him to silence. She let him stew a few seconds before continuing. "I'm not sure alerting Baron Ortega is the proper thing to do. If his son hasn't mentioned how the AWC and probably the MBA are conniving, or at least criticizing, behind his back, I'm not sure it is our place to do so. And we have no proof of anything more. Such as fratricide."

Elora paused again, as if considering what more to say.

"What is it, Elora? There's something you're not telling me."

"The MBA has refitted IndustrialMechs," she said bluntly. "To protect their property, they say. Those infernal devices can be turned against the rioters—or legitimate military forces."

"Then it might be rebellion?" Legate Tortorelli looked stunned. "It all makes sense. The MBA uses their 'Mechs against my forces to gain power. If the Baron resists, they kill him and install the Baronet."

"But we can't prove it, and to say a word to the Baron might endanger us all."

"No! I have the forces to fight even refitted IndustrialMechs. It would be a fearsome battle, but they won't seize power that way!"

"You're the commander to do it, Calvy. You have experience fighting against BattleMechs off-world. But

15

HQ of the Legate
Mirach
26 April 3133

"**E**mergency meeting," barked a colonel. "Hurry up!"

Manfred Leclerc turned and looked to the officer, thinking the order had been addressed to him. A half dozen senior officers walked quickly to the elevator at the end of the hall, flashed their passes to the guard, and were admitted in threes and fours. The rest waited impatiently for the express elevator to go to the Legate's briefing room and then return for them. Manfred joined the small knot of officers waiting to be whisked forty stories up to hear what Tortorelli had to say.

Another officer, an infantry major, turned and looked at Manfred, giving him the once over from boots to collar insignia. His gaze stopped there.

"You're not required to be at the meeting, Captain," the major said.

Manfred looked around, thinking the officer spoke to someone else. When he realized he was being addressed, he said, "I'm senior officer, First Cossack Lancers. Unless there's some reason, I should be in on the briefing."

The major and three others showed their IDs to the guard sergeant. Manfred followed, only to have the guard thrust out a hand and gently push him back.

"Sorry, sir, not you. Your clearance isn't sufficient."

The infantry major flashed Manfred a nasty grin as the doors hissed shut and the elevator launched itself for the conference room.

"Who's supposed to attend? I just transferred in."

"I know, Captain Leclerc." The guard was an immovable object.

Manfred backed off. He didn't like the noncom touching him the way he had, but the sergeant was only following orders. That didn't make Manfred feel any better. The Mirach security force was small, considering the size of the population, and the addition of the FCL significantly augmented the military's power.

He knew better than to make a scene. Instead, he found a desk and settled down behind it as if he belonged there. Less than an hour later, the elevator doors opened and began disgorging the officers who had attended the Legate's emergency conference.

Manfred pretended to be hard at work on a stack of papers, but he never even read what they were. His full attention fixed on the loose-lipped officers. He kept from grinning when the infantry major stopped not a meter away to talk with a tank commander.

"I tell you, Captain," the major said to the woman. "You'll have every last one of your Behemoths in the field before autumn."

"It didn't sound that bad," the captain replied. "A few malcontents, nothing more."

"You didn't hear what the Legate said—try to understand what he meant."

"You mean about possible rebellion?" The tanker captain laughed and shook her head. "He's being paranoid."

"Legate Tortorelli's not paranoid," snapped the major. "He might be overly cautious, but he's not crazy. Watch what you say, Captain Mugabe. That might be taken as insubordination or even treason."

"Sorry, sir," Mugabe mumbled. "I just don't think we have to worry about the MBA, not the way the Legate is. They're looking for profits, not insurrection."

"They're converting those hunks of scrap for a reason," the major said. "Be sure your unit is ready to move out at an instant's notice. It'll take quick response and heavy artillery to put down a rebellion led by the Governor's own son."

Manfred perked up and almost spilled his pile of paperwork. He hastily bowed his head again to keep everyone from noticing how he eavesdropped as the major stalked off to speak with even more senior officers. Manfred looked up and started to say something to the tanker captain, then held his tongue. She was a commander of the Behemoth IIs that had been so thoroughly trounced by Austin Ortega during the war games. Bringing himself to Captain Mugabe's notice would serve no one. If anything, his usefulness depended on him remaining invisible.

Manfred saw the lieutenant whose desk he had appropriated coming from the elevator. Even junior officers had been summoned to the Legate's emergency meeting. That cemented Manfred's notion of what was happening. He might be a captain and in command of the First Cossack Lancers now, but that would change quickly. The FCL was being dismantled, one lance at a time, sent on detached duty, elements assigned to other units, until their cohesion was destroyed. Manfred had heard rumors that he was to be reassigned to a test group—a nonexistent test company with no mission. That meant he would do nothing but ride a desk and turn in reports about nothing that no one read.

Manfred smiled a little at the notion of such an assignment. It would be perfect for what he had to do.

It was all he had expected when Governor Ortega had ordered him to Tortorelli's command. But he had not expected the Legate to mobilize against the populace, claiming Austin was leading a revolt. That was so absurd Manfred wondered why everyone wasn't laughing the rumor into oblivion. He suspected Elora had something to do with it—more than something.

He got up, started toward the elevator and then stopped at a major's vacant desk. He activated the comm-unit, punched in a series of numbers, counted to three, then disconnected.

Manfred wended his way through the office and down to the garage, where he found a cycle. He scribbled his name on the checkout sheet, climbed on, and roared off.

Manfred loved the rush of air against his face. The sense of danger made his breath come a little faster, just as the scent of weeds growing along the road leading into Cingulum reminded him of his parents' farm when he was growing up. All he did was cut weeds, or so it had seemed then.

Manfred's nose twitched just a little. He realized that times had not changed much. Then, the tenacious plants he had chopped down were ankle-high bind-weed and the taller blue-gray grasses. Now he worked at weeds in the Governor's garden.

He took a curve in the road at high speed, skidded, and then stopped, watching the road behind. He was the only traffic on the beltway circling the city. A slow line of vehicles made their way inward toward the skyscraper complex he had just left, but no one followed him along this road. Manfred fumbled in his pocket and donned a pair of glasses. A few seconds' adjustment let him scan the ruddy sky for any trace of airborne spy devices. The IR lenses caught heat reflections off a few metallic slivers, but Manfred decided they were high-flying airplanes. He had no sense that he was being followed or electronically monitored.

He gunned the cycle back to a full-throated roar and raced off. Time worked against him, but he had to be certain no one saw whom he was meeting.

Around Cingulum he ran, taking corners at breakneck speed, then slowing and speeding up at random intervals to throw off anyone trying to track him. He doubled back more than once, stopped, and then took a spoke road into a decrepit section of town where he watched from cross streets, and always, always, he used the IR detection goggles. In the field they were good for spotting enemy battle armor and motorized equipment. Here they warned him of aerial spies.

Only when he was sure he wasn't observed did Manfred Leclerc pull into a dingy, garbage-littered alley and lean the cycle against a wall. He dusted himself off, stepped into the street, and walked directly to a small bookstore sandwiched between larger businesses. He went inside, resisted the urge to take a final look out into the street to see if anyone noticed him, then went to the clerk behind a long counter running three-quarters the length of the store.

"I'd like a history book," he said.

"History is a dusty subject," came the answer. "Perhaps you'd like something else." The clerk looked bored and never glanced up at him. He was reading a book of his own.

"Then I'll buy a cookbook."

The man lifted his chin, silently pointing out a staircase leading to a second floor, reached under the counter, and pressed a button. He went back to his reading without saying another word.

Manfred hurried up the steps, aware of the intricate wiring and electronics along the way. He opened the door at the head of the stairs, slipped inside quickly, and shut it behind him with a profound sense of relief. He had made it without being seen.

"You worry too much, Manfred," Sergio Ortega said.

"Sorry to take so long, my lord. I had to be sure no one noticed I'd left."

"Unless I miss a guess, you are completely off the radar screen in the Legate's headquarters. That makes it easier for you to get away often, as you will have to if we are to finish this scheme quickly." Sergio sat in a comfortable chair, a book perched on the arm. Manfred sidled around to read the title. A book of essays on pacifism written by a Terran named Bertrand Russell.

"I overheard a few officers talking after an emergency conference," Manfred said with some bitterness.

"To which you were not invited, I take it." Sergio laughed. "Don't feel left out, Manfred. I'd've worried if you *had* been included."

"I suppose you're right, sir," Manfred said. "An infantry major spoke with a tank commander about a call-up against civilians. The major bragged how battle armor could take out any rioter."

"Bravado, nothing more. I can't believe Tortorelli would use battle-armored troops against demonstrators after I've warned him against such a move."

"He's concerned that there is a rebellion brewing, Sergio, one powerful enough to overthrow the government."

"Insurrection? And the leader . . . ?" From the way Sergio sat a little straighter, Manfred saw he had the Governor's complete attention.

Manfred hesitated, then said, "Your son. With the backing of the MBA and their converted Industrial-Mechs."

"Austin is going to overthrow me?" Sergio's good humor slowly evaporated as he considered this. "He's a hothead and we don't agree on how to handle the demonstrations, but he'd never lead a revolt."

"I don't think so, either, Baron," said Manfred.

"No, of course he wouldn't. He's a good boy. But he has a stubborn streak in him and he doesn't believe I'm doing a particularly good job running the world at the moment. I want to keep him out of this ruckus as much as I can until he gets more experience, but that might not be possible if Tortorelli thinks he is leading a revolt."

Manfred said nothing as Sergio argued with himself, finally deciding that Austin would never sanction rebellion, even if he thought it strengthened The Republic's grip on Mirach. That's what Sergio ended up saying aloud.

Manfred worried that the Governor didn't sound as if he truly believed it. Deep down, they both knew

Calvilena Tortorelli was capable of ordering troops against civilians, whether out of fear or cupidity did not matter, and that was something Austin would oppose with all his heart and soul.

16

*Industrial Giants manufacturing plant, outskirts
  of Cingulum*
Mirach
30 April 3133

"The Governor's not planning to cut his spending on
other projects, is he?" asked Marta Kinsolving. She
tried to sound nonchalant, but Austin Ortega felt the
tension in her question. Her brown eyes fixed on him,
making him a little uneasy about having to lie to her.

"The budget is set for the coming fiscal year," Austin said, carefully choosing his words. He wasn't lying
about that. He simply didn't know what his father was
going to do because he was not privy to the actual
workings of the government or how his father came
to his decisions. Two things were certain, though. Because of his pacifist leanings, Sergio Ortega was not
inclined to spend more on military procurement, and

Austin had wrangled a tour of another plant under false pretenses.

Austin wasn't sure if he wanted to see what military capability the MBA might be developing or if his purpose was to see Marta again. She was a benign splinter in his mind, always obvious, yet not doing anything to fester. Try as he might, Austin could not find evidence that Marta had arranged Dale's death. The trail of guilt went to the technician loading the live rounds and abruptly stopped there. When the inventory had been delivered to the field, one crate had been mismarked; the tech actually thought she had given the tank commander dye-marker warheads. But how the crates had become confused— or switched and the labeling altered—was something Austin had failed to determine. There was one soldier in the supply chain he had been unable to identify, but pursuing the lead had proved difficult because his father had kept him so busy with small, time-consuming chores.

The only chance he had of proving to his own satisfaction that Dale's death was anything more than the officially reported accident was to dig around in Marta Kinsolving's businesses to eliminate her and the MBA as suspects.

She and AWC had profited immeasurably by Dale's death. The contract Sergio Ortega had announced helped offset the loss of revenue from the HPG net failure and gave AllWorldComm a position that challenged the Ministry of Information for eventual influence over Mirach. The Span-net proposed by AWC would connect citizens directly, doing away with the need for scheduled newscasts vetted by Lady Elora. A single flip of the switch on a handheld unit would connect to any news provider, and the small cost for maintaining such a service would ensure that dozens of competing private companies would flock to set up their own direct-transmission news operations.

The Ministry of Information might still control a significant portion of the data flow, but Elora's stranglehold would slip when the citizens found other, more diverse sources for their information.

Austin didn't know if his father realized it, but Sergio had significantly reduced his own power by providing this new conduit of information. Although Lady Elora seldom followed the script as Austin would have written it, she paid some lip service to supporting the Governor and his policies.

Not enough, not anymore, Austin thought, distracted from Marta. Would it be better for the Governor to seize the news services or to give wider access, as he was doing? Austin wasn't sure how Marta, the MBA, and all the other factions on Mirach would use this direct pipeline to every citizen. He hoped Marta meant it when she said AllWorldComm was interested only in supplying the equipment and that content could be someone else's bread and butter.

He wished his father confided in him more, rather than treating him like a minor functionary. Not for the first time Austin wondered what it would be like if he had remained with the First Cossack Lancers, even serving under Legate Tortorelli's direct orders. He felt he had a flair for being a soldier. He certainly felt adrift working as an aide-de-camp for his father.

He hoped poking around MBA-affiliated factories, such as this new IndustrialMech assembly plant, might prove useful. How, Austin wasn't sure, unless it gave some clue about Dale's death, but he needed to keep busy. And he had talked Marta Kinsolving into being his guide through the Mirach Industrial Giants factory.

"I hope the project clears all the fiscal hurdles," Marta said.

"What project?" Austin asked before he thought about how such a question made him appear. He had to stay more alert and not let his thoughts wander.

"The Span-net, of course," Marta said. "We'll have operational relays on all four moons within two weeks and cheap full-spectrum broadcast capacity for whomever your father approves."

The Span-net would help direct attention inward, to how well others on Mirach were doing rather than making comparisons, probably created out of sheer vacuum, with other planets.

"Will only MBA companies be able to contract for transmission time?" he asked.

"Since we are such an encompassing group, I'm sure many will. But the licensure won't be limited strictly to members."

As long as "many" means more than the Ministry of Information, Austin thought. From Marta's expression, he saw she meant what she said.

They reached the entrance to the huge assembly building. Stretching a hundred meters inside were ranks of MiningMechs in various stages of assembly. The ones nearest were almost complete, standing six meters high with a rotary drill on one arm and a giant scoop weighing down the other. Such a machine could bore into a planet and clean out a stope with relentless efficiency.

"Are these units going to Nagursky?" he asked. Austin studied the lines of the 'Mech nearest him. Squat and vaguely menacing, the 'Mech wouldn't take much refitting to become a deadly fighting machine. It was nothing compared to a real BattleMech, but there weren't any in the Mirach armed forces. He and

Dale might have trained endlessly in the simulator, but it was only play.

"I'll see," Marta said. She drew out a small hand-held unit and spoke rapidly into it. She tucked it back into a pocket and said, "Ben Nagursky's got eight on order."

"Eight!" This startled Austin. "Is he expanding his mining empire that much?" Austin knew enough about MiningMechs to know this many could ream out the interior of an entire mountain in a few weeks.

Marta gave a small shrug. "I can't say. We work together for the common good of Mirach industry, but plans for our individual companies are not shared, except in general terms. He might have a new strike waiting to be exploited. Nagursky wouldn't make such a find public until ore began coming out of the ground and he had a market to announce."

Austin felt she wasn't telling the complete truth. He hesitated to brand her words a lie, but they carried a feel of . . . untruth.

"That phone. The portable one. Is that part of your Span-net?"

"Here," she said, pulling it out of her pocket and handing it to him. "Use it like a standard phone. Or you can punch one of those small blue buttons for news reports, weather, that sort of information."

"Fair, twenty degrees, wind from the north at ten kph," reported the phone when Austin thumbed the weather information button.

"The news available to Span-net is still sketchy, but when the moon stations are finished and the entire world is under a decent reception footprint, there'll be more," Marta said. She obviously thought more of this small communications device than she did the looming 'Mechs on the line.

The truth is mightier than the 'Mech? he wondered. That was hard for him to believe; it sounded too much like something his father might say.

"Do you mind if I take one for a test drive?" Austin asked.

"Keep the phone," Marta said.

"Not the phone. One of those." Austin pointed to a MiningMech standing at the end of the assembly line.

"It might not have been checked out yet," she said.

"Who do I contact to find out?" Austin held up his phone, giving her the goad to reach the plant supervisor. Marta showed him how to use the device by dialing up the super. Austin spoke to the supervisor for a few minutes, then tucked the phone into his pocket.

"All settled. The super said I could take one out, as long as I didn't redline the equipment."

"They only have internal combustion engines," warned Marta. "Not a fusion unit like on your simulator."

Austin had to laugh. AllWorldComm had manufactured most of the simulator equipment and all the software. This was something Marta knew well.

"Have you ever piloted one before? A real one?" she asked.

"I . . . know my way around one," Austin said, again not quite telling the truth. He had trained in battle armor, in every mobile unit available to the FCL, and in some of the Legate's heavier tanks, but other than the simulator, Austin had never piloted a 'Mech. Any 'Mech.

"That's good. It requires considerable experience to control one," Marta said. "There's no need for lateral agility in an industrial model, so the controls give you forward and back, not much lateral movement. The arm controllers are the most extensive, but they're easier to figure out than autocannon loaders. The one on the right controls the drill and the other, on the left, the scoop."

"I might dig or drill a little, to test out the handling," Austin said, his heart racing a little faster. He should have found an IndustrialMech to try out much earlier. He and Dale could have really enjoyed themselves with mock dogfights.

His enthusiasm muted a little as he thought again of his brother, but Austin walked quickly with Marta to the 'Mech. She appeared to know her way around the metal giants as well as he did. The auburn-haired woman smiled.

"I was quite a tomboy when I was growing up. I know everything there is to know about a 'Mech. Even if I hadn't been fascinated when I was younger, I'd still know quite a bit about them. I used to oversee all simulator software design work at AWC before I moved into management."

He kept forgetting how capable she was. Her technical expertise was only one of the traits that had propelled her to such a position of power in such a short time. The other CEOs in the Mirach Business Association were much older than Marta.

"Here," she said, rummaging about in an envelope taped to the wall behind the 'Mech he eyed with such admiration. "The activation codes."

"Thanks," he said, glancing at them. The sequences were simple, but then, these 'Mechs were still in-factory, with neurohelmets unprogrammed. Once they were put to work in the mines, Nagursky's drivers would imprint their own neurohelmets and reprogram their access codes to something far more difficult to crack. Nagursky wouldn't want just any employee jumping into a MiningMech and taking it for a joyride.

Like Austin intended doing now.

Grinning like a fool, he stripped off his jacket and let Marta help him into coveralls. He looked around for a cooling vest but didn't see one. He asked.

"You won't need one. This is an internal combustion 'Mech. Remember? Cooling fins carry away most of the heat when there's sufficient airflow above ground. Right now, the wind's blowing at ten kph. Remember?" She tapped his pocket where he had stashed the phone.

"In the mines," she went on, "they use huge ducted fans to keep air circulating over the 'Mech's exterior. The pilot never gets that hot."

"Still," Austin said, "it must turn sweltering after an hour or two."

"You won't be out that long," she said positively. Marta made a big deal of looking at her watch to remind him she had a company to run.

"Why don't you go on and see to your business?" he offered. "You've gone out of your way to show me the factory. I appreciate it but don't want to take up more of your time."

"Industrial Giants policy is that I have to check you out if I checked you in. By the time I could get someone to pass along the authority for you, you'd be back from your little jaunt. You won't be out more than five minutes," she said, her eyes boring into him. Austin knew an order when he heard it. Marta had set the time limit for him to run the 'Mech.

"I'll hurry," Austin said, wanting to pilot it the rest of the day. He scampered up the ladder welded on the left leg, opened the rear hatch, and slipped into the cockpit. He slipped on the neurohelmet and shivered as little as it matched his brain waves to appropriate systems on the 'Mech. The minor programming would have to be erased and the neurohelmet completely recalibrated later, but Austin supposed that Marta didn't mind. He peered out the polymer window and felt on top of the world, even if this wasn't a BattleMech. It was close enough.

After orienting himself, he felt confident enough to run down a checklist. For a BattleMech such lists ran long pages. The MiningMech was snorting fumes and shuddering, ready to ramble, with only one page of instructions because it lacked complex weapons systems.

"Good to go," Austin announced. When he got no reply, he hunted for the radio and found it inoperative. A few more seconds jiggling switches told him communication was out of the question. It was dead.

Austin jumped when his phone rang. He fumbled it from his pocket and heard Marta's voice. "Go on, take it out onto the test range and put it through the paces."

"What's wrong with the onboard radio?" Austin asked.

"Most MiningMechs don't use a radio," Marta explained. "There's no reason to unwind a couple klicks of comm coaxial cable to hook into the cockpit unit."

Austin tried not to kick himself. MiningMechs were designed for use underground and didn't have standard radios. If communication was needed, the unit was hardwired with the base more like an intercom than a radio. It would be like being on a tether, the coaxial cable unreeling behind as the 'Mech cut its way along mine shafts.

"All right!" He reached the last item on the checklist, closed the hatch, and then secured his safety harness. The hatch sealed with a hiss and the internal air supply began feeding into the enclosed space.

Austin grinned like a fool as he stared out the polymer window. He was strapped into a 'Mech and ready for action. He put his feet down firmly on the pedals, gripped the joysticks, and eased the ponderous machine forward. As the 'Mech strode from the assembly building, Austin experienced a flash of fear. Something wasn't right. The 'Mech didn't respond properly. Then he calmed. He was used to quicker BattleMech sims. There wasn't any reason for this one to race along at sixty kilometers per hour or agilely dodge. It was built to hunker down, drill, and scoop. That was it.

Austin still was thrilled by the sensation of immense power at his beck and call. He looked down on the world from his lofty perch in the cockpit. Lined up outside the assembly building were non-'Mech military units destined for service in the Legate's army. APCs and a few scout vehicles were parked and waiting for drivers to whisk them off to their duty stations. But they were low-slung and impotent compared to the MiningMech. The immense strength in the legs sent a chill up Austin's spine. On impulse, he activated the right-hand drill. It whirred futilely. There wasn't a drill bit installed yet.

He switched to the left arm and made spastic scooping motions until he found the precise rhythm. He dug a trench five meters long just beyond the rows of vehicles until he had proved to himself that he was in full control. Austin let out a whoop of glee and straightened, towering two stories above the ground. He looked out across the test range from his lofty vantage point and set the 'Mech into motion, lumbering along at about the speed a man could run. He might not have the sophisticated viewing equipment of a true BattleMech, or even the IR and other radar ranging gear of the military units, but he didn't need them for this trial run. The pitiful sensory equipment and his own keen eyesight were all he needed as he kicked the 'Mech to greater speed.

To meet the demands placed on it, the engine noise whined upward to the supersonic range, but Austin ignored it. The simple readouts showed he wasn't near maxing out the systems.

When the needles approached redlining, Austin reluctantly backed down the power. He was hurrying along at almost ten kilometers per hour and totally wrapped in his own feelings of power when he heard the phone's small chiming sound. He used his thumb to press the activator button, then recoiled when Marta's voice exploded from the small speaker.

"Austin!" she screamed. "Answer! Answer, dammit!"

"I'm here," he said, holding the phone away from his ear to keep from being deafened. He couldn't figure out how to lower the volume. "What's wrong?"

"The test range supervisor reported a rogue 'Mech on the field with you. It's homing in fast, and it looks like it's out for blood."

"What do you mean?" Austin shook the phone, as if it might provide him with a more logical report if he punished it enough.

"No one knows who's in that 'Mech. No radio response. All we know is that it's outfitted for battle, Austin. Get away from it. Turn around and get back as quick as you can."

"It's too late for that," he said. Austin spotted the other 'Mech now. A brown dot moved against the dirt of the test range, but it grew fast—and responded even faster. Austin knew the other 'Mech had detection and ranging equipment from the way it swung about and homed in on him.

His 'Mech staggered as a series of blows knocked it sideways. Austin struggled to keep the MiningMech upright. It took him a second to realize an autocannon had fired on him and the hammering sounds came from rounds hitting his 'Mech. A large section on his left torso had been damaged, but the 'Mech still functioned. He hunched over to present a smaller cross section for the other 'Mech to fire at, then found himself under missile attack. The salvo whined above and around him, but two found his right arm and blew it off.

Austin grunted as he fought to keep the 'Mech upright. If he tumbled over, he knew he was dead. Autocannon fire and more missiles would end his life in a flash. He couldn't even eject. Such safety devices weren't included in a basic MiningMech.

For some reason the mental image of an escape pod ejecting while the MiningMech burrowed deeper into the ground amused him. Then all humor fled. Another blast from the 'Mech's autocannon damaged his right leg, slowing him considerably.

Austin made a quick assessment of his situation and saw it was hopeless. He had no armament worth mentioning that would combat a converted Industrial-Mech. Sucking in a deep breath, he tromped hard on the pedals, jerked at the controls, and pushed the engine to overload to drive directly at the other 'Mech. His frontal assault took the enemy pilot by surprise just long enough for Austin to get a glimpse of what he faced.

The AgroMech had been extensively refitted with autocannon and two missile launchers. Something had gone wrong with the launchers. Austin saw thin tendrils of black smoke twirling away from the unit mounted on the AgroMech's right shoulder, betraying a serious malfunction. If the other pilot tried firing another barrage, one or two of the missiles might reach Austin. The rest would explode, causing a fiery suicide.

Austin forced his 'Mech forward at top speed, in spite of increasing accuracy by the AgroMech's autocannon. Smoke filled his cockpit, choking him, but Austin had no choice but to get as close as possible. If he tried to run, the other 'Mech's autocannon would blow him to metallic bits.

The impact of his MiningMech crashing into the other snapped his head back. Austin recovered fast. He brought the digging scoop up, then drove it at full power as if he scraped once more at the ground. Huge blue sparks leaped away when the digging edge crashed into the other 'Mech's leg.

This was the only chance he got at damaging his opponent. Dozens of rounds from the autocannon blew away the top of Austin's 'Mech. Hot air and cloying dust began to fill the cockpit. He could hardly see, much less control his 'Mech. But he had to keep fighting if he wanted to survive.

He guessed where the AgroMech had to be and charged again through the dust cloud. Austin knew his gamble had failed when the surge of heavy depleted-uranium slugs cut off his 'Mech's legs just below the knees. His 'Mech whined in almost human agony as metal tore away. Then the engine hit a crescendo that was unsustainable. The 'Mech died around him in metallic pain.

Austin felt the ponderous machine toppling to the side and was powerless to stop it. The impact against the ground rattled his teeth and caused him to see a collapsing black tunnel for a moment, but he never quite lost consciousness.

"Austin, Austin! I'm coming! Are you alive?"

"Hanging in there," he answered Marta on the phone. Somehow, it had bounced around the cockpit and had come to rest beside his head. He pressed it to his ear. "What do you mean, you're coming?"

At first he thought he heard an explosion. Then he realized it was the crash of metal against metal relayed by the phone. Whatever Marta had done, it had stopped the incessant hammering of autocannon rounds into his disabled 'Mech.

Through the clouds of dust whirling around like a tornado, Austin caught sight of an APC grinding into reverse, then launching forward again to smash into the AgroMech. The armored personnel carrier didn't have anything to fire, so Marta was using it as a battering ram.

And he saw the AgroMech turn an arm toward her. Smoke belched from the autocannon as they fired.

"Marta!"

Austin realized that warning her was pointless. If she didn't know the autocannon fired at her, she was already dead. He frantically worked the controls of his MiningMech, hunting for something that still functioned. The digging scoop swung in a wide arc parallel with the ground and caught the AgroMech's metallic ankle.

Metal twisted and the hot burning smell of tortured steel filled his nostrils. Then there was only silence.

Austin hung in his safety harness, too stunned to move. Slowly pulling himself together, he hit the releases on the web straps and fell almost a meter, cutting his hand against ragged metal. He got his feet under him, ducked around cracked polymer plate that had once been his window, and tumbled to the ground.

He had hoped to breathe easier outside the devastated 'Mech. He was wrong. The dust, the smell of burned metal and cordite and something more that sickened him, was worse outside. Austin wiped his mouth after retching, then staggered forward, fearing what he would find.

"Marta!" He saw the APC flipped onto its side. Flames lapped fitfully at the exposed skeleton where it had been ripped open by vicious autocannon fire.

"I'm all right," came the woman's choked voice.

She pulled herself out of the rear emergency hatch and flopped to the ground. Austin knelt beside her. She was bruised and bleeding and filthy, but she spoke before he could.

"You look a mess," she said.

He realized he was in no better condition. Somehow, that struck him as funny. Then hysteria seized him until tears ran down his grimy cheeks.

"Sorry to lose control like that," he said, holding his sides. They ached from laughing so hard. Austin swiped at his eyes, then found the AgroMech.

"You really did a number on it," he said. "You rammed it head-on."

"The digging claw on the MiningMech finished the job," Marta said.

"Finished?" Austin said grimly. "It's not finished. Not yet."

He stumbled across the chopped-up field to where the AgroMech lay smoking. As he approached, he saw how it had been extensively refitted for battle.

He picked his way through piles of smoldering scrap metal and pulled the cockpit hatch all the way open. The cockpit was empty and the enemy driver had fled. Kicking his way through the debris, he hunted for the neurohelmet.

"What are you looking for?" asked Marta, peering in from behind.

"The identity of the driver," Austin said. His heart sank when he saw how badly the neurohelmet had been damaged. He held up a few wires and the melted helmet itself. Destroyed beyond forensic recovery. "There's no way this can be used now to match brain wave patterns." He turned and saw Marta's expression.

"Do you know who this 'Mech belonged to?" he asked. She didn't have to answer. He read the answer on her face.

17

"What would Manfred be doing there at all?" Austin
Ortega stared at his father in disbelief. The Governor's office was bright with sunlight but so deathly
quiet that Austin could hear the hammering of his
own heart. "He hasn't gone rogue, has he? Being
transferred to the Home Guard didn't please any of
the FCL, but this would be treason. Unless—" He
stared at his father, realization dawning.

"Manfred is a loyal aide," Sergio said in a neutral
tone.

"You knew he was at the plant, driving 'Mechs for
the MBA. Why didn't you say something to me?"

"There's no need for you to become entangled in
this."

"Marta Kinsolving is involved, too," Austin said, piecing together a jagged puzzle. "She didn't want to tell me that was Manfred's refitted 'Mech, but I got that much out of her."

"She, with the MBA, are cooperating fully in my investigation of this situation," Sergio said. "Please, Austin, do this for me. Don't get involved."

"I *am* involved. That wasn't Manfred in the 'Mech. It couldn't have been. He had no reason to come after me."

"Someone else piloted the refitted 'Mech," Sergio said, "and his identity is still a mystery. He covered his tracks well, destroying the neurohelmet. However, there's no reason to believe he singled you out to kill. He was probably intent on destroying the IndustrialMechs being manufactured. You chanced to be on the test range, and he decided to demolish an operational 'Mech."

Austin tried to digest the idea of his father, Manfred, and Marta Kinsolving being in a clandestine partnership. Whatever the purpose, it had little or nothing to do with Span-net. Some other strategic purpose was being hidden from him.

"You'll only endanger Manfred's life if you keep searching for answers to this, Austin."

"Is it tied in with Dale's and Hanna's murders?" he asked. Austin spoke before he thought, but as the words rushed out, an electric thrill ran through him. On the face of it, this was absurd. Three unconnected assassination attempts, two successful and the third failing only through outrageous luck and Marta Kinsolving's quick action.

"Don't drive yourself crazy," Sergio said more sternly. "Who could have known you were going to the Industrial Giants plant? No one but Ms. Kinsolving knew you were even going out in a 'Mech, and she did everything possible to rescue you. Now drop it. Trust me to do the right thing."

"I want to talk to Manfred," Austin said. "Where is he?"

Sergio's response was interrupted by the insistent buzz of the intercom. He passed his hand over the actuator. "What is it?"

"My lord," said the secretary, "Legate Tortorelli is here to see you. He says it is urgent."

"Send the Legate in," Sergio said.

Too much remained to be discussed. Austin started to argue, but Sergio lifted his hand and cut off any further exchange. Austin glanced over his shoulder as the office doors whispered open and Legate Calvilena Tortorelli marched in, jeweled medals bouncing against his chest with every stride. Tortorelli came to a halt in front of the desk and even clicked his heels.

"Governor Ortega!"

Austin saw what the secretary had failed to mention. Lady Elora trailed the Legate at a discreet distance and stopped just inside the office. She smoothed her already wrinkle-free red silk dress over her thin frame, struck a pose, and waited. Austin couldn't help looking around, but the Minister was alone.

"Well, Legate? What is it?" demanded Sergio. "I was in the middle of an important conference with the Baronet."

"It is good he is here, Governor," Tortorelli said, not bothering to look in Austin's direction. "A full investigation of the incident at the 'Mech factory is being conducted."

"By your authority, Legate?" asked Austin. "Isn't it unusual for the Legate to conduct an investigation into a civil matter?"

"Not when an AgroMech outfitted with autocannon and LRMs is involved. That is a serious matter."

"What have you found?" asked Sergio. He and Austin locked glances. Austin fumed. Then he tensed when the Legate answered.

"We know who was responsible, Governor. He is an officer in my command."

"What?" Austin and Sergio cried out simultaneously.

"I am sorry to inform you that the attempted assassination was conducted by none other than Captain Manfred Leclerc."

"What makes you think the captain had anything to do with this?" asked Sergio.

"Extensive comparison of equipment in the 'Mech cockpit shows he was the driver."

"The neurohelmet was destroyed beyond any chance at identification," Austin said. "I saw that for myself."

"There are other things. Access coding, other things," Tortorelli said. "We are certain he is responsible and I have informed the civil authorities, but so far, they are at a loss to find Captain Leclerc. I have empowered military intelligence to begin a search. Technically, since he was on active duty, Leclerc falls under military jurisdiction. With the evidence accumulated so far damning him for this atrocious act, he will find few allies. We will arrest him soon, Governor."

Austin was at a loss for words. He looked from Tortorelli to Lady Elora, whose slight smile told him she was the driving force behind the accusation against Manfred.

"I find these charges incredible," Sergio said, "but I am sure the captain will address them fully in court."

"He didn't do it," Austin spoke up. "He's my friend."

"The evidence goes against your, umm, feelings," Lady Elora said in her soft voice. The words cut like a knife with a serrated blade. "There were his fingerprints on the AgroMech controls. No one else's were there."

"No one's?" asked Austin. "Not even a tech? Isn't that strange? It takes a team of trained technicians to field a 'Mech. And a pilot would wear gloves."

"I misspoke," Elora said. "I'm sure there were other fingerprints—Leclerc's techs. There were only the captain's prints on the controls. Perhaps he touched them without gloves on. I know you thought he was your friend and this must shake certain beliefs, but there is more evidence."

"What?" asked Austin.

"Witnesses seeing him preparing the refitted Agro-Mech," the Legate said. "We are interrogating them now."

"You have the investigation well in hand," Sergio cut in, again glaring at Austin to keep him silent. "Keep us informed, Legate."

"The Ministry of Information is doing as much as possible, also, Baron," Elora said. "Captain Leclerc's likeness is included on every newscast, along with details of why citizens should turn him over to military police."

"Not the civil authorities?" asked Austin.

"Or civil authorities, though everyone anticipates arresting Manfred Leclerc will be dangerous and better handled by military action."

Lady Elora's emerald green eyes danced with merriment. Austin saw that she considered this meeting to have gone her way and herself to have won.

"I'm sure everyone is doing their duty as they see it," Sergio said. "Forward any report to me marked EYES ONLY, if you will, Legate."

"Consider it done, my lord." Tortorelli turned and followed Lady Elora from the office. Austin closed the doors behind them.

"There's no proof," Austin said angrily. "They're making it up. Elora is making it all up!"

"This is the last time I'm going to say this, Austin. Don't butt in. Let this play out. You don't have all the facts."

"Yes, sir," Austin said, having no intention of ignoring a friend in danger. Manfred Leclerc was a decent man. Austin had to help straighten this out—and find out what intrigue his father was involved in. He had the uneasy feeling that Sergio knew more about Hanna's and Dale's deaths than he was letting on.

He quickly left the office, closing the doors behind him. Tortorelli and Elora had already vanished. Austin considered following the Minister, then knew it would do him no good to spy on her. She was the expert at such things. Whatever he saw or overheard would be exactly what Elora wanted him to know.

"Damn her," Austin exclaimed. Office workers turned at his outburst. He smiled weakly and waved them back to work. She was the master spy, always rooting about for news. She might have had him followed to the 'Mech factory, or she might have known earlier of his visit, since it had hardly been a state secret. He took a deep, settling breath.

Austin had to find Manfred Leclerc before Elora whipped up a vigilante mob, and knew only one place to begin his search. Stride lengthening as his resolve hardened, Austin left the Palace. He needed to don some camouflage before the hunt.

18

The huge unwinking disk of the springtime sun splayed across the western horizon, confusing the eye with strange crimson wavelengths and allowing twilight to sneak in to claim the rugged land for night. To the north, glaciers had retreated forty thousand years earlier, leaving behind steep valleys with rounded bottoms and more minerals than could be mined in any man's lifetime. To the east a plain stretched to the Marabot Ocean. This ragged plain was all that looked familiar to Austin Ortega. As a child, he had hiked there and knew how deceptive it could be. Small ferocious animals snapped at unwary hikers' ankles and the dearth of water made a trek of any distance hazardous. Southward lay the capital of Cingulum, the city where Austin had been born.

Mirach was a cold, obscure world ignored by most of The Republic, but to Austin it was home. Savage weather, wan sun, oceans dotted year-round with icebergs—it was the perfect training ground for a warrior. In spite of this, Austin felt he had been shortchanged. He wasn't a warrior, not like Dale had been.

Stop that, he thought. It did no good dwelling on what he thought were his shortcomings. If he didn't stay positive about uncovering the information he needed, he would certainly fail. Austin wasn't going to let Manfred Leclerc take the fall for the attack at Industrial Giants.

This set off a new circuit of thoughts. He had to prevent his friend from being used as a pawn in Elora's power game, but there was more to his mission. Austin reluctantly admitted he wanted to prove he wasn't useless to his father. Sergio Ortega was a decent man, a great man in many ways, who had guided Mirach through good times and bad. But he was pigheaded and never admitted he was wrong. Austin couldn't convince his father that a good Governor was not only beneficent, but also able to rule with an iron hand when necessary. The demonstrations across Mirach were growing in violence now, and yet Sergio had failed to quell them.

A battalion of battle armor patrolling the cities would do the trick, Austin thought. That would keep the hotheads from whipping up the fear that threatened the stability of an entire world. Seeing companies of the Legate's finest marching through the capital would also put an end to Lady Elora's verbal tinkering. No riots, no paranoia about being cut off from the rest of The Republic, and she would become a toothless tiger.

But Sergio continued to counsel Tortorelli not to deploy troops. His one concession to restoring order had been to send out the police, but Austin saw this as too little, too late. The police had no stomach for trying to control the uncontrollable.

Austin snapped back from his reverie when he almost missed the turn in the road. He careened through the curve, fighting the controls and finally righting the car. Then he opened up the throttle and whirred along to the barracks at better than two hundred kilometers per hour. All too soon, he saw the rotating blue and yellow lights atop the guardhouse and knew he had to slow down. More than a klick away, he took his foot off the accelerator. Speed peeled away like layers of an onion, bringing him to a reasonable pace by the time he could make out the individual guards on duty. Austin braked and brought the car to a halt beside the guard standing duty on incoming traffic.

"Sir, good evening," the guard said. She bent over and peered into the car. "Just you?"

"Returning from R and R," he lied. Austin had pulled out his uniform from storage, the one he thought he would never wear again, and had put it on for this charade. Although he was no longer entitled to wear the black-and-silver, it surprised him how *right* it felt.

"What unit?" she asked, frowning a little.

He started to say he served under Captain Leclerc, then caught himself. Even if Manfred hadn't been in serious trouble, that wouldn't have been an acceptable response. The FCL was being broken up, the soldiers deployed to smaller units all over the continent of Musasalah. Some of the scuttlebutt he had overheard between the FCL guards still at the Palace detailed how some of the First Cossack Lancers were even being sent across the planet to the other continent of Ventrale to garrison research outposts. Any cohesion in the FCL would be completely erased within months.

Austin figured that was Tortorelli's intent: destroy the Governor's bodyguard and leave him vulnerable. Any element of the Legate's force sent to protect Sergio Ortega wouldn't have the devotion, the loyalty, the take-a-bullet dedication Manfred had instilled in the FCL.

"On detached duty with the Legate's staff. Liaison with Governor Ortega's office." Austin fumbled in his pocket and pulled out his legitimate ID. It said nothing of military standing but had the official seal and his father's signature at the bottom of the card.

The guard took the ident-card and peered at it under the bright guardhouse light. Then she ran it through a verifier. Austin held his breath until he was sure the guard wasn't calling up his full dossier.

"Go on in, Lieutenant," she said. "You know the way to Colonel Armitage's office?"

"To the command office? Of course," Austin said, "but I have to stop at the barracks for a few minutes."

She stepped back, saluted, and waved him on in. He realized then that he had passed one final, small test. It was good that he had come out here several times with Manfred, Dale, and the other FCL officers for training seminars. Austin refrained from flooring the accelerator. He drove slowly into the tangle of narrow streets, hunting for the proper crossing thoroughfare. When he found it, he turned in and pulled over.

Austin jumped from the car, made certain his uniform was in order, then entered the front door of the barracks. Two men lounging around looked up but, once they saw his FCL uniform insignia, hastily turned away. That gave him an idea of the status of Manfred's former unit. Insulted by this pointed disregard, he made his way upstairs to the rooms allocated to the FCL. Or what remained of them.

The first three he checked were empty, but in the fourth he found a veritable fountain of information. Master Sergeant Dmitri Borodin was like a spider in the middle of a web. Every vibration, no matter how tiny, became a full-fledged rumor in a single telling. He was just the man Austin wanted to see.

"Master Sergeant, as you were," Austin said. Borodin looked up from the tech manual he studied intently, startled.

"Lieutenant, didn't know you were here. Most all's out and about tonight."

"Pulled punishment duty again, Sarge?" Austin laughed as he perched on the edge of the desk where Borodin struggled to make sense out of the material. Austin reached over and looked at the title. "Must have been a dandy. Not black-marketing again, were you?"

"It was only meant to be a prank. Didn't mean no harm, Lieutenant. Honest. That major's behind was only slightly singed. Hardly noticed it, 'specially after he got the hole in the pants fixed."

Austin wished he could hear the entire story, but he was on a mission. Dale's death, his own brush with death, Manfred's indictment—all were more important than a passing diversion of what had to be a funny story.

"You didn't come out here for my stories. How are you faring since the . . . exercise?" Borodin asked. "Damn shame about your brother. He should have been in armor . . ."

"I'm getting ready to transfer back," Austin said, hoping to spark a comment from Borodin. He wasn't disappointed.

"Reckoned that might be what happened, what with Dale dead and Captain Leclerc up to his neck in hot water. We need all the leadership we can get, not that

there's many of us left. I do up the roster, you know."
Borodin looked at him, as if expecting comment. Austin wasn't certain what the master sergeant hoped he would say.

"I wish I could help Manfred," Austin said. "He's a fine soldier, no matter what they say about him."

"You heard the rumor, too? That he's run off to hide in Cingulum and do nothing but start riots? Pure garbage." Borodin's voice lowered. "I support Aaron Sandoval all the way, but as Lord Governor of a Republic Prefecture, not any other way."

Austin said nothing. There was more making the rounds in the barracks than he had expected. Soldiers generally held themselves above political concerns.

"No, Lieutenant, I tell you, Sandoval's a respectable fellow, brave and true as a tempered steel blade, but he's got my loyalty only as long as he follows in Devlin Stone's footsteps."

"I can't believe Manfred—Captain Leclerc—would support any opposition to the government."

"Might not, but that's not what some are saying." Borodin cleared his throat. "I know you and the captain are friends and all, but I got to know where his true loyalties are."

"Manfred supports The Republic all the way," Austin said without hesitation. He straightened a little when he saw that wasn't the intent of Borodin's nascent question. "You think Manfred's sold out to somebody else?"

"Not me, Lieutenant, not me," the sergeant said, not wanting to condemn an FCL officer after Austin had so strongly spoken his praises. "But the others, now, they don't know him so well. But is there any chance he might be running with the MBA?"

Austin knew he had to be careful answering this.

He knew a fraction of his father's plans, and they seemed to involve Manfred training in the MBA's modified 'Mechs.

"The Mirach Business Association? What does a trade group have to do with Manfred?"

"Now you're insulting my intelligence, Lieutenant." Borodin looked as if he wanted to spit.

"Never, Master Sergeant, never. Fill me in." Austin glanced over his shoulder to the open doorway to be sure no one eavesdropped on them.

I'm getting too paranoid, he thought. He turned his attention back to the sergeant and tried to quash the feelings of being spied on.

"Well, sir, rumor has it that the MBA is outfitting IndustrialMechs. Lots of them. Like the AgroMech that almost did you in. It had missiles, didn't it?"

"I can't say if there are more than a few refitted IndustrialMechs, but the one that attacked me was packing. But I refuse to believe Manfred was piloting it, no matter what Tortorelli or the Ministry of Information say."

"Some say that he was in the cockpit, sir. Some." Borodin fixed him with a gimlet stare. "You wouldn't go against your own father. I know that, but the grapevine says maybe you and the head of the MBA are conspiring to overthrow him."

"I am loyal to my father, to Mirach, and The Republic," Austin said forcefully.

More than this, he couldn't see Manfred doing anything but supporting The Republic. If the captain drove a 'Mech for the MBA, it had to be with the Governor's full approval and for some reason other than overthrowing the government.

Austin felt a small shiver when he realized other schisms were possible when Lady Elora and Calvilena

Tortorelli were mixed into this brew of conspiracy. Austin was sure something Hanna had told his father about Lady Elora had brought about her death. Elora had made little secret of her contempt for the Governor, but how far would she go to oppose him? Would she be willing to kill him?

How did he find the right threat to follow? Too many factions meant Mirach stood on the brink of a vicious civil war that could split it into several blocs, each fighting the other. It could take decades to pull such a politically sundered world back together.

"Yes, sir, it's possible the captain was out there on the test range when you tried out the MiningMech. The MBA gave orders for him to kill you."

Austin had to laugh. "Then that probably means Marta Kinsolving knew nothing about the attack. She saved me."

"She saved you by ramming the AgroMech, didn't she? Now that's a poser, unless there's argument in the MBA ranks about how to seize power."

"That doesn't make much sense, does it? Too many rumors and not enough facts is the real problem, Master Sergeant."

"Yeah, I guess so," the sergeant said, his forehead furrowing at the complicated situation. The problem with conspiracy theories was the myriad possibilities inherent in them. Anything could be proved—or disproved. Lack of evidence became proof.

"I'm glad one rumor is put to rest."

"That doesn't mean the MBA isn't getting ready to field all those converted 'Mechs. Who'd be a better pilot to lead them than Manfred Leclerc, especially considering how he's been treated?"

"One man in a 'Mech, no matter how good, cannot stand forever against trained infantry and battle armor," Austin said. "It would be a hard fight, but sheer numbers would eventually overwhelm a BattleMech." Many of their unit maneuvers had been designed to prove this, not only to the soldiers of the FCL but also to Tortorelli. "Has the MBA been recruiting pilots for their refitted 'Mechs?"

"Not really," Borodin said. His tone didn't convince Austin he was telling the truth.

"Not that I'm interested, but where might the MBA approach a soldier about strapping down in the cockpit of a 'Mech? Think of the firepower compared to what we use! Autocannon, missiles, what a weapon that would make." He saw the dreamy expression on Borodin's face. Such a romantic vision appealed to the sergeant.

"They wouldn't find any recruits here," Borodin assured him. Austin waited. Heavy silence fell until the sergeant grew uneasy. "Not that I know anything, mind you."

"You're a topflight tech, Master Sergeant. Getting your hands on a refitted 'Mech would be a dream come true. Almost as big a dream come true as me piloting one."

"Might be, if you have a thirst, you might stop at the Borzoi after midnight some night."

"Some night," Austin said slowly. "I'm usually busy."

"Might be a good time to go tomorrow night," Borodin said. "For a nightcap. Nothing more."

"Nothing more," Austin said. "Unless I chance upon an old friend so we can reminisce."

"You might do that, too," Borodin said uneasily. He buried his nose back in the tech manual, then turned away so his back was to Austin. If he had written it across the wall in meter-high red letters, the sergeant couldn't have signaled the end of their conversation any more clearly.

Austin left the no longer garrulous Borodin, made a circuit of the adjacent rooms without finding any others from the FCL, then returned to his car and drove back to Cingulum. This time the drive was slower to give him time to think as three of the planet's four moons snaked across the dark sky above.

19

The Borzoi Tavern was decorated as a Russian hunting lodge, complete with stuffed animal heads on the wood-paneled walls and long oak tables stained with beer. On closer inspection, Austin Ortega saw that the stains were designs embedded permanently into a plastic surface and the animal heads were as artificial as the Russian motif. A bear of a man with a bushy beard worked behind the long bar, his dark eyes roaming endlessly as if they were radar dishes searching out enemies. He kept his hands below the level of the bar, making Austin worry a bit about what he might be holding.

"Good evening," Austin said to the barman, who only nodded to him. The bartender kept his hands hidden from sight. "Stormy night, isn't it?"

A stunstick was one thing, but a large-caliber pistol was something else, if the huge man chose to fight. Austin could outrun a man intent on stunning him but had found dodging worked better than running when his opponent carried a firearm. And that was the way Austin felt inside the artificially cozy tavern—if not surrounded by enemies, then by suspicious people who were not in the least friendly.

Or it might just have been that he was so keyed up that everyone looked suspicious. He tried to calm down, but it wasn't easy.

"Seen worse storms this time of year," the bartender said. Austin decided conversation wasn't too likely and went to the back of the long room to sit at an empty table. Both bartender and barmaid ignored him.

He wasn't here to drink. He was following the hint given him by Dmitri Borodin. He shrugged off his coat and draped it over his chair.

He lounged back and found his mind drifting. He smiled as he remembered better times with Dale, when he had been a recruit standing before Manfred for the first time and, in his haste to dress, had forgotten to zip his fly. He recalled the terror and outright exhilaration he had felt in the MiningMech as he battled the AgroMech on the test range. Those memory fragments were peculiar ones he couldn't quite fit together. Extreme fear and equally extreme gratification. He might have been killed at the 'Mech plant, but he had been doing what he had been trained to do. And he had been in a 'Mech, even if it had not been modified to carry weapons. Austin had felt complete piloting a real 'Mech.

When the stroll down memory lane began to stumble into such odd paths, he grew restive. Austin forced himself not to look at his watch, but he was sure he had been in the Borzoi for at least fifteen minutes. Past midnight now.

Nothing had happened. The bartender didn't even shout at him to order or leave, not that the business was particularly good; the Borzoi was empty of anyone else but the staff. Still, what business likes loiterers? Not being forced to order or getting chased out told Austin he was on the right track. Then it hit him. *He* had to initiate contact, and he had been given the key.

"Can I get a nightcap?" Austin called to the bartender. The man's bushy eyebrows rose slightly. He leaned over the bar and talked in hushed tones with the barmaid.

"You want anything else?" the bartender asked.

"Just a nightcap." Austin kicked himself for not speaking up sooner. Borodin had given him a code word and he had not recognized it as such. He should have realized, if these were Manfred's friends, they would require recognition signals. They wouldn't know otherwise that he wasn't bringing the authorities with him.

The barmaid went about her chores, disappeared into the back room, only to return with a tray of glasses a minute later. Another ten minutes passed and Austin half stood when a man bundled like a mummy against the night came in from the street, the gusty wind sneaking inside until the door slammed against the storm. The staff greeted him warmly, all gathering around to talk to him as if he were a long-lost relative, but Austin saw the barmaid cast a furtive glance over her shoulder in his direction. Whatever the newcomer said to her involved Austin.

He wished now that he had come armed. For all that, he wished he had worn battle armor. Finally giving in to his nervousness, Austin checked his watch and saw he had been in the Borzoi for almost twenty minutes. It was time to go. He had hoped Manfred might show up, or someone who could help him get in touch with his friend. Borodin's recognition code hadn't amounted to anything. Austin hadn't even got a drink out of it.

As he came around the small table, the bartender barked, "We don't close for another hour. Sit down, tovarich." The man's voice was gruff, but Austin heard no menace in it, so he sank down and put his hands on the table in front of him. Waiting became increasingly difficult.

Suddenly his eyes went wide and he shot to his feet.

"Manfred!"

The customer at the bar pushed away a heavy scarf from his face.

"Go on, advertise it to the world." Manfred Leclerc laughed to take the sting out of his rebuke. "You need to learn restraint when it comes to espionage."

"Spying? Is that what this is all about?"

Manfred seated himself beside Austin and leaned closer so he could speak in an almost inaudible whisper.

"I'm not a spy and I didn't try to kill you, but you know that. Your father told you as much. The way you came tonight shows you probably ignored him when he told you not to get any more involved."

"You're my friend, Manfred. It looks like you need help—almost as much as I need answers."

"I'm your friend forever, Austin, for all time," Manfred said, reaching out. He pressed his hand into Austin's arm. "I'm glad you didn't swallow that line Elora put out about me trying to kill you."

"There wouldn't be any reason," Austin said.

"What happened? I've reached the point of believing even Borodin might have ulterior motives."

"Dmitri?" Manfred laughed. "That's rich. Dmitri is about the most transparent man I've ever seen. Everything is wide-open with him. He serves faithfully and well. Don't ever mistrust him."

"Who tried to kill me? And have you learned anything about Dale's death?"

"Slow down," Manfred said. He glanced back at the barmaid. She shook her head. "We've only got a few minutes before they find us."

"Who?" Austin was genuinely perplexed.

"Someone with great power who might have forged an alliance off-world that we need to fight," Manfred said.

"Elora?"

"Of course Elora," Manfred said. "I thought you understood more of this. You'd better stand clear and let your father's plans unwind."

"I want to help. Did she kill Dale? Hanna? Are you saying she framed you? How?"

"That 'Mech *was* mine, but someone hijacked it," Manfred said. "That's why my fingerprints were all over it. I'd spent hours going over it with the techs." He stared at Austin. "I wouldn't have had the time away from observation if the FCL hadn't been transferred and Tortorelli so intent on disbanding us. I was given pointless assignments and no one checked up on me."

"That's why my father was so intent on getting rid of the FCL? To give you access to the MBA 'Mechs?"

Manfred nodded. "If the man who hijacked the 'Mech was careful piloting it after replacing the access code cards, he might have only smudged my prints from a training mission I ran earlier that morning."

"Whoever piloted it was experienced."

"I'm not sure who the driver is, but I think I can identify him. Besides whipping the 'Mechs into shape, I've been busy nosing around. Getting evidence against him is something else, since he seems to change his name more often than he does his underwear. A real shadowy character. One of Elora's henchmen is my guess."

"But he knew how to pilot a 'Mech," Austin protested.

"He might be a cashiered BattleMech pilot from off-world. One thing is for sure: he has no trouble killing."

"What about Marta Kinsolving?" Austin asked. "How does she fit in?"

"You can trust her," Manfred said. "We've come to work close together." Austin's expression prompted Manfred to continue. "I'm training the MBA's pilots, and yes, your father knows. He doesn't approve of such dangerous equipment being built, but I'm keeping its use in check. I assure you, Austin, we're all trying to keep Mirach from boiling over into civil war."

Austin thought about what Manfred had said. He knew he should obey his father's wishes—and take Manfred's advice—but he feared that what he thought was so important might be ignored.

"Dale?" Austin asked, afraid of the answer. "Did Elora have him killed?"

"I don't know," Manfred said, "but I'll wager at any odds you want to give that she ordered a henchman to drive the car through the sidewalk café and kill Hanna. The car might have been aiming for Dale, too. When it missed, he was killed during the training exercise. If I'm right about Elora's henchman being militarily trained off-world, that could explain how he blended in so easily to replace the marker missiles with live rounds."

"What did Hanna tell my father that got her killed?" Austin asked. "She must have told Dale, and that got him killed. Elora probably thinks I know it, too. She'll keep sending her goons after me and I don't really know a thing."

"You deserve to know," Manfred said, "but I promised your father to keep you out of the loop. It's for your own good. Borodin should never have given you the code word to reach me, either."

"He's a good man," Austin said. "And he knows I won't quit. You do, too."

"I've got to speak to your father. Can you arrange it? I tried reaching him through our usual channels but found that Elora was tapping them. She's becoming more aggressive in her spying."

"Usual channels?" asked Austin. "I don't understand."

Before Manfred could answer, the barmaid reached for a pitcher of beer, let out a yelp, and then spun about, the beer arcing away from her body and spewing into the face of two men entering the Borzoi Tavern.

"MPs! They must have followed you," rasped Manfred. "Get out the back way. They might be after you, too."

"We need to stay in touch," Austin said. The barmaid continued her wild spin and smashed the glass pitcher into the head of the leading military policeman. He staggered into the second MP, but both were shoved out of the way as three more pushed their way inside. No matter how the barmaid tried to slow the newcomers, they evaded her and went directly for the rear of the tavern.

"North side of the Czar Alexander Fountain," Manfred said. Then he kicked his chair spinning across the room, forcing the MPs to vault over it. He took the opportunity to run for the storeroom, duck inside, and slam the door. Austin heard a lock secure the heavy wood door.

He had no idea what Manfred meant, but he could figure it out later. Austin stood and started to call to the MPs, to slow them down. The one nearest him, a woman with a savage scar running the length of her left cheek, locked eyes with him. He knew in that instant Manfred had been right. They came not only for the renegade guard captain but for him, too.

The MP fumbled to draw the stunstick thrust through her broad webbed belt. Austin's brain kicked into high gear. He saw that all the MP needed to do was activate the electric prod and fall toward him. He'd have no chance of avoiding the rod, and the lightest touch would paralyze him for several seconds.

He caught the edge of the table, straightened his legs, and heaved. The wood table upended and crashed into the woman, causing her to drop the stunstick. Austin considered fighting the MP for it, then knew he didn't stand a chance in hand-to-hand with her.

Grabbing another chair, he flung it into the tangle of military police, then darted for the rest rooms. The MPs weren't fools. They had to know dangerous fugitives might try to escape through windows or out back doors. Austin hoped Manfred had found some secure hidey-hole or a secret way out.

The small windows in the rest rooms opened into an alley where other MPs undoubtedly awaited a foolish exit. Austin jumped to the washbasin, caught an air vent grating in the ceiling, and used his weight to yank it down. He pulled himself up and wiggled into the tight space as the MPs burst in after him.

He had only seconds—less!—before they would notice he had chosen an aerial getaway route. Twisting like a snake, he reached a branch in the filthy ductwork and saw a way out. A fan spun sluggishly above him, pulling out stale air and sending it into the stormy night. Austin knocked away the frame on the fan and tumbled onto the roof.

Luck was with him. The flat roof was deserted. He scrambled to his feet, slipped, went to the edge, and saw his chance. He retreated a few paces, then ran for all he was worth. At the edge of the roof he launched himself outward over the street to land on the top of a truck just pulling away from the roadblock the MPs had set up. From the cab came angry shouts and the driver pulled over.

Before the driver could exit to see what had crashed down on the top of his truck, Austin slid across and jumped off the far side, using the truck to shield him from the MPs. He caught his breath, then walked quickly down an alley away from the truck. The driver shouted and heavy booted feet echoed down the street, telling him he had only a few seconds before they spotted him.

Austin ducked down behind a stack of crates as a light beam cut through the night, seeking him out. He heard the MPs arguing; then the beam vanished. Straining to hear, Austin waited for sounds that would tell him they were coming down the alley after him. After an eternity, he peered around the crate. The truck had driven off and no one was in sight patrolling the street. He brushed himself off and hurried away.

He had escaped. But now what?

= 20 =

Ministry of Information, Cingulum
Mirach
3 May 3133

"What went wrong?" Lady Elora asked. She fought to keep her voice level, but the man irritated her. He stood in front of her desk, smug and self-satisfied, and he had failed.

No one failed her. Twice.

"Relying on military police proved to be a mistake," he said. The man who had been a waiter, a technician loading missiles, and an IndustrialMech pilot was still dressed in an MP uniform. "It's only a matter of time before they are found. As angry as the MPs were at the beating they took, neither Leclerc nor Ortega will live long enough to be interrogated."

"I know where Austin Ortega is," Elora said. "He was observed returning to the Palace an hour ago."

"Then I can leave this uniform on and take care of him before dawn." The man shrugged. "With the guards Tortorelli assigned to the Palace, I could walk past them without any trouble. With this uniform, I could get them to help me slit the Baronet's throat."

"And how will you find Leclerc?"

"That, Lady Elora, is my secret, but I have ways to unearth anything. Anything at all." He crossed his arms and looked at her as if this were his office and she was the menial.

Secrets, fumed Elora. *What do you know of secrets?* She leaned back and considered him. He had proved useful twice. But now?

"I see you are thinking about removing me," he said without any sign of fear in his pale blue eyes. Elora hated him for those eyes. Her mother had spent years describing the man who had fathered her, until Elora had a perfect mental image of the raping sadist. The Clansman who had sired her had eyes this color. There the resemblance ended. He had been so large and physically powerful in her mother's fierce reminiscences of the rape. This man lacked stature, which was perfect for his job of assassin. No one remembered a man who looked like this. No one remembered ordinary.

The Clan blood flowing in her veins might be dilute, but she had vowed to make up for that while still a young girl. Her mother's hastily arranged marriage to a young landowner from Ventrale had provided her daughter with legitimacy and nobility, but Elora still railed against her fate. Not good enough to be Clansworn? Over and over she told herself that genetic engineering could not matter as much as determination. She would show them her greatness by turning over the entire planet to Kal Radick.

Of course, she'd received no response to the communiqué she'd sent via DropShip so many weeks ago. He didn't know who she was, but she'd show him. In a way, it didn't matter to her if he even acknowledged such a fine gift. Conquering a world using words and carefully spun schemes would be reward enough for her. She would know she had deposed Ortega and made a fool of Tortorelli, then grabbed power.

But if Radick offered her the planetary governorship in his new order, she would not turn it down. She would show him and the Steel Wolves that even a drop of Clan blood was enough to triumph.

This nothing in front of her had failed. It troubled her that he read her so expertly, but he had survived on several worlds using his wits.

"You have to prove your worth to me," she said. "I would be a fool to waste a valuable asset. I would be equally foolish to permit a flawed one to survive."

"I kill to make my living. I also find out things," he said, grinning wickedly. "You've worked your way up in the Ministry of Information by character assassination and double-dealing."

"*This* is the best you can do? All you needed to do was ask anyone in the Ministry. They all hate me—and all could give detailed recitations of every person I stepped on as I came to my current position." She kept her face impassive as she saw the expression on his face. He thought he held a trump card.

"You've contacted Prefect Radick about giving him control of Mirach," the man said. "Reports say Radick is no longer loyal to The Republic, and you plan to take advantage of this shifting allegiance. Mirach would be a different world under Clan domination."

"You spin fanciful tales as well as fail in what should have been simple assignments," she said.

"Your childhood was spent battling an inferiority complex. You were a bastard child with endless ambitions to prove herself, to have someone to respect, if not love, her." His smile broadened even more. "I like that."

"That I am a bastard of a Clan warrior?"

"That you have ambition. I hold no store by their genetic program."

"Yes, you fought against them, didn't you? That's where you learned to pilot a BattleMech. But you were a coward who fled rather than engage in combat and were stripped of your command." It was Elora's turn to grin. "I find out things, too."

"Just so we understand each other," the man said. His smile had melted into a scowl now.

"I understand you well," Elora said. "You failed to kill Leclerc, who is now in hiding and probably teaching MBA pilots to use their modified 'Mechs. That will make my coup that much more difficult to achieve. You also failed twice to kill the Baronet, so what information he might carry is still a threat."

"His brother and the reporter, they were the ones to fear. Austin Ortega doesn't know anything that can harm you."

In a rush of intuition, Elora knew the source of the man's background data on her: Hanna Leong's files. After killing her, he had searched the woman's files and read what she had discovered.

"Was there anything about an air transport crash?" Elora asked.

"What? I don't understand."

"No, you wouldn't," Elora said. She took a small pistol from her desk, aimed, and fired a single deadly

21

Palace of Facets, Cingulum
Mirach
3 May 3133

"**F**ather, listen to me," Austin Ortega said angrily. "They weren't trying to arrest Manfred and me. They were trying to kill us!"

"I don't think so, Austin. Not only had I told you to let the matter lie, you met him in secret. How would it have looked if the MPs had caught you, along with Manfred?" Sergio Ortega stared at his son, colorless eyes unfathomable. There was a hint of worry but not the way Austin expected. His father was more upset by the bad publicity of the Baronet being caught with a renegade officer than he was over the unfairness of it.

"They were military police, not civilian officers," Austin said. "They killed the people in the Borzoi and set fire to the tavern to cover their crimes."

"I read the official legate's report on the incident," Sergio said. "There's no evidence that the MPs did anything wrong. It was the bartender, this Pavel Orndorff, who set fire to the place. They have surveillance video of it happening." He shook his head sadly. "You could have been killed. You and Manfred."

"I can take care of myself," Austin said, trying to keep his anger in check. "You can't treat me like a child."

"You're not a child, but you're behaving like one. Just for one instant consider the possibility that I know more about what's going on than you. If you keep blundering into business that's not your own, I might not be able to save you."

"I don't need saving. Tell me what you're planning. Why don't you remove Elora? You know she doctored those surveillance tapes to show whatever she wanted. I'm sure, Father, that the bartender wouldn't set fire to the place and kill himself. That's a cover-up."

Austin saw the shift in his father's expression and didn't like what it might mean.

"You can't send me off-world or to Ventrale or wherever far away to get rid of me. I swear, Father, I'll be back. You *have* to take me into your confidence."

"You've shown you don't deserve it," Sergio said coldly.

"I do, Father. My fitreps in the FCL were always tops. I'm a quick study. I can find out what happened to Dale and Hanna if you let me."

"You'll do as you're told," Sergio said, his anger flaring now. "People have died needlessly because of your ill-conceived rendezvous. Leclerc is on the run and is hiding who knows where. That alone makes it more difficult for me to act against Elora and to stop the rioting."

"This isn't fair," Austin said.

"There is no such thing as fair. I thought you'd learned that by now. You're on my staff to learn. Keep quiet and do so." Sergio shook his head once to forestall more argument. He leaned over and touched the annunciator button on his desk. The tall carved wood doors swung inward on their silent hinges.

Only the doors were silent. A gabbling crowd pressed through from the Armorer's Chamber to shove against the Governor's desk.

"Governor Ortega, what can you tell us about your son's involvement with the traitor Manfred Leclerc?" shouted a reporter Austin had seen briefly on an early Ministry of Information newscast.

Austin stepped to one side, shocked at the ferocity of the questioning. Somehow, through the crush of reporters representing most news purveyors on Mirach, he saw the only one who counted. Lady Elora stood toward the rear of the Armorer's Chamber speaking quietly with her director. The harried rat-faced man held a small control panel rather than using a full-scale one. From the amount of sweat on his wrinkled forehead, Barnaby obviously had trouble performing the intricate maneuvers with the cameras that Elora demanded.

For a brief instant, Elora's emerald eyes locked with Austin's. He thought a flicker of a smile danced over her thin lips, and then her amplified voice boomed over the din of other questions. There was no doubt about how she used her position as Minister to best the others technologically.

"Governor Ortega, is it true that your son evaded

arrest last night after consorting with a known traitor?"

"Ladies and gentlemen, please," cried Sergio. "This is my office. I will answer your questions in the conference room. Not here."

Austin looked for guards to move the crowd from the outer office, but none were in sight. He maneuvered his way around the group of reporters and gave the secretary instructions. The man corralled five others from the Governor's office staff and began to herd the reporters out and down the hall. They went more willingly after Elora made a point of leading the parade. Austin found his way back to Sergio as the crowd dispersed.

"You need the FCL guarding you," he said. He thought his father started to say something, then stopped. A mask of calm settled, the mask he always wore when dealing with difficult situations. Austin envied him in that moment. He couldn't find composure when his best friend was running from the authorities and he had no idea who had murdered his brother.

Worse than such turmoil was his father refusing to trust him.

"Thank you," Sergio said, eyes forward. Austin wasn't sure if the Governor thanked the secretary and the others or him. He didn't ask as he followed at the proper two steps behind as they went to the conference room. The Governor's protocol officer ought to have prepared for this, but Austin hadn't seen him in days. More to the point, as Minister, Lady Elora should have helped control the news flow instead of being in the forefront of blowing up the dam.

The tumult hit Austin the instant he stepped onto the dais with his father. A hundred questions from a hundred mouths all vied for supremacy, but one came through loud and clear.

"Why was the Baronet consorting with a known felon?" Elora might have asked the question, but she didn't. She didn't have to because this was the single query they all wanted answered.

"My son Austin was attempting to get Captain Leclerc to surrender to authorities when this incident occurred," Sergio said. "He had almost convinced Leclerc of the folly of remaining a fugitive, when heavy-handed officers of the Legate's military police interrupted. Leclerc was scared off by their unnecessarily violent entrance into the tavern."

"Isn't it true that your son fled with the traitor Leclerc?"

"You play fast and loose with our legal system by such unproved accusations. Manfred Leclerc deserves his day in court. When he is arrested, his guilt or innocence will be determined."

"Then you don't deny that your son consorts with traitors and killers?"

"Next question, please," Sergio said. Austin wanted to say something to defend himself but saw his father's clenched fists and how he struggled to remain calm.

"One last question, Governor Ortega," Elora boomed, drowning out the other reporters. "How do you respond to the recent off-world communiqué from both Prefect Radick and Lord Governor Sandoval expressing 'no confidence' in your ability to perform your duty as head of Mirach's government?"

The room fell silent. Then the other reporters babbled their own questions.

"Why haven't you told us of this message from the leaders of The Republic, Governor?" asked one. "What are you hiding?" asked another. "What else aren't you telling us?" The noise rose to a deafening pitch. Even if Sergio had answered, no one could have heard him.

Austin fought to protect his father as the reporters surged forward with their shouted questions. Elora was Minister of Information and had flatly stated that not only had the Governor lost the confidence of the two most powerful leaders in the Prefecture, but he had also committed what was quickly becoming the ultimate crime: not revealing communications from other worlds immediately. The fall of the HPG built new conspiracies at every turn.

Austin had almost forced back the reporters when he heard Elora's final cut.

"Since the leaders of Prefecture IV have lost confidence in your ability to lead, Governor Ortega, when will a replacement be named?"

Austin felt as if he had been hit in the belly with a sledgehammer. Elora's scheme was transparent. There wasn't a replacement because the Lord Governor had not lost confidence in Sergio Ortega. But Elora could make a strong case for Legate Tortorelli leading a military coup until a civilian replacement arrived.

Which it never would.

She would disgrace the Governor and then put her toady in Sergio's place. Retaining the powerful position as head of the Ministry of Information, Elora would control Mirach completely from the shadows. Tortorelli would retain his post as Legate, giving him military and de facto civilian authority.

All the reins of power ran to her grasping fingers.

"Father, this way," Austin said. Sergio let his son guide him from the conference room into the hall. To Austin's surprise, Dmitri Borodin and four other soldiers he did not recognize hurried toward them. All five were dressed in the forest green Home Guard uniforms.

"Nobody's allowed out, Austin," Borodin said, putting up his hand to stop Austin from leaving.

"It's a mob scene in there," Austin said. "Help the Baron back to his office—"

Borodin looked grief-stricken as he stepped away from the other four. In a low voice he said, "We're here to make sure Governor Ortega doesn't try to go anywhere *but* his office. Those were Legate Tortorelli's orders, straight from his own lips before we came here from the barracks."

"That's an outrage!" Austin cried.

"Don't argue," Sergio said. "It's not worth it, son." He went directly back to his office trailed by two guards, leaving Austin behind with Borodin and the other soldiers.

Austin seethed at such injustice. His father was a Baron, Governor of Mirach, and was being treated like a prisoner. Then he settled down and realized that Borodin was a good soldier and followed orders, even if they ran counter to his own loyalties.

"Thanks for what you've done so far," Austin said. "Can I count on you later?"

"You can count on me, sir, but the patrol with me," Borodin said uneasily, "they're all loyal to Lord Governor Sandoval—if he declares for the Federated Suns. Every time a DropShip lands, there's stories. They're sayin' Sandoval's trying to take back FedSuns worlds, and there're some who'd just as soon have it that way." This was a shock to Austin, too concerned with the local situation to even consider what might be going on in the rest of the Prefecture, especially with the HPG net down. The FedSuns was one of the older states from which Devlin Stone had taken worlds to build The Republic. If the rumors were true—and Austin had no way to be sure that they were—then Mirach was in more trouble than he'd realized. And where did the Envoy from Sandoval, Parsons, stand? "They don't exactly trust me, knowing I prefer The

Republic, but it's gettin' hard, Lieutenant, it's getting real hard, to keep thinkin' The Republic's the right way to go.''

Austin saw the two with Borodin overheard and grinned. This would be reported to the officer of the day.

"Carry on, Master Sergeant," he said, as if he were still Borodin's commanding officer.

"Wait, Lieutenant; I got more orders coming in." Borodin pulled out a small radio and pushed it close to his ear. "Come on," he said to the two soldiers. "We're shutting down the news conference. The Governor's incommunicado from now on, by order of Legate Tortorelli." Borodin cast an anguished look at Austin, then silently mouthed, "Get out of here," before leading his small squad to the conference room.

Austin wondered if the next order from Tortorelli would be to arrest everyone in the Palace. This was as close to a coup as there could be without shots being fired. And he had warned his father about turning over the FCL to Tortorelli's command.

Feeling vindicated did little to ease the fear growing like a cancer in Austin's gut. With Tortorelli shutting off the Governor and his staff from the reporters, Lady Elora would be the only source relaying government news to the public. Austin knew what those reports were likely to say after she had openly charged the Governor with being a traitor.

He took a side corridor and quickly lost himself in the maze of the Palace. This had been home for all his life and now it felt as if he walked an alien landscape, terrain as odd and deadly as the plains outside the Blood Hills Barracks.

Austin rounded a corner and came to an abrupt halt. In an alcove not five meters away Marta Kinsolving held a Span-net device to her ear and spoke rapidly into it. Austin caught only snippets but went cold inside when he caught the gist of her conversation.

"Marta!" he called. She looked up, startled. She hastily clicked off the phone and shoved it into her pocket.

"I've got to go," she said, spinning away from him and walking as rapidly as she could without running. Austin was under no such polite rule. He caught up with her before she reached the door leading to the small snow-crusted park south of the Palace.

"I heard what you said to Manfred," he said. "You can't do this."

She faced him squarely. Marta's face hardened and she set her jaw.

"Protect yourself, Austin. I know the orders Tortorelli just gave. He and Elora have finally made their move and we can't let them succeed." She pulled away and dashed into the mazelike hedges in the south park. Austin hesitated for a moment, then ran after her. If he didn't convince her to call off the rebellion, the entire planet would be plunged into civil war.

22

Cingulum
Mirach
3 May 3133

Austin Ortega sprinted and dived into Marta Kinsolving's limousine as the door closed. The woman looked up in surprise at the unexpected intrusion.

"Austin!" Marta scowled at him. "You shouldn't meddle, Austin. What do you think you can do against the Legate?" she asked tartly. "Get out right now and go protect your father."

"Tortorelli won't hurt my father," he said. "He won't even imprison him until he's moved his forces and Elora has whipped up even more fear and made a transfer of power plausible. The majority of citizens still support the government," Austin said. His heart hammered and his mouth had turned to cotton. He had listened to his father prattle on endlessly about "key moments" and "turning points in history." He had never believed such phenomena existed and had thought even if they had he would have nothing to do with them. Austin realized how wrong he was. The destiny of his world hung in the balance now, this very instant. Even more worrisome, what *he* did mattered most.

"You don't know anything," Marta said. She reached to signal the driver, but Austin caught her wrist.

"Even a lance of refitted AgroMechs won't stand against the Legate's combined forces," he said. Austin knew he had hit the target by the way Marta blanched.

"Don't try to stop us," she said, recovering some of her poise. She yanked free of his grip but made no move to alert the driver again. "You, of all people, should see what's going on. Mirach is facing a civil war that will destroy us. The riots are only a prelude to the troubles falling on our heads like a runaway DropShip."

"It's Elora's doing," Austin said. "A blind man can see that Tortorelli's her pawn. She plays on the lack of HPG communication. She's responsible for fueling the street demonstrations with fear and paranoia, but the only way she can get rid of my father is through Tortorelli. She's chosen a weak tool for that job."

"Not as weak as you think. He's issued a full mobilization order, but he's not doing the planning this time. It won't be an easy victory like you had in the war games he tried to impress Parsons with."

"So you're saying it's Elora's strategy?" Austin knew Tortorelli had expert field commanders. Given decent orders and unleashed, they were a match for any on-planet opposition.

"The MBA is right in fielding 'Mechs to protect

ourselves. Ultimately we'll be protecting the people—
and your father's government."

"But think of the slaughter," Austin said. He surprised himself. He was beginning to sound like his
father, arguing against the refitted 'Mechs rallying
against the Legate's forces. "Your modified 'Mechs
can do incredible damage to Tortorelli's troops, but
the collateral damage could be bad, especially if fighting takes place in the city." He wanted to save Mirach,
but not at the expense of the lives of the populace.
"Even if Manfred's worked with your pilots, they can't
have gained enough experience to prevent wholesale
destruction when they engage troops in battle armor
supported by tanks."

"What do you suggest?" she asked, leaning back.
Marta wasn't at ease but was willing to listen. Austin
counted that as progress.

"You need a wedge driven through the middle of
Tortorelli's force. Psychological warfare, and not military action, is your only chance. I've spoken with a
few noncoms and know their loyalties are divided."
Austin didn't itemize exactly how divided that loyalty
was nor that he had talked to only one noncom. Master Sergeant Borodin sounded like an island of fealty
in an ocean of confused allegiances. Out of that confusion, Austin had to build a new loyalty for the Baron,
but Elora had to be countered forcefully. With Sergio
Ortega bottled up, he could not be the rallying figure.

"Are you that wedge?" she asked bluntly.

"No," Austin said. "Dale would have been, but he's
dead. I'm liked but not as respected as Manfred
Leclerc among the FCL. We need to find him and
reestablish his role as leader."

"Easier said than done," Marta muttered. "Elora
has turned him into a criminal. Having him in com-

mand of the FCL again won't be enough, especially if it becomes a rebel unit in the midst of the Home Guard."

Austin hoped that Tortorelli had not had enough time to fully deploy the FCL soldiers yet. A strong leader like Manfred at the head of a strong unit like the FCL might sway some of the soldiers in the Home Guard. Austin slumped a little, knowing he was grasping at straws. But the alternative to weakening Tortorelli's forces was unleashing the MBA 'Mechs. He didn't think Marta understood the potential for extreme destruction by the mechanical juggernauts.

"We need to talk, you, me, Manfred," Austin said. "Call him and—"

"I can't reach him," Marta said. "He calls me."

"I know how to contact him, but I don't have the resources to help him when I do."

"What do you have to do to get in touch with him?" she asked.

Austin felt the swirl of intrigue all around. He wasn't sure he trusted Marta fully, but he had no choice with his father under Tortorelli's thumb, the FCL being dismantled, and Manfred on the run. Manfred would know what to do once they talked this through.

"North side of the Czar Alexander Fountain," he said.

"What's that?" Marta came out of her own deep thought. "Oh. How you contact Manfred." She instructed the driver to change destination. The massive limo swayed slightly as it took a corner at high speed. Otherwise, Austin had no sensation of movement as they raced through the increasingly war-torn capital.

"He's lucky to have a friend like you," Marta said suddenly.

"And a patron like you. How did you get him to train your refitted IndustrialMech pilots?"

Marta shrugged, her brown eyes drifting away from Austin for a moment. Then they came back to fix on his.

"Manfred is quite an impressive man. In many ways." A small smile came to her lips.

Austin understood then how the captain of the FCL and the president of the Mirach Business Association had come to trust one another. He had overlooked the simple notion that there was more to the world than politics.

A red light flashed on the padded console arm beside Marta.

"Czar Alexander Fountain," she said. She changed the polarization on the window next to Austin so he could look out. The huge white limo drove several times around the fountain with its towering twenty-meter-high sprays and intricate, lacy veils of tumbling water before Austin spotted the message.

Anyone passing by on the sidewalk circling the fountain might think it was only graffiti, but Austin recognized the scrawl immediately as a locator code used by the FCL during maneuvers. He deciphered the relative position and passed along instructions to the driver. The section of town where they headed looked as if the war had already been fought, leaving behind only destroyed buildings and fearful inhabitants.

Austin drummed his fingers nervously, worrying that Manfred might be dead amid this rubble. The limousine braked to a smooth stop.

"This is it, exactly four kilometers from the fountain," the driver said on the intercom.

"Here," Marta said to Austin, opening a small panel

in the door, revealing a 10-mm pistol. He took it, jacked a round into the chamber, and held the weapon for a moment to savor the feel and balance. He didn't recognize its make, but the operation was obvious enough.

"The clip has a mix of bullets," Marta said. "Every third round is an explosive round. The others are armor piercing."

"Couldn't cut through too much," Austin said, staring at the compact weapon. Then he reconsidered. Marta wasn't the sort to make idle boasts.

"At close range, a full clip of those will severely wound a soldier in light battle armor."

"I doubt it will come to that right now." Austin slid from the limo and found himself in a strange world unlike the regal elegance of the Palace of Facets or the starkly utilitarian FCL barracks. Scents of rotting garbage and death assaulted him as much as the sight of burned-out buildings and bodies partially buried in the rubble, no one even trying to dig them free.

Austin leveled the pistol and set off, looking for the next set of instructions from Manfred—if the captain was still alive.

23

Ministry of Information, Cingulum
Mirach
3 May 3133

"What do you mean, you lost contact?" Lady Elora's green eyes turned colder than jade as she glared at Calvilena Tortorelli. "Aren't the devices I loaned you adequate, or were the operators inept?"

"Please, Elora, don't be like this," Tortorelli said, moving about the Minister's office. He picked up knickknacks and replaced them after only cursory examination, making Elora angrier by the instant.

"How should I be, Calvy?" she asked with venom dripping from every word.

"They'll turn up again. Where could they have gone? After all, Kinsolving has a large communications company to run and those dreary MBA meetings to attend. And who cares about Ortega's worthless son? The Baronet does nothing but run hither and yon. He's completely lost in the world of political infighting that you and I are so adept in. It was a fine idea I had separating him from the FCL, although I suspect he is hardly a soldier, either."

"You forget who spearheaded the FCL attack during your so-called military exercise," Elora said. She wished she didn't need him to command the Home Guard. The civil unrest could be subdued quickly when he unleashed his forces, but it would come at a huge and bloody cost. Elora smiled faintly. She would be sure to assign the blame later where it belonged, after she was sure Mirach would be another shining jewel in the Clan's sword hilt and her true worth was recognized.

She rocked back in the chair behind her vast desk. Her eyes swept across the flat expanse. Newly embedded in the surface, angled by clever lenses to follow her as she swiveled about, were a half dozen different projected images monitoring not only what was on-air but also the faces of her directors and producers as they worked. She reached forward, the ring on a bony finger clicking slightly as it touched the desktop, and brushed across a slight depression. The array of monitors changed, giving her a view on the world outside the Ministry of Information.

Tortorelli prattled on, citing how quickly the Baron had been isolated from all support, and taking credit for clever ploys she had suggested. Let him think he was in charge and not being groomed to be the eventual scapegoat. Elora was more intent on watching the renewed wave of rioting in the streets. Cingulum was torn apart by a dozen disturbances. Stripping police, support from Governor Ortega had been difficult because she had done it slowly, incrementally, so no one really noticed, least of all Sergio Ortega. He knew he was a toothless tiger now but could do nothing to retrieve control because he had lost the means of enforcing his orders.

The police had become looters and rioters themselves when Elora had planted rumors of manpower cutbacks, punishments, and huge salary cuts due to declining planetary revenues. Mirach's economy had not weakened appreciably, but without the HPG to furnish second-to-second comparisons with other worlds in The Republic, gullible people would believe anything she told them because the news spoke to them directly every day, every night. She controlled the news and would the Minister of Information ever lie?

Elora almost laughed at how she had reported fighting on Achernar and set off another round of riots in Cingulum. She had heard only rumors from DropShip crews, but it sounded better—and served her purposes more—to report huge loss of life as if it were literal truth. Let the whispering spread.

"Can you be certain Kinsolving and the Baronet are not going to be problems?" she asked. "What of that renegade captain of yours?"

"Leclerc?" Tortorelli finished his circuit around the room, fingering all the small statues and objets d'art, then stopped in front of the huge faux window looking out across the city. Elora reached out a bejeweled hand to change the view to gauge Tortorelli's reaction, then stopped. He didn't care that he stared at a cleverly contrived monitor.

"You didn't arrest him at the Borzoi. Your military police have been equally incapable of tracking him since his escape."

"The Borzoi?" Tortorelli frowned, trying to recollect the name.

"The tavern where the MPs failed to kill him and young Ortega."

"Was that the name?" Tortorelli shook his head. "Some officer I didn't authorize was in charge. I am sure he was disciplined for his incompetence. It's in the report my staff filed."

Elora laughed and the Legate had no idea why. Tortorelli stood on the spot where the bogus MP officer's blood had been spilled by a single shot from her pistol. She had arranged for his body to be dumped at the edge of a riot and no one had noticed or cared. One day the Legate would suffer the same fate. But not today. She still needed his authority.

Elora considered all the possible replacements for Tortorelli after the Governor was deposed. Prefect Radick would undoubtedly follow her guidance in the matter, since it would leave him in control of Mirach.

"Are you any closer to capturing Leclerc, Calvy?" She lowered her voice to a husky whisper to erase any hint of criticism. She had always been told she could catch more flies with honey than with vinegar, though her need for an insect like Tortorelli was strictly circumstantial. He was already caught and when his usefulness evaporated, he could be quickly swatted.

"My best officers are working on finding him. He might be hiding in Havoc."

"They'll never find him there unless you move in adequate military power to level what buildings are still standing." Havoc was the name her own newscasters—in private—had given to a particularly ugly section of the city. Nothing but burned-out buildings and dangerous refugees filled the ten-square-block area.

"That might not be a bad idea. Thank you for suggesting it to me, Elora," the Legate said.

Elora had just set into motion the next step in her plan to marginalize Governor Ortega further and paint Legate Tortorelli as a bloody-handed butcher. She had to fight against overconfidence, but the time was almost at hand to contact Prefect Kal Radick and invite him to this fine world.

24

Havoc, Cingulum
Mirach
3 May 3133

Austin jumped at every small sound. Most were caused by rats and other scavengers feeding off the carcasses littering the streets—or what was left of the streets. Entire buildings had collapsed. He could picture in his mind's eye how the fronts would crumble and fall onto demonstrators, unable to escape because of their numbers. Then the remainder of the building, weakened to its foundations by fires, would slowly follow in a stately, almost majestic orgy of demolition.

His nose twitched at the scent of death and decay and dust, but he kept moving cautiously through the destruction. Austin clutched the small pistol Marta had given him so hard his hand turned sweaty. He kept thinking that the first two shells in the magazine were armor piercers, the third an explosive round. He concentrated so hard on that, he didn't hear the man creeping up from behind.

Austin jerked around when a tiny *pop!* sounded and a brilliant white star illuminated the area from a height of almost ten meters. His eyes swept around and up to the burning spot on a third-story window ledge, then dropped back to the silently stalking dark form. His pistol lifted.

"Halt or I'll fire!" he called. When the man hunting him did not stop, Austin fired. Once, twice. Both rounds hit squarely in the center of the man's torso. Austin saw flesh and blood sail away from the impacts, but the man only hesitated. He looked at his chest, touched the two small round wounds, then grinned.

Austin started. The man confronting him was missing all but two teeth, but most frightening were the sunken eyes, mad and manic. No shred of sanity remained.

Austin fired a third time. This time the round detonated and sent blood and body parts into the air like water from the Czar Alexander Fountain. He recoiled, dropped to one knee, and used his free arm to cover his head as the grisly rain cascaded down. When Austin looked up, he fought to hold down his rising gorge. Hot blood had splattered in lumpy puddles as it fell on the street around him.

"Killing isn't quite as sanitary as it is in a trainer, is it?" came the calm question.

Austin swung around to face the new threat but quickly elevated the muzzle away from Manfred Leclerc.

"I don't know why the first two rounds didn't stop him," Austin said, his voice cracking with strain. "I hit him. I saw."

"They were armor-piercing rounds and went through him like a laser through vacuum. Where'd you get the pistol?"

Austin knew that wasn't Manfred's real question. He really meant, why are you carrying a weapon whose capabilities are a mystery? Manfred was always the commander, always the instructor.

"We've got to get out of here," Austin said. "Marta Kinsolving—"

"Marta!" The look on Manfred's face confirmed all he suspected.

"She gave me the pistol. She's back there in her limo. We've got to get you into hiding where—" Austin stumbled when another white-hot pinpoint blossomed above him, this time from the other side of the street.

"What was that?" Manfred asked, rubbing his dazzled eyes. "I was looking almost directly at it when it blew up."

"Come on," Austin said, realizing what Manfred did not. "Don't say a word. Just follow me. Fast!"

The two set out at double time. Austin wasn't sure he remembered the way back through the tumbledown buildings but felt the need to show Manfred he wasn't a complete idiot stumbling over his own feet. Austin had always thought of himself as an expert soldier, but this brief excursion in Havoc convinced him there were soldiers and there were soldiers. Urban warfare hadn't been his military specialty.

He preferred the cockpit of a 'Mech to being on foot, without armor, with a small but potent weapon that was inappropriate for the mission.

"There's the limo," cried Manfred, breaking into a dead run. Austin followed at a slower pace, winded from the dash through the ruins. He blinked as another of the brilliant white points flared a dozen meters beyond the limousine. He caught himself against the side of the car, looked behind, and realized he and Manfred had attracted a considerable amount of attention. A small crowd of haggard, almost skeletal men and women dressed in rags trailed them, as if they were magnets pulling iron filings. Austin thought to shoot at them, then lowered the pistol and swung into the back of the limo. It would have been a mercy for the people, but it was wrong to murder those he was sworn to protect.

Manfred and Marta sat side by side, their thighs pressed together tightly. Other than this he would have thought they had just met, given how they kept their eyes locked on him and their hands to themselves. He dropped into the seat opposite them and said, "Can we get out of here?"

The words hardly escaped his lips when he was thrown forward by the sudden acceleration. Manfred caught him and gently pushed him back into the soft leather-upholstered seat.

"I'm glad to leave," Austin said. "How'd you survive there, Manfred? That place is terrible. I've got to tell my father and do something."

"He knows," Manfred said. "Other, more pressing problems need to be taken care of first."

"But—"

"Austin, be quiet," said Marta. "Did you notice the small explosions back there?"

"What were they?" Manfred asked.

"Remote surveillance cameras. Tortorelli might have ordered them installed, but any picture has already made its way to Elora. Count on it," Marta said.

"Why did they blow up?"

"AllWorldComm makes them, so I can locate them.

I might not be able to tap into their encoded signal, but once I know where they are, I can send a radio spike that will blow out the electronics. And I did."

"What are we going to do?" Manfred said. "Tortorelli and Elora both know where I am—and that puts you in danger, too."

"While you were out sightseeing, I contacted my security chief. There's no way we can hide you, not on Mirach. We're going directly to our company's launch facility," Marta said. "A DropShip is taking off soon. You can hide out on Kuton."

"I'm not leaving Mirach, not now!" Manfred protested.

"She's right," Austin said. "We need a leader and that's got to be you. If we don't split the Legate's forces somehow, he will seize complete control."

"You're talking mutiny, treason," Manfred said. "I don't think so, Austin. Not enough troopers in the Home Guard would go along."

"If you don't try, there won't be any stopping Tortorelli and Elora," Marta said. "Austin's convinced me that the MBA can't put those refitted 'Mechs into the field without them causing terrible collateral damage."

Manfred stared at Austin for a moment, as if seeing him in a new light. Then he nodded slowly. "He's right, if he's been arguing that. The 'Mechs can defend your plants, but they'd be at a real disadvantage if you tried to field them offensively against soldiers in battle armor. Property damage in the city would be awful, and every soldier a 'Mech killed would be a loyal Mirach citizen following what would appear to be legitimate orders from the Legate."

Austin sank back in the soft seat and felt every ache and pain in his body.

"That was clever leaving the message on the fountain," he said to Manfred. His friend smiled and nodded once. Austin got the message. Shut up.

He watched Manfred and Marta pressed so close together in the spacious limo, trying to appear as if they hardly knew each other, but since he was looking, he saw the glances and the small, furtive touches. He almost asked if Marta would accompany Manfred to the moon.

"There it is," Marta said, the window polarization changing to show the DropShip field. "Let's hope we've stayed one step ahead." She looked at Austin and pursed her lips. "You should go with him. Your life's in as much danger as his."

"I need to get my father out among the people where he can speak freely, without having every word censored by Lady Elora."

The limo drove to the far side of the field where the smallest of the ships stood. Austin fancied he could see the DropShip quivering in eagerness to launch, but that was only his imagination. If anything, there was less activity around it than around its larger companions across the field.

"I'll release the security ring," Marta said. She leaned across Manfred, who did not mind at all, and took out a small Span-net phone from the armrest console. Marta fiddled with it a few seconds and gave the authorization codes that would allow them to approach the DropShip this close to launch.

"I feel as if I'm running away," Manfred said. "There's got to be a better way for me to rally support. If I'm on Kuton, it'll make me look like a coward." He took the phone from her and tucked it into his pocket.

"I'll check to be sure everything's in order," Austin said, wanting to leave Manfred and Marta alone for a moment. He climbed out of the limo, looked around, and then walked toward the DropShip to stare up at its bulk. From a distance it had looked small; this close, he estimated that it towered more than a hundred meters. Lights from around the field caught the shining exterior and turned it silvery, with darker markings declaring that this was an AllWorldComm cargo vessel. Austin sucked in a deep breath, tasted the airborne metallic tang of reactants used as fuel.

Austin saw Marta hurrying toward him, but Manfred remained in the limo.

"Anything wrong?" he asked.

"No, he's coming. He's taking care of some last-minute business."

Austin frowned when he saw Manfred using the phone. From the expression on his face, it looked as though whomever he spoke to must have given him disturbing news. Manfred looked around as if he expected to see MPs swarming over the field, then hastily broke the connection when he noticed Austin watching him.

Who'd he call? Austin wondered. He started to ask, but Manfred rushed past him.

"Hurry," Marta said. "The less time we take, the less likely Elora is to know what's going on." Manfred's arm snaked around Marta and he pulled her close to kiss her. Then he released her, slapped Austin on the back, and ran for the far side of the DropShip, where the small elevator would take him to the midships entry port.

"We've got to get out of here fast. The ship's on schedule for launch in five minutes." Marta hesitated, shot an almost shy smile in the direction of the DropShip, and climbed into the limo, Austin immediately behind her.

The limousine roared off at top speed, heading for a line of concrete control bunkers at the far side of the field.

"I've tapped into the field control," Marta said, putting the feed from the bunker onto the limo intercom. "We'll be well out of blast range."

Austin caught his breath as the countdown neared its end. "Engines ignition," the controller intoned. "Five, four, three, two, one, liftoff."

Austin leaned forward anxiously, barely able to make out the DropShip through the rear window. A sudden flare illuminated it and made him squint, in spite of the polarization.

"There he goes," Austin said.

Then words failed him. The DropShip had risen less than a hundred meters, still building speed, when it exploded.

=== 25 ===

AWC DropShip launch pad
Mirach
3 May 3133

The accusation of treachery came unbidden to Austin's lips, but the instant he saw Marta's stricken face he knew she had no part in the explosion and Manfred's death.

"Find out what happened," Austin said, pushing aside his shock to take command. "The control center must have telemetry."

"I . . . yes, of course. The controllers." With a shaking hand, Marta pressed in the access code that linked her directly with the DropShip launch bunkers.

Austin looked outside. Chaos reigned. Technicians ran about, shouting, gesturing, blaming one another, getting emergency equipment out to the crash site.

"We've never had a cargo DropShip blow up on us.

Ben Nagursky had a few, but those were test vehicles. These . . . these were all nothing but workhorses. They're supposed to be dependable, reliable." Marta savagely threw down the phone. "No answer. Come on." She piled out of the limo and led the way to a nearby bunker. Austin pushed through the technicians inside so Marta could speak to the launch director.

"Dr. Penrose, what happened to the cargo launch?" demanded Marta of a pale-faced, still shaking woman.

"I can't say. Everything read in the green, Ms. Kinsolving," the launch director said. "But the sudden loss of thrust and the explosive nature of the accident makes me think the DropShip was sabotaged."

"Someone sabotaged the ship? You mean a bomb of some kind?" asked Marta. She ground her teeth as she waited for the information. Austin knew better than to say a word.

Dr. Penrose pointed to a screen with a razor-sharp glowing line across it. "Here it is. A millisecond before the ship itself exploded, there was a major concussion inside, right by the fusion reactor. We're going to have to look for trace evidence and find out what kind of explosive was used. If we can figure out what was used, we can start building a case for who is responsible for this. Whoever it was, they were good enough to breach our security, and they know something about DropShips."

"The Legate would have access to all kinds of explosives," Austin said in a low voice. "Anyone with military ID could justify inspecting a ship leaving the planet."

"Seal the area," Marta said decisively. "Question everyone. I want the saboteur located."

"Ms. Kinsolving, something like this takes time, planning," Dr. Penrose said. She cleared her throat. "It's likely that whoever did this is already long gone."

"You don't know that. We have to try. If we come up with nothing, then we'll decide what to do next."

Marta pushed aside a tech and commandeered a comm-link. Within a few seconds familiar faces appeared on the screen. Austin recognized Dr. Chin in the top half of the screen and a sleepy Benton Nagursky in the lower section.

"Pseudosecure link," Marta explained hurriedly, as much for Austin's benefit as to inform the other MBA directors. "We have reason to believe that the Legate sabotaged a DropShip. We're starting an investigation now." She swallowed hard and then added, "Manfred Leclerc was aboard."

"Do you want us to authorize use of the 'Mechs?" asked Dr. Chin.

"Yes," was all Marta said. The other two touched controls out of range of their cameras and the screen went blank.

"You can't attack Tortorelli," Austin said in exasperation. "I explained why that's foolish. This might be the very opening Elora is looking for!"

"I know, but Manfred was on that ship." Tears flowed unashamedly now. "I don't know if he could have rallied the military as you hoped," Marta said, "but he would have done the best he could."

"He was as strong a supporter of The Republic as anyone I know," Austin said. "And he was my friend."

"I'll get full telemetry records," Marta said, her shoulders squaring. "It doesn't matter what destroyed the DropShip, but we can get evidence of who ordered it and let everyone who'll listen know."

"We already know that," Austin said.

"Elora's moving sooner than we feared," Marta said in a low voice. "If we aren't to continue paying the price for underestimating her, we have to act. Now!"

26

**Ministry of Information, Cingulum
Mirach
3 May 3133**

"Yes," Lady Elora gloated, grinning ear to ear. She laughed and then leaned back in her comfortable desk chair, relaxed for the first time in days. Looking past Legate Tortorelli, she took in the fake view of Cingulum. With a careless pass of her hand over an IR controller, she changed the window so that it became sunrise. Then she activated another control, one that set into motion a new series of attacks on the MBA. The time was finally right for power to be transferred on Mirach.

The sudden light from the faux window brought Calvilena Tortorelli upright. He stared at the magnificent scene.

"It's not supposed to be dawn," he said, frowning as he worked on the solution to this conundrum.

"That's not the same direction it was a few minutes ago. That looks eastward now." He brightened. "Ah, you sly fox. You're changing the projection just to please me."

"I can't put anything over on you, Calvy," Elora said. She spoke mechanically as her mind raced along a dozen different paths, all leading to power. With a major AWC shipment to Kuton destroyed, Marta Kinsolving's plan to oust her monopoly was, if not ended, then at least delayed. But now it didn't matter. Fate had put Manfred Leclerc on that transport, and with his death, the MBA lacked an effective pilot-commander for their refitted IndustrialMech fighting force. More than this, Leclerc's death meant the dissolution of the FCL. The last unit loyal to Governor Ortega had lost its leader and rallying point.

"Everything is looking up, Calvy," she said. "The dawn of a new day."

"But it is still so late."

She glanced at the video feed from the lone camera recording the furious salvage operation at the DropShip launch facility. Another screen showed a coded message confirming, rather redundantly, that the package had been delivered. Finding someone to execute the sabotage had been easy; getting the military-grade explosives for this particular job had been even easier. Elora knew that Tortorelli's forces were factionalized. Finding someone loyal to him, against Baron Ortega, and stupid enough to believe the lies of an attractive and powerful woman had been an entertaining project, and quite successful. Of course, her need for such people was at its end. Now matters could be taken to a larger stage, where events were decided not by one well-placed pawn, but rather by a savvy and dangerous queen.

"An impressive package. I didn't think this man had

it in him, quite frankly," Tortorelli said softly. Elora jumped. She had not realized he had drifted around the room on his nervous quest to touch every knick-knack and had stopped behind her chair. He laid a hand on her bony shoulder. "If you are going to order troops from my command in my name, tell me. I can ensure a successful mission. Neither of us has any love of Sergio Ortega."

"You're right, Calvy," she said, tossing back her mane of red hair and looking up at him appraisingly. Perhaps he wasn't such a fool, after all.

27

"There's no hope," Marta Kinsolving said. She bit her lower lip until Austin saw beads of blood well around her sharp white teeth, but the woman remained ramrod straight as she studied the photos of what remained of the DropShip. "Any radiation leakage?"

"Some but not as much as I feared," Dr. Penrose said. "Initial reports say that the fusion plant has a very manageable breach, and that's being taken care of now. The size of the explosion was more a result of heat touching off combustible chemicals on the DropShip, and they worry me more. Those fires on the field will burn for several days. Contamination of the area is significant." Penrose hesitated a moment, looked from Austin back to Marta, then said, "Ma'am, what did you mean, 'There's no hope'? Hope for what? You knew the instant of the explosion that we couldn't salvage anything from the 'Ship."

"I counted on the equipment being sent to Kuton," Marta said, not lying very effectively, or so thought Austin. "Now more than ever we need the relay station."

"Of course, for Span-net," Penrose said. The woman stood only 155 centimeters tall, but Austin felt the power wrapped tightly within her. She was no one's fool and did not believe Marta's explanation. A new DropShip could be prepared in just days. The financial burden was huge, but a megacorporation like AllWorldComm would bear it, since the return on establishing the world-bridging Span-net was greater.

Marta turned toward him, her brown eyes pools of sadness.

"Is there anyone to notify? Manfred never mentioned family."

"The FCL was as close to family as I ever heard him mention." The desperation of the hours following the DropShip crash were now replaced with quiet frustration—for them. He and Marta had Manfred's loss to bear in silence.

"Ms. Kinsolving, you might want to see this," called a technician working at a bank of monitors. The screens flickered endlessly from one scene to the next. How anyone could decipher the visual morass was beyond Austin, but the man in the center of the screens homed in on one specific view. A few seconds of fiddling brought the same newscast up on all the monitors.

". . . our sources report that the Mirach Business Association has denounced The Republic and is currently negotiating an alliance with Jacob Bannson."

"That's a lie!" raged Marta.

"The other 'cast, the one on-air now, that's what I wanted you to see, Ms. Kinsolving," said the tech. "This was a recorded 'cast from a couple hours ago." The screens flowed like oil on water and firmed on Lady Elora's angular face. She looked as grim as Austin felt.

"Citizens of Mirach," Elora said solemnly, "what should have been a day for celebration has become one of peril. Less than an hour ago, the Ministry of Information received its first transmission from Prefect Kal Radick concerning the reestablishment of the HPG network."

The hush that fell on the room erupted a second later into pandemonium.

"Quiet!" bellowed Marta. "Why wasn't I told of an HPG comm?"

"It never happened, that's why," Dr. Penrose said, hastily checking another bank of recording instrumentation. "We might have been up to our asses working to salvage that cargo DropShip but I'd never let anything as important as an HPG message from off-world slip by. It never happened, Ms. Kinsolving. I swear it."

"The lying bitch," Marta growled.

"I want to hear what she's saying," Austin said. He stepped closer to the screens, but Elora's words were drowned out by the tumult in the command bunker. He cocked his head to one side and listened hard. There had to be a way to turn her lies against her, no matter how clever she was.

"Prefect Radick has declared for the common citizen," Elora went on, her voice aquiver with excitement now. "He will support a populist movement intended to depose tyranny. In this pursuit of maximum freedom, he urges every citizen to obey only Legate Tortorelli until the reins of government can be passed successfully to those more capable of leadership."

"Civil war, that's what she's declaring," Austin said. "She's trying to get the populace to back Tortorelli—and her—when the two of them move against my father." Austin closed his eyes for a moment and knew what would happen as surely as if he watched it unfold.

The military he had hoped to split into factions would be securely in Tortorelli's command. Manfred was dead. Dale was dead. Sergio Ortega was being held incommunicado in the Palace. Lady Elora controlled the news.

The only credible opposition to the coup would be mounted by the MBA's converted IndustrialMechs. As potent a force as they would be, Austin knew the combined might of an entire planet would be flung against them.

Austin saw nothing but disaster on the horizon. He lacked the experience of Manfred Leclerc or the charisma of his brother, but someone had to marshal the forces believing Mirach could survive and prosper under The Republic. His mind raced.

The people of Mirach had been told the net was working again—and would believe anything Elora told them.

"You look panicked," Marta said.

"I . . . no, not that. There's so much swirling around that it's hard to decide what I ought to do. I've got to go to the Palace and get my father away. If he can prevent even a few of the soldiers from following Tortorelli, he must do it."

"Your father has been mighty passive, so far. He might have other plans," Marta said.

Austin felt nothing but contempt for his father. The

old man's finest days were gone and he now faced nothing but disgrace. His elegant words would not stop the missiles and lasers arrayed against him by the Legate. This was a coup, not a debate. The loser died.

"We've got to stop Elora and Tortorelli somehow," Austin said. "Can you jam her newscasts? AWC probably built the equipment. Your technicians know it better than anyone else could."

"You don't understand, Austin," Marta said. "Elora's already told the world that she received an HPG communiqué from Radick. *She* is the anointed, as far as they are concerned. The riots came from fear of isolation, of not knowing what is going on throughout the Prefecture. She has established herself as the oracle who can tell them not to worry."

"And what to do," Austin finished bitterly. Marta was right. "Elora's way ahead of us."

"No one will protest when the Home Guard is sent to seize our companies, because the people think Radick is backing Tortorelli to the hilt. The power of belief that the HPG is up again will drive them to destroy us, unless we use the 'Mechs."

Austin saw no way out. The MBA could negotiate now, hope that Elora was merciful, or they could send out their ultimate weapons in an attempt to break the Legate's military power.

Elora would never be lenient.

Everyone lost. Everyone but Elora.

Marta snapped orders and began marshaling her forces and those of the Mirach Business Association. As her attention focused on the immediate needs of protecting her plants and workers from the mobs that were undoubtedly on the way, Austin backed away, then slid the heavy bunker door aside and stepped into the new dawn.

28

"**H**alt!"

For an instant, lost in thought as he was, Austin Ortega didn't realize the guard meant him. He had lived in the Palace all his life until he moved to the FCL barracks for service with the unit. The situation had changed and Austin had foolishly ignored it in his haste to see his father.

"Austin Ortega, aide to the Governor," he said, reaching for his ID. Austin was shoved back against a wall and looked down the muzzles of two rifles.

"Keep your hands where we can see them," the guard said.

"The Governor's my father. Don't you recognize me?"

"Get the captain of the guard. We caught him," the soldier immediately in front of Austin said.

Austin looked around and saw gun emplacements where none had been before just inside the southern entrance to the Palace. Rifle barrels bristled from behind massive carved stone columns, and from the distance came the click-click of heels marching along the marble corridor.

"What's going on? I demand to see the Governor!" Austin knew his words fell on deaf ears. He only bought time to think. If the captain of the guard had been summoned, that meant he would be frogmarched to a cell away from the Palace. "I—my belly!" Austin screeched, doubling over and clutching his midsection.

As he bent, he got his head away from the rifles for a split second. This gave him the chance to drive forward, burying his shoulder in the gut of the soldier in front of him. The other two tried to cover him, to shoot him. Austin didn't give them the chance. He knocked one soldier into another, spoiling her aim. Kicking out like a mule, he caught the third guard on the kneecap. Bone crunched like stepped-on plastic and then triggered a loud scream of pain. The confusion of this shriek gave Austin the chance to keep moving, spinning, grabbing, hitting with short, quick punches that dazed and bewildered.

By the time all three soldiers were sprawled on the floor, Austin had a rifle securely in hand. He fired the instant he saw an officer's insignia rounding a column five meters off. The bullet ripped at the stone and sent sharp fragments flying like angry bees.

The brief, fierce scuffle had drawn the attention of the soldiers in the gun emplacements. They swung their automatic weapons around and opened fire, but

Austin was already dodging among the pillars, using the massive limestone columns to protect his back. Even so, the heavy rounds whined past his head and kept him bent over until he reached a low railing. Without breaking stride, Austin vaulted the steel rail and fell almost four meters.

The landing jarred him, but he recovered fast. He had to if he wanted to stay alive. Their insignia indicated that these were Legate Tortorelli's personal troops, and Austin decided they were under orders from Lady Elora, whether they knew it or not. He cursed his own self-absorption at barging in as he had done. He knew his father wasn't allowed to communicate with anyone outside the Palace; people trying to contact him would be stopped, too.

The small passage took a right turn into darkness. Austin had come this way many times before, he and Dale having discovered the passage when they were youngsters.

Running his hand along the cool stone, he found it harder than he expected to find the depression he sought; then he remembered he had been only fourteen the last time he had used this secret route. Austin hunted lower on the wall, found the spot, and pressed hard until the wall slid back silently. Austin slipped inside as a hail of automatic fire rattled along the tight passage. He shouldered the door shut and leaned against it, breathing hard. He heard angry cries in the narrow passageway as the guards wondered how they could have missed him, quickly blaming one another for what had to be a mistake.

Austin felt his way through the darkness. He and Dale had left flashlights here years before, but Austin didn't take the time to hunt for something whose batteries were probably dead. Depending on old memories, he worked steadily beneath the Palace through the maze of tunnels once designed for servants and other service personnel.

A small, lighted rectangle above told him he was close to the exit he wanted. Austin took the stone steps three at a time until he pressed his eye against the panel and looked out into the corridor leading from the conference room to his father's office. If there had been a secret way into the Governor's presence, he would have taken it, but he and Dale had never found such a path when there had been all the time in the world to explore. Now Austin felt time crushing him.

A squad of Tortorelli's soldiers marched past, perfect parade ground troopers all. Clutching the rifle, he made sure a round was chambered, then forced open the ancient latch and stepped into the corridor.

Ten quick steps brought him to the Armorer's Chamber. He turned grim when he saw all the weapons on display had been ripped from the walls. The office staff was gone. Although it was early, a few should have been on duty.

As elegant as the Palace of Facets was, the Baron was still being held in solitary confinement. Austin worried for a moment that he'd have to break his father out of some prison cell that Tortorelli—Lady Elora—had consigned him to, but the instant he reached the inner office door, he knew Elora had held off making her final move against the Governor.

The Baron looked up as Austin came in and closed the door.

"You shouldn't have come, Austin. I told you to stand down."

"I'm here to get you out, Father."

"You're armed," Sergio said. "Put that down. It's not going to help."

"You've got to get out of here and establish a government-in-exile. You need to appeal to as many of the Legate's soldiers' loyalty to The Republic as possible, split his force, regain some control."

"Not with force!" This brought Sergio up. His eyes shot sparks as determination was reborn. "You have to learn, Austin. Violence does not accomplish anything."

"Thinking like that's got you bottled up and unable to do your job. How can you protect the citizens of Mirach when Elora controls the communications in and out of your office? How can you govern if Tortorelli won't let you step into the corridor without being surrounded five-deep by his soldiers?"

"You don't understand," Sergio said. "I still wield considerable power. I need to be here where I can use it."

"Use it, then!" cried Austin. "Stop the rioting. They killed Manfred, you know."

Austin blinked when he saw that his father didn't react as he had expected. Such news ought to have shocked him into action, into the realization that Tortorelli and Elora were playing for keeps and would destroy friends and family to seize power.

"The DropShip launch," Sergio said, his colorless, fathomless eyes fixed on his son. "You were out there, weren't you? You and Marta Kinsolving?"

Austin hardly trusted himself to speak. But he finally got out, "Manfred was my friend. There weren't enough pieces left by Tortorelli's sabotage to give a decent burial."

"An eye for an eye? Is that the only way to prevail? I don't think so," Sergio said.

Austin held back his angry retort as a thought struck him.

"Why haven't they deposed you by now?" Austin

began pacing like a caged animal in the Central Zoo as he rolled the notion over and over in his mind. "What do you still control that they can't take from you?"

"Moral authority, my position as Governor of Mirach," Sergio said. "And one other thing."

He beckoned Austin closer and held out a Span-net phone. Sergio punched up a news report that had not gone through the Ministry of Information. Austin's eyes widened when he heard the news.

"Jerome Parsons has returned," Sergio confirmed.

"The Lord Governor's Envoy?" Austin was not sure if this was a help or hindrance.

"He'll land in sixty hours. Elora and Tortorelli dare not seize power because of his cargo."

"What's he have?" asked Austin, curious now.

"Envoy Parsons is bringing a BattleMech."

29

Museum of Modern Mirach
Mirach
4 May 3133

Austin Ortega hunkered down as a squad of green-clad infantry double-timed it through the museum rotunda as they hunted for him. He had left his father's office almost an hour ago, Sergio following. When a dozen soldiers had approached from down the Great Hall, his father had created a diversion, keeping the guards away and giving Austin the chance to escape. Austin had been reluctant to leave his father behind but thought he was safe enough for the time being in light of Jerome Parsons' unexpected return. Austin knew that tenuous safety could vanish at a whim. He had to work out a plan to rescue Sergio from Tortorelli's soldiers.

The only place he could think of to hide until such

a plan came to him was the museum on the Governor's Park grounds. And once in the museum, he had gone directly to the walkway looking down on the BattleMech.

He let out his pent-up breath when the squad leader finally herded the soldiers away from the *Centurion* and into another wing of the museum. The echoes from their boots faded down distant hallways, then grew louder again as they returned.

Austin waited as the officer down on the rotunda floor snapped orders.

"Close the museum. Lock it down. No visitors. Do you understand your orders?" The officer pushed his face close to his sergeant's.

"Yes, sir," the noncom said. "The museum's empty. We'll lock it up right away."

"See to it; then return with your squad to the east wing of the Palace. We won't stop hunting until we find the fugitive."

The sergeant stood at attention until the officer stalked off, then hustled his squad outside. Austin heard the large outer doors lock. He was alone in the vast museum, thanks to a sloppy search by the soldiers.

He stepped back into the bright lights, went to the railing, and looked at his father's old BattleMech.

Austin still felt a quiver of excitement seeing *Sergeant Death*.

"A 'Mech," he said aloud.

He stared at it and knew he was daydreaming if he thought he could turn the *Centurion* into a true weapon against Tortorelli's forces. *Sergeant Death* had been mothballed and on display for years—for longer than Austin had been alive.

Why not? he asked himself, scrambling over the railing and going to the rear of the fifty-ton BattleMech. He had nothing to lose. With it, he had a chance to chase off Tortorelli's troops and rescue his father. If the BattleMech couldn't be resurrected, he was no worse off for the attempt than he was now.

Austin remembered how he and Dale had sneaked down here when they were youngsters and climbed into the cockpit, pretending they were mighty warriors like their father.

He also remembered how their father had ordered the cockpit sealed to keep them and other would-be MechWarriors like them out. In spite of this, the fusion power plant had been kept hot at the museum curator's request. The curator had wanted to keep the *Centurion* in a condition as close as possible to its original state: a metal dreadnought that had fought for Devlin Stone and The Republic. For this tribute Austin was now very glad.

How long before Elora decides to kill Father? Austin wondered. He had no idea why Jerome Parsons brought a BattleMech to Mirach, but such a fighting juggernaut had to disturb the balance of power. If he put it into Tortorelli's hands, everything was lost. If Parsons gave the BattleMech to Sergio, the Governor might be loath to use it properly, but it would show the people the extent to which Lord Governor Sandoval supported Sergio Ortega, no matter which government Sandoval was loyal to. That might be enough to sway both the people and the military forces Tortorelli—and Elora—counted on.

Austin couldn't come up with any personal motivation for Parsons to use the BattleMech for his own ends. The Envoy would throw his considerable support to either Elora or the Baron. If Parsons backed Elora, Austin needed the *Centurion* to oppose them.

Austin gripped the supporting scaffold, more decorative than functional, and scaled it quickly, reaching the platform behind the cockpit. He sucked in a deep breath and held it when he saw the problem facing him. The 200 Nissan fusion power plant might be intact and ready to drive the *Centurion* out of the museum, but the cockpit hatch had been welded shut. A small spot-weld opposite the hinges held it more securely than any lock ever could.

Dropping to sit with his feet swinging over the edge of the scaffold, Austin stared at the weld. Without a cutting torch or a laser, there was no way to open the BattleMech.

"A laser," he muttered to himself, peering down at the BattleMech's chest. The *Centurion* still had one forward-mounted Photec 806c Medium Laser. For reasons of space in the display, the rear-facing laser had been removed. In the right arm rested the Luxor autocannon, and the LRMs were torso-mounted. The missiles had long since been taken to a warehouse for fear of deterioration in either their warheads or their propellant, but the forward laser on the torso was intact and the autocannon had not been tampered with. He'd need ammunition for the D-series autocannon, but that wasn't an insurmountable problem. Behind the museum were long rows of warehouses where the museum archives were stored. He remembered seeing case after case of armor-piercing ammo stored there.

Let's see if I'm as smart as I think. Austin slid down the BattleMech's upper arm, caught himself, and straddled the thick wrist with the cold metal between his legs. He leaned over toward the chest, opened a small technical access panel, and checked the leads running to the laser and saw they had been disconnected for the sake of safety. The ends shone from heavy red plastic insulation. While it rarely happened, sometimes a static charge could build and randomly trigger the terrible power of the laser. Mirach's sun was known for its sporadic and violent ion storms that caused just such static buildup. Inside the museum's walls, an accidental laser discharge would have been catastrophic.

Luck's still with me, he decided. He didn't have to waste time disconnecting the leads for what he had in mind. Wrestling the power leads around, he climbed back to the cockpit.

Austin stripped off a few centimeters of the red insulation from both leads and held one thick cable in each hand. He placed one bare wire against the spot-weld, then turned his face away as he shoved the other live lead down. The power intended to fire a laser discharged through the steel ring, melted the spot-weld, and chewed a deep hole into the cockpit hatch. The sudden flare and spattering of molten metal caused Austin to jerk away.

Not perfect, but it'll do, he thought, squinting at the glowing ring surrounding the cockpit hatch. The crude cutting torch had melted away almost fifty centimeters of the hatch and its seal. This was a small price to pay for access. Austin kicked the hatch open and peered into the cockpit he knew so well. His heart beat a little faster as the musty, stale air escaped and the smell he remembered so well came back. Before, he and Dale had pretended. His brother had always chided him for picking this model *Centurion* for simulator training. Now his training had to pay off.

Careful of the live power leads, he shinnied back to the BattleMech's arm and the access panel. Austin had some training in weapons preparation, and it stood him in good stead now. He still wished he had some of the expert weapons technicians in the FCL to aid him, but reconnecting the bare leads proved easier than he had anticipated. Less than twenty minutes later, he had reattached the leads to the laser.

With the fusion plant hot, he had laser capability.

Austin returned to the cockpit, entered the hatchway, and slid around to sit in the command chair. It was smaller and tighter than he remembered, but he had been eight the last time he had been here. Only a single indicator light burned a baleful red, showing the power plant was on standby. Not bothering to strap himself down, Austin began working across the control panel, waiting for lights to flicker on to green and meters to indicate power levels.

Laser at full charge!

Power flowed into the systems and myomer muscles hidden under tons of armor began contracting, bringing the *Centurion* to arthritic life after so many years. He was feeling good about his progress when he was thrown back into the padded chair as *Sergeant Death* lurched slightly. He knew the problem and its cure. He reached around and drew out the neurohelmet, carefully putting it on, securing it with a chin strap. The usual tingle on his scalp and deep inside his brain did not come.

The neurohelmet had lost its programming over the years.

Austin reached down, turned on the proper systems, juggled power levels, and then leaned back, letting the BattleMech's automatic systems align themselves with his brain waves. Programming the neurohelmet required for maintaining balance and aiding movement would take hours, perhaps days, especially without a trained technician to help.

Austin stretched out and made himself as comfortable as possible. He wasn't going anywhere as long as the Legate's soldiers hunted for him. What better way to pass the time than to program a BattleMech to respond to his commands?

30

Ministry of Information, Cingulum
Mirach
7 May 3133

"Those fools have looked everywhere," Calvilena Tortorelli said with some irritation. He stood with his back to Lady Elora, staring at the clever deception of the projected city skyline.

She shook her head in amazement. Although he knew he stared at only an image of Cingulum, that didn't sap his enthusiasm for all that went on above in the sky or down in the streets. Elora had chosen recordings from the fall more than thirteen years earlier when she had finally moved into this office as Minister.

"Calvy, darling, you need to assign more troops to finding him."

"More?" The Legate flared uncharacteristically. He

spun, fire in his eyes. "Austin Ortega danced into the Palace past my personal guard—supposedly the best I have, my bodyguards!—and spoke to the Governor for more than ten minutes before disappearing again. Just like that!" He snapped his pudgy fingers. "He vanished under the nose of my best unit."

"He's lived in the Palace all his life. He knows all the hiding places, Calvy. He's hiding like a cockroach in the walls. The Baronet isn't our biggest problem." On the list of impediments to claiming the world for the glory of Kal Radick, Austin Ortega was only third or fourth. She had mistakenly thought the Governor was passively obeying. More than the quick rendezvous with his son, he also maintained secure communications from the Palace. Try as she might, she had been unable to stop him. At first she had tried to find his agents by trying to tap his lines. That hadn't worked and now the damnable Jerome Parsons was returning. Her opportunity to put Sergio into solitary confinement was lost. How would she ever explain the situation to Parsons if Sergio wasn't on hand to greet him again?

Dead? Parsons was no fool. He would want to know the circumstances. Only if Sergio cooperated could they endure another visit by the Envoy. And she had to find out why Parsons brought a BattleMech to Mirach. The best reason she could think of was that Parsons brought it as a gift. Let Sergio make a fine speech—and then let Tortorelli accept the powerful fighting machine for his Home Guard.

Then it no longer mattered what Sergio said or who he contacted.

Sergio Ortega was toothless, thanks to his foolish acquiescence in transferring command of the FCL. His once capable guard had been dismantled and scattered all over Mirach. Elora couldn't help smiling as she thought of the fate of their captain. Manfred Leclerc had been blasted into ions with the destruction of the DropShip. That simple act of sabotage alone had advanced her cause dramatically.

But Sergio Ortega kept his secret comm lines, no matter how closely she spied. She would have ordered him to a prison cell if it hadn't been for Parsons' return. Mirach needed more than a Governor. It needed the same Governor the Envoy had spoken to on his prior visit.

"What of the MBA?" Tortorelli asked unexpectedly. The change in subject forced Elora to refocus.

"They have Mining-, Agro- and other Industrial-Mechs all refitted. I've sent reporters out to gather better intel on their armament and disposition, but they are stonewalling me. Agitating the populace against the MBA isn't enough now. If you can get the BattleMech Parsons is presenting to you into the field quickly enough, it can destroy the MBA modifieds in short order."

"When does Parsons land?" Tortorelli asked.

Elora checked her screens and saw a countdown running. She smiled broadly.

"Within the hour," she said. "We will greet him as he lands and find how he wishes to transfer control of the BattleMech. If he insists that the Governor be present, I'm sure we can find some way to convince Sergio."

"Drugs? For all his prattling about being a pacifist, he is still quite a fighter," said Tortorelli. "Threats of physical violence would not work."

Elora listened with half an ear. Sergio's cooperation could be coerced. She plotted his fate after Parsons left Mirach. It might take a few more spurious messages on the supposedly resurrected HPG net to settle the citizens, but after they came to believe all had returned to easy, quick communication between the worlds of the Prefecture, *then* Sergio Ortega would be discovered to have sabotaged the net again.

Or perhaps she would blame that annoying son of his.

"Should I call out my guard? A few companies of battle armor? As a tribute, of course."

"To meet Envoy Parsons?" She shook her head. A strand of fiery red hair drooped down; she brushed it away impatiently. "That won't be necessary. The crowds will behave because I've told them he is here to celebrate the reestablishment of the HPG."

"Why's he back so soon? He hardly left."

The question startled Elora. She had been so occupied with Sergio, his son, and positioning the MBA where she wanted them that she had not considered this. It was certainly worth finding out.

"The size of the reception at Mirach DropShip Field should be molded to fit the occasion, Calvy," she said, wondering if a few companies might not be necessary to keep a man bringing a BattleMech away from the truth.

Her quick, long, ring-burdened fingers clicked as she worked. Her eyes narrowed when she received her response.

Jerome Parsons refused to acknowledge any communication from her.

31

AWC DropShip launch pad
Mirach
7 May 3133

"Guidance locked in, Ms. Kinsolving," came the excited call from the landing-field director. "You want me to query again, to be certain?"

"There's no need," Marta Kinsolving said. She was puzzled why Envoy Parsons had specifically refused to land at the Mirach DropShip Field and had vectored in on the much smaller AWC facility. It was a mystery, but Marta was more concerned that the debris from the destroyed cargo 'Ship was hauled out of the way before Jerome Parsons landed than she was about figuring out his motives.

Marta's phone jangled. She almost shut it off to keep from being bothered but on impulse accepted the call. Sergio Ortega peered up at her from the small vidscreen.

"Marta, good to see you," said Sergio Ortega. "It's good to see anyone. I don't have much time before the guards take me away."

"They wouldn't do that, Baron," Marta said. "Elora might have whipped the populace into a froth over bogus HPG transmissions, but forcibly removing a Governor is more than she wants to tackle right now."

"If it weren't for Parsons returning, I'd have followed my own course by now. I'm tracking him to your field. Are you prepared to televise his arrival?"

"The Ministry of Information is blocking AWC frequencies," Marta said.

Sergio snorted in disgust. "AllWorldComm built most of the Ministry's equipment. You know how to circumvent it. Jam *her* signal. I give you official approval. It's necessary you show everyone that the Lord Governor's Envoy is avoiding Tortorelli and Elora."

"I understand, Baron," she said. "We'll do everything we can to transmit what's really happening here."

"Keep this line open as long as possible," Sergio asked. "I'd like to see firsthand what Parsons is up to."

"What Lord Governor Sandoval is up to, you mean," Marta said. "Parsons doesn't exhale without explicit orders."

"You underestimate him. Don't. But on one point you're right. Parsons is loyal to both Sandoval and The Republic."

Marta hesitated to say anything more, distracted by alarms and lights flashing throughout the control bunker.

"Baron, I'm switching you to multiple images, on the field and at the reception area. Parsons' DropShip has touched down." Marta didn't wait for acknowledgment. She shot from the chair and hurried to the heavy door, where she waited impatiently until poisonous vapors from the DropShip's landing blew away.

Marta walked out onto the field, head high and wishing she had a couple of the MBA modified 'Mechs behind her as honor guard. Meeting Parsons without any idea why he had returned so soon after his last visit was troubling. She took the steps up to the observation platform two at a time and stepped forward to wait for the Envoy to emerge from the DropShip. The gusty winds died, but Marta experienced chills running up and down her back.

"Are you tracking, recording, and transmitting?" Marta asked, switching her phone connection to the control bunker. "What's going on? I can't quite make it out through the vapor over the field."

"Ms. Kinsolving, the cargo bays are opening."

The crunching and grating of one hundred tons of metal could not distract her from the sheer, overwhelming *presence* of the BattleMech emerging through the haze. She had watched the refitted IndustrialMechs practice their war games, and they were impressive.

The *Atlas* towering fifteen meters awed her.

"Greetings, Ms. Kinsolving," boomed a voice she hardly recognized as Jerome Parsons'. It came from a speaker back on the DropShip. "Excuse the moment of drama but I find it is always useful to capture attention before speaking."

"Y-you've got mine, Envoy," Marta stammered, assuming he had a directional mic aimed toward her. She took a deep breath and checked that her commlink was still transmitting, not that anyone could do anything if this Behemoth took a few more strides forward and squashed her.

"This is an *Atlas* BattleMech, equipped with a Gauss rifle, two Extended Range Large Lasers, one in each arm, and two torso-mounted SRM launchers."

"Impressive, Envoy." Marta knew Parsons would have a battle-trained MechWarrior in the cockpit, unlike the men and women who struggled to pilot the MBA's modified 'Mechs.

The BattleMech stirred slightly, as if impatient to begin destruction. Ozone from electrical discharges in its ECM Suite made her nose wrinkle and eyes water, but nothing detracted from the overwhelming impression made by the mountain of stark power that was the BattleMech.

"Why do you bring this here?" she asked.

"For demonstration purposes, Ms. Kinsolving. Lord Governor Sandoval wishes everyone on this planet to know of the devotion to The Republic shown by the Mirach Business Association and your personal commitment to both Mirach and the rule of law."

"Demonstration?"

"The 'Mech is yours to command, Ms. Kinsolving. For a while."

Marta stood stock-still for a moment, then thumbed her phone to reconnect with Sergio Ortega. He still used his secure Span-net phone to monitor every instant of Parsons' arrival.

"Baron," she said softly into her phone, "what do you think?"

"You know what I'd do with the BattleMech," came the Governor's answer.

Marta cleared her throat and addressed Parsons in a clear voice. "I'd like the *Atlas* to restore civil order in Cingulum. No more rioting. No more looting. Keep violence to a minimum."

"As you command."

The BattleMech turned slowly, took inertial guidance bearings on the distant city, and then gathered speed until it was rushing along at its full sixty-five kilometers per hour. As the BattleMech vanished from sight, Marta checked her phone. Static. Lady Elora had finally jammed the signals from both the AWC DropShip launch pad and the Governor.

Marta shuddered when she realized this was the opening shot. Sergio Ortega would never condone the use of the BattleMech against Tortorelli's troops due to his philosophical leanings, but nothing prevented Elora and Tortorelli from pitting the Legate's entire military might against the BattleMech. It didn't matter to them if Cingulum was laid entirely to waste, if they came out the victors. Parsons and Lord Governor Sandoval had chosen sides, and the Legate and Minister were obviously in the wrong faction. The showdown had come sooner than anyone had thought.

In that, Marta knew, might lie the salvation of Mirach—or its destruction.

32

Palace of Facets, Cingulum
Mirach
9 May 3133

"**W**e've got an important mission ahead of us, Master Sergeant," Sergio said grimly to Dmitri Borodin. "How many of the old FCL are in the Palace?"

Borodin grinned from ear to ear.

"More'n you might think, Baron. Don't know how it happened," Borodin said with a wide grin, "but I just happened to be writing up the duty roster, and more than half of the best of the best are here instead of somewhere else." Borodin laughed self-deprecatingly. "Then there's me."

"You've done so much already, Master Sergeant. Alerting me last week to the missing explosives helped more than you could imagine." Sergio touched his Span-net phone but did not pick it up. "Have you found where Austin went?"

"He lit out and just vanished, Baron, after you told him the Envoy was coming back. Can't blame him. Tortorelli's guards were out for blood because he made them look so bad. I been huntin' and askin' around for the last couple days." Borodin shook his head. "It's like the ground opened up and swallowed him."

"But there hasn't been even a rumor that Tortorelli's troops have caught him?"

"Not a whisper. If anything, just the reverse. Quakes been comin' down from on high because of everyone's failure to find the lieutenant. The Baronet, I mean, Governor."

"That's all right," Sergio said, knowing the master sergeant thought of Austin first as an officer. He knew his son could take care of himself, but wished he were here now, just as he wanted Manfred Leclerc at his side. Sergio had long since learned, though, that he could not always get what he wanted.

"Remove any of Tortorelli's guards who won't help defend the Palace," Sergio said. "Don't kill them. Lock them up in the east-wing cellar. The wine cellar doors are thick and impossible to open without explosives if you lock them."

"What? Let them have your good wine, Governor?"

"It'll keep them quiet," Sergio said, liking the way the sergeant thought. "Seize control of the heavy machine guns Tortorelli placed at the doors. If you don't have enough FCL soldiers to man them all, fall back into the Palace corridors until you can defend junctures in the halls with the troops you do have. I can give you a map, if you need it."

"Governor, I been guardin' you for goin' on three years. There's not much of the Palace of Facets me and the rest haven't explored, just to know where danger might be, mind you."

"Don't worry about destroying the Palace. Keep yourselves safe."

"Governor, we'll keep ourselves safe, you and the Palace, too." Borodin snapped a salute and hurried off, bellowing orders as he went. Like a Pied Piper, he drew soldiers dressed in the drab green of Tortorelli's infantry from odd corners along the Great Hall. Sergio recognized them all as having been in the First Cossack Lancers. This part of his plan had worked well.

Tortorelli had got careless assigning troopers because he thought all those at the Palace were loyal to him. Sergio intended to have made significant progress toward neutralizing him and Lady Elora Rimonova before the Legate realized anything was wrong with his pet prisoner.

Sergio closed his eyes for a moment and then pushed regrets away. He had ignored Elora and her ambitions and it had almost cost him his world. By the time he realized she intended to wrest Mirach from The Republic, she had grown far too powerful to simply remove. Worse, Sergio had never confirmed whether or not she had forged an alliance with Kal Radick.

If these so-called Steel Wolves descended on Mirach because of her, Sergio feared nothing would be left but Elora's ambition. As matters now stood, Lord Governor Sandoval had declared against Tortorelli and Elora, sending his Envoy with a BattleMech to restore order. And Kal Radick had not been heard from at all.

Sergio knew a show of force by Sandoval's BattleMech would never succeed, not in and of itself. More had to be done, and he needed to be free of his gilded palace/prison guards now to do it. He had allowed the First Cossack Lancers to be transferred away to free Manfred Leclerc to work with the MBA and watch their 'Mech program closely. The transfer had the added advantage of lulling Elora into a false sense of complacency, thinking he was unprotected and vulnerable.

But he had lost so much. His older son. Hanna Leong. He had never believed Elora would go to such lengths. Everyone had a blind spot. Misjudging her repeatedly was far too easy a trap for him.

Sergio dropped into his chair and picked up the Span-net phone Marta Kinsolving had given him, using the most sophisticated encryption equipment AWC had, intending to place the call he had started earlier. He put down the phone when Master Sergeant Borodin rushed back to report.

"All secure, Baron. We got a dozen from the Home Guard to join us. Me or at least two FCL vouch for them."

"That's good enough for me, Master Sergeant," Sergio said.

"You see the newscast she's putting out?" Borodin spoke as if the words burned his lips.

Sergio quickly viewed what the Ministry of Information was broadcasting. He sucked in his breath at the sight of the *Atlas* trapped in downtown Cingulum, surrounded by heavy tanks and badgered by battle-armored troops. The BattleMech strove to contain the Legate's forces without destroying the buildings—and killing the populace—but Sergio knew that was an impossible mission. Either the horrific fighting machine used its weapons or it would be repeatedly attacked by heavy tanks and battle-armored troops trained to harass and bring down even such a fierce fighting machine.

Sergio knew he had indirectly hampered the BattleMech's deployment by insisting that deaths among the civilian populace—and the military—be kept to a minimum, but they were all citizens of Mirach.

A monitor on his desk flickered as Elora's face appeared. There was a wild look about her he had never seen before, reminding him how dangerous it was to corner a rat. Trying to escape, the rat might fight more ferociously than anyone expected. He had to allow her a chance to back away and stop the carnage.

"Surrender, Sergio. You cannot possibly win. Save lives," Elora said. Sergio heard the bluff in her voice.

"There must be some reason you want me to surrender, Elora," he said. "If all went your way, you'd ignore me. Or kill me. What's wrong? Is there a chance the BattleMech will break free and come to the Palace to stand guard? That would show the people of Mirach that the Lord Governor still supports me."

"I'm trying to save your miserable life, Baron," Elora raged.

"I won't give up," Sergio said. "I've ordered my personal guard to defend the Palace and the sovereignty of my office. My only regret is not understanding the depth of your ambition earlier. So many have died needlessly."

"Too little, too late," she sneered. "If I know you, you probably ordered the soldiers not to shoot, to try to bore my soldiers to death."

"Yours?" Sergio asked mildly.

"Are you going to give up, Baron?"

"No."

"The Legate's best tank battalion will reduce the Palace of Facets to a hundred-meter-high pile of debris."

He glanced over at Borodin. The master sergeant looked grim as he listened to a radio report. He silently mouthed, "They're bringing up the Behemoths. South of the Palace."

"This is your only chance, Baron. All you have to defend yourself is a few traitors with rifles."

"There might be more," Sergio said. "The *Atlas* is on its way to the Palace."

"The BattleMech is trapped," Elora said, sneering. "So are you. And both of you will be destroyed completely!"

The line went dead.

Sergio swallowed hard as he stared at the news broadcast. Elora was right about the BattleMech. The *Atlas* tried to elude the Condor tanks pecking away tenaciously at it—and it couldn't. Even if the Mech-Warrior put the 'Mech into full power and headed for the Palace, it could never arrive before the Behemoth moving up inexorably from the south opened fire.

"Master Sergeant Borodin," Sergio said, "prepare to evacuate the Palace."

"Evacuate, sir? No! We're here to protect it—and you."

"Unless you want to face a tank with hardly more than a rifle, you'll do as you are ordered. Leave. Now. Retreat."

Borodin's sputtering reply was cut off as a shell from the leading Behemoth slammed into the outer façade of the southern entrance. The resulting concussive blast shook the huge Palace and destroyed most of its communications equipment.

Sergio Ortega leaned back in his chair, watching an external camera's view of the tanks advancing, firing as they came. They would get the range soon enough and the end would come.

So be it. He would die before surrendering the government of Mirach to Elora.

33

Lady Elora felt flushed, her translucent skin ruddy now with the rush of excitement. She sat on the edge of her chair, leaning forward intently as if she played some gigantic musical instrument. Her desk had come alive with lights, indicators flashing warnings and OKs, a dozen views of the city and the skirmishes being fought.

Is this what it feels like to have power, real power? she wondered. Her fingers flew like jeweled birds across the array as she guided one unit after another into battle and supplied tactical intelligence to Tortorelli's forces.

She positioned a Behemoth II Tank and ordered it to fire on an APC carrying former FCL troopers to the Palace. The heavy laser lashed directly into the side of the armored personnel carrier and snuffed out the lives of a dozen fighters.

The enemy, she gloated.

"I say, how's it going? You are deploying according to the battle plan I gave you?" Calvilena Tortorelli turned from his position in front of her office window. Elora had left the tranquil city view on the screen and this pleased the Legate, although it had no bearing on the death and destruction actually stalking Cingulum. The thought flashed through her mind that the citizens were much like him. Give them pretty pictures and they would sit for hours, content and willing to be guided in whatever direction she chose.

It was time for The Republic to lose Mirach. Kal Radick would provide far better rule. And he would receive it because of her.

"Everything is going well, Calvy," she said. "Do you want to see?" With almost savage glee, she transformed the cityscape into the transmission from a camera mounted at the corner of a building in downtown Cingulum. Tortorelli rocked back as a dozen missiles burst in front of his face with hellacious force.

Elora had to switch to another camera because the one she had activated had been destroyed. From farther down the street she focused on the advancing *Atlas*.

"The BattleMech," Tortorelli said with a hint of fear. "Parsons should have placed that in my command. But such a slight doesn't matter, not really. My soldiers have been trained to bring it down, and it's not giving a bit of trouble to them. Why, it's not even fighting back!"

"Its pilot doesn't want to destroy any more of the city and its people than necessary."

She didn't add that it was too late for the Battle-Mech to save itself. With careful movement she had ringed it with heavy artillery and tanks. A few Condor tanks made swift attacks, only to dart back before the BattleMech's heavy lasers could take them out. But the *Atlas* was doubly limited. It couldn't use the incredible power of its Gauss rifle, nor did it have jump jet capability. Stuck to plodding along at ground level, it was hindered by the closeness of urban buildings its pilot had been ordered not to destroy.

Elora had practically ignored Tortorelli's strategic plans in favor of her own. She was no fool. The ebb and flow of battle was laid out in front of her as clearly as could be. What was needed and what was impossible were obvious in a flash, thanks to her constant flow of intelligence about the battle, the enemy, and the position of the Legate's forces.

"I'm keeping up the propaganda barrage. Kinsolving's techs aren't able to jam my transmission. If she had succeeded in activating the relay stations on the four moons, it might have been a different story. But on the ground, the Ministry of Information has the technological muscle to make the people believe anything we want them to!"

Tortorelli looked at her strangely. Elora realized her voice had risen to a screech, and she was acting erratically.

"We are so close, Calvy. You are such a brilliant tactician."

"Strategist," he said absently. "The overall battle plan is strategy. How it's accomplished is tactics."

Lady Elora ignored him. Her mind raced ahead to the eventual success over the BattleMech. Should she try Parsons as a traitor and execute him, or would it be better to send him packing back to Aaron Sandoval? Definitely the latter. The message would be clearer that way. Mirach, under the guidance of Kal Radick, had destroyed a BattleMech. The planet was off-limits from now on to Republic forces if they didn't want to face the same punishment.

Possibly the battle itself would make the decision for her. Jerome Parsons might be killed, either in combat or by Marta Kinsolving's sycophants.

A new river of intrigue flowed around Elora as she considered the benefits of announcing how Kinsolving and the MBA had murdered Sandoval's Envoy. She had already broadcast how Sergio Ortega had again destroyed Mirach's HPG station. It hardly mattered if many believed the wild claim, as long as some did. All this might be enough to wrest control of Mirach's industrial sector from the triumvirate that now ran it. Elora could control not only the military and civil authority, but the mining, manufacturing, and agricultural might of the planet.

Authority, power, and wealth!

"You don't want to do that," said Tortorelli.

"Why not?" Elora's fierce green eyes fixed on him. *How did he know what I was thinking?*

"You'll box in the tanks. They'd either have to waste ammunition blowing their way through Havoc or swing far around and fritter away valuable time doing an end run. If they did that, the BattleMech could get free and establish a defensive position at the Palace."

"The *Atlas* could fight there without fear of destroying any of the populace," she said slowly, considering the merits of what the Legate said. Elora relaxed when she realized Tortorelli had been commenting on the skirmish raging in the city and not on her political engineering.

"It could certainly defend the Governor until battle

armor could be brought in, should that be Parsons' intent." Tortorelli paused, then continued. "Ask him to surrender."

"Parsons?"

"No, no, my dear. Ask Sergio to surrender. He would do it to prevent more bloodshed. You know how squeamish he gets. I do think he really believes all that pacifistic nonsense he spouts. Tell him to hand over the government immediately or there will be even more bloodshed."

"Only he can stop it," Elora said, keying in exactly to what Tortorelli meant. This was the Governor's Achilles' heel. He might have been a fierce fighter in the days of Devlin Stone, but he had lost the will to fight and he believed anything could be negotiated.

She would show him how politics really worked. Words were fine, but a barrage of missiles or a laser blast produced more dependable results.

"No, wait—he won't surrender," Tortorelli said, as if this was a major revelation for him. "He will see his own martyrdom as a stronger statement that will unite the people against us. The Baron might be right; yes, he just might be right. But I don't think so."

He reached past Elora and got a command line to his battalion commander.

"Captain Mugabe, full attack. Hit the Palace with all you have."

"Sir!" came the reply. "Repeat your order, please."

"Destroy the Palace of Facets," Tortorelli said decisively. "Take no prisoners."

"Understood, sir," came the reluctant reply. But Tortorelli saw Mugabe obeyed. She was his top tank commander. She moved into position rapidly and her Behemoth fired a Gauss round that crashed into the Palace's facade with horrific results.

"He won't surrender," Tortorelli repeated. "Did I

do right, Elora? Should I have ordered the Palace and everyone in it reduced to rubble?"

"I can announce that he has already surrendered," Elora said, more to herself than to the Legate. This appealed to her. When she moved in with her cameras, any fight on the Governor's part would then appear to be violation of a truce.

"Yes, that is splendid. There isn't much time left for him, so do make it sound sincere," Tortorelli said. Elora fixed him with her cold stare. Was he being sarcastic? She couldn't tell because he turned and went to the screen so he could watch the destruction moving like a tsunami across Cingulum. Tanks sniped at the *Atlas*, and battle-armored soldiers continued their persistent attack, in spite of increasingly heavy losses from the BattleMech's crushing feet and sweeping arms as it tried to escape.

But nothing matched Elora's feeling of accomplishment when fifteen minutes later, her news anchor interrupted the live-action fighting to read the report of Governor Sergio Ortega's unconditional surrender.

The stage was now set for victory. If the Baron fought, he would be seen as treacherous. If he didn't, he died.

34

Here goes nothing, Austin Ortega thought. He had
worked steadily for five days and had programmed the
neurohelmet to respond to his brain waves, then had
set access codes to permit him to fully power up the
BattleMech. He had brought ammo from a warehouse
and, using a small, motorized carrier, had struggled to
load LRMs stored in an underground bunker. Several
technicians would have done such work, but Austin
had relied on his own training and a considerable
amount of innate talent.

And he had invested more physical exertion than
he cared to think about, every muscle in his body
aching. It had been a hectic, strenuous five days.

Sergeant Death had gone from an inert tower of

metal to a reborn fighting machine in less than a week under his careful ministrations.

It just goes to show what a sturdy 'Mech the Centurion is, he thought with a sense of accomplishment. Then a moment of grief washed over him. Dale had been wrong about the old BattleMech.

"This is for you, big brother," Austin declared. He fastened his neurohelmet, strapped himself in, and gripped the joysticks. His feet pressed into the pedals and *Sergeant Death* came alive. A heavy metal foot moved forward and crushed down, destroying the marble floor in the rotunda. As the BattleMech swung about, an electrical junction box at floor level exploded amid a shower of sparks and loud whistles and electronic screeches. Austin piloted the *Centurion* forward, crashing through the western wall of the museum without breaking stride. Lath and bricks fell all around, creating small clicking sounds against the metal hull.

Visual observation vanished amid the dust cloud he created. Austin switched to instrumentation. He was pleased to see that the targeting and ranging equipment was operational. When he powered up the Corean Transband-J9, he was disappointed to hear only static. Austin had hoped to contact the *Atlas*, coordinate an attack, and establish an unbreakable defense around the Palace.

Adjusting the targeting radar, he saw that the *Atlas* was more than twenty klicks away in the city. Small flares around the other BattleMech showed how furiously Tortorelli's medium tanks engaged it. The *Atlas* MechWarrior depended on surgical shots at the Condors and ignored what Austin saw as the real goal: the Governor.

"*Centurion* to *Atlas*, come in *Atlas*. Do you read?"

Austin tried several different channels, all offering no response. Before long, he gave up trying to contact Sandoval's pilot. It took increasing attention on his part to step past displays on the museum grounds and not destroy everything as he stormed toward the kilometers-distant Palace.

Austin worked on his ranging displays and sucked in his breath. The Legate might have most of his military might pitted against the *Atlas*, but enough moved in fast on the Palace to seize it. Or to destroy it and anyone inside.

Austin had hoped his father had successfully escaped during the past few days, but seeing this much firepower coming to bear argued against it.

The worst sort of war—civil war—blossomed like an evil weed all around him.

The flash of laser cannon filtered through his optics from the direction of the Palace, followed closely by the gut-shaking thunder of a concussive blast from a Gauss rifle round. Tortorelli had dispatched a Behemoth tank to spearhead the attack.

They want my father dead, he realized. Elora and Tortorelli weren't going to capture him, put him on trial as a traitor, and have a public execution. They wanted him removed from power permanently. Now. Austin took some satisfaction from this. It meant the MBA and the *Atlas* were giving more resistance than he had expected. This also chilled him because it meant Elora and the Legate no longer worried what Jerome Parsons might report.

Myomer muscles protesting from lack of movement over the years, *Sergeant Death* lumbered off, waveringly at first, then with growing stability. Austin settled in and found driving the venerable 'Mech easier than his training in the simulator. But that was as it should be. Problems were thrown fast and furious in the computerized version to test his mettle and train him for any problem that might crop up in actual combat.

Feeling as tall as the ten-meter *Sergeant Death* and twice as invincible, Austin kicked into top speed and headed directly for the expansive grounds surrounding the Palace. The ranging and targeting computer swamped him with input.

Sensory overload got worse when warning bells sounded an instant before a laser rocked him. Sheets of molten steel boiled up from his armored torso. He instinctively turned to keep the attack from concentrating on a single spot. Austin craned about and saw the source of the attack. A combined attack force had been driving hard to reach the southern Palace gates and had come across him instead. A VV1 Ranger Infantry Fighting Vehicle raced toward him, its machine guns chattering impotently as its four lasers raked him viciously.

Austin was hardly aware of the mental process he went through before his right hand spat a deadly burst of autocannon rounds that raked along the ground and hammered hard into the Ranger. His left index finger curled back and ten LRMs lashed out.

The Ranger shuddered under the impact of the salvo and then slumped to one side. Austin launched a second barrage that blew the vehicle apart. Without thinking, he immediately targeted two APCs behind the Ranger. Repeated fire from his autocannon took them out quickly.

He swallowed hard. Those personnel carriers had been loaded with human beings. He might have known some of them—some might have been former members of the FCL. Then Austin found himself fighting for survival. A company of battle-armor-clad soldiers surged forward, intent on swarming around the *Centurion*'s legs and destroying his capacity to walk, using their lasers and LRM 5s.

He kicked as if he had stepped in something sticky and sent a few of the soldiers flying, but Austin saw their unrelenting attack was succeeding. Heavy projectiles, explosives, even laser assault—all chewed away at his armor and eventually damaged some of his sensors. He had less to fear from loss of the StarGuard III armor than he did from loss of his controls. The soldiers expertly nipped like terriers at his most vulnerable spots.

Austin fired the autocannon and mowed down a rank of battle armor and infantry moving toward him. He lifted the sights and locked on to a medium Condor tank. Another long burst blew it up. Then he swung about, only to stagger heavily.

A Gauss rifle round from the Behemoth caught him squarely in the center of his armored chest. He stepped back and the step became a stagger. His head spun as he fought to hold the *Centurion* upright. As he struggled, he triggered the autocannon. He started to step forward, but a stream of shells hammered his right leg. He saw damage warnings flashing all around him, but the right leg was the most serious. Austin loosed another hailstorm of autocannon rounds and still he was under attack. The Hauberk-battle-armored soldiers fired their SRMs directly into his vulnerable leg. Salvos of fire ripped away armor, tore armor, blasted armor. He got a few of the soldiers but not enough.

His *Centurion* had taken too much damage to the right leg. He toppled to the ground with a bone-jarring crash as it gave out under him.

Stunned for a moment, Austin finally blinked his

vision back to focus on his targeting screens. Soldiers in Hauberk battle armor rushed forward, intent on destroying him with laser and missile.

He flopped about onto his back, lifted his right arm with the autocannon, and . . . nothing. Austin cried in frustration and jerked back hard on the trigger that should have sent deadly kilos of depleted-uranium shells ripping through the ground troops.

Nothing. The autoloader had jammed.

Digging in his heels and kicking up a huge dirt cloud, he tried to swing about on his back and use his torso-mounted laser on the soldiers before they reached him. He would not be Gulliver to their lilliputian might.

And Legate Tortorelli's troops wouldn't simply tie him down. They would kill his *Centurion*; they would kill him.

Austin fired his laser and ionized a wide corridor through the dust cloud. He fired his laser again and again.

Then nothing happened for a third blast that would have taken out a squad of soldiers.

"Damn, no! Don't do this to me!" he raged. The charging unit on the Photec laser indicated a short. He could get the weapon on-line again but had no idea how long it would take for even a partial charge.

He changed tactics, concentrating on getting to his feet rather than fighting.

He sat up and almost got his feet under him when *Sergeant Death* was rocked by another missile barrage. He crashed back flat on the ground, seeing nothing but the sky above. Austin refused to give up and die. His father needed him. The Republic needed him. He couldn't let Elora triumph.

With a sweep of his arm, he knocked away two

infantry soldiers and rolled onto his side. From this view he saw death staring him in the face. A Condor lowered its cannon and began the firing cycle that would send a torrent of shells into the middle of the *Centurion* cockpit.

35

Palace of Facets, Cingulum
Mirach
9 May 3133

The distant thunder of detonating missiles brought back unpleasant memories for Sergio Ortega. The entire Palace shuddered down to its foundations as Condor tanks sighted in, trying to penetrate the defenses Master Sergeant Borodin had established, but Sergio knew even the cleverest, toughest defense gave way eventually under severe enough punishment.

He had thought his days of being a warrior were past.

"To murder thousands takes a specious name, / War's glorious art, and gives immortal fame." Those ancient words echoed in his head. And it would be Elora whose fame was sung. He had been a fool to think she would hesitate to attack once Envoy Parsons

arrived with the BattleMech and placed it in Marta Kinsolving's command—for "demonstration purposes." He had not considered a cornered rat and its similarity to his Minister of Information.

The *Atlas* had precipitated the fight for control of Mirach, not discouraged it. Elora had felt the jaws of a steel trap clamping down on her ambitions and had to act or be imprisoned. Sergio saw that now and wished he could replay some of the events that led to her subverting Legate Tortorelli and believing she could seize power.

Sergio closed his eyes for a moment and felt the distant tremors come up through the floor and shake him anew. Sergio was alone in the vast halls now echoing only with memories and autocannon fire. Borodin and the others still loyal to him and the ideals of The Republic were on the battle lines, fighting and undoubtedly dying.

He glanced at the screens and saw the rapid approach of three tanks, one Behemoth and two Condors, then recoiled when his field of vision filled with a monster metallic foot coming down to block the advance.

"The *Centurion*!" he cried. Sergio's colorless eyes widened. Only one person could pilot the Battle-Mech—his old 'Mech—so competently. "Austin, no, don't fight. Don't risk your life," he cried in exasperation.

Sergio worked frantically with the comm equipment. He knew the frequency used by the *Centurion* as well as he did his own face in a mirror. For almost four years he had lived in the cockpit, fighting for The Republic. Never since the day the BattleMech was placed in the museum did he think he would use these settings again.

He found the proper frequency to contact Austin, but time had run out. Sergio watched in dread as the *Centurion* toppled over and the tanks closed in for the kill. The *Centurion*'s autocannon had jammed and the sole remaining laser shot sparks, betraying some fatal internal short circuit.

"Austin, come in. Austin!" Sergio decided communication with the BattleMech was not in the cards and tried to find another frequency. It took what seemed an eternity to lock in the carrier signal. The short IFF beep-click-beep told him he had located his son's only chance for salvation.

"Home in on my signal," he said in a choked voice. "Hurry. Please, hurry." Sergio Ortega sank back in his chair, eyes on the monitors, following the battle on the Palace grounds intently, all else forgotten.

36

Ministry of Information, Cingulum
Mirach
9 May 3133

"It's all going according to plan," Lady Elora said, her lips pulled back in such an extreme smile that she looked like a death's-head with red hair. "Parsons' BattleMech is trapped in the center of the city where we can nibble it to death."

"Ah, yes, unable to move because of their silly rules of engagement," Calvilena Tortorelli said as if dismissing the notion out of hand. "They try to preserve life when the sole purpose of the BattleMech is to destroy it. Foolish. Ever so foolish."

"My, that is, *your* tanks have circled it. No matter which way the 'Mech turns, it is being hit hard. If it retreats, the tanks will pursue." She stared at the video feeds pouring in from a dozen different angles.

Huge gouts of molten metal exploded from the surface of the *Atlas*, blown off by barrages from half a dozen tanks.

"Is it Envoy Parsons who decreed that the Battle-Mech wasn't to use its weapons where civilians might be lost, or was it Marta Kinsolving?" Tortorelli stroked his chin as he pondered this point. "I find it difficult to believe she, as leader of the MBA, cares if we slaughtered everyone in the city, but the structural damage, now, that might bother her. If AllWorldComm doesn't own a considerable amount of property in downtown Cingulum, I am sure other MBA members do."

Elora hardly listened to him arguing with himself. What difference did it make if Parsons or Kinsolving had given the foolish order for the BattleMech to only defend rather than to attack? The result was the same. The full might of Mirach's military fell like a sledgehammer on the 'Mech. No matter that it was still functional. They had trapped it, forcing it to play a defensive role while the Legate's best tank commander drove to remove Sergio Ortega at the Palace of Facets.

Soon it will be his tomb, Elora gloated.

Elora chuckled as she authorized transmission of pictures of the *Atlas* being hammered by Legate Tortorelli's forces along with hearty congratulations for the soldiers. Offers of vast rewards to infantry and battle-armored troops if they brought down the BattleMech were made public, giving yet another way of gaining honor.

But no individual would claim the reward. The heavy tanks would eventually blow off enough armor to expose the MechWarrior to the killing blast.

No quarter asked, no quarter given, she thought as she stared at the bank of monitors popped up all over her desktop.

"Yes, yes, definitely. The battle is going well," Tortorelli said, as if he had won an argument. "I planned carefully. There ought to be another medal in this for me. Yes, there should."

He began strutting around her office, posturing and practicing his speeches. She wasn't sure when he had slipped away from reality, and it hardly mattered. She had needed his authority to put the entire military of Mirach into motion against the Lord Governor's Envoy—and against Governor Ortega.

She partially turned in her chair to face other monitors gleaming atop her desk. She panned around the vast bucolic grounds of Governor's Park and saw two light tanks moving in ahead of the ground troops, all supported by the heavy Behemoth II. It would be a combined-forces assault on the Palace because Sergio had turned it into a fortress using defenses put into place by the Legate.

Elora's elation mounted again when she saw how the field commander deployed her force, the main battle tank at point with the lighter Condors in an echelon formation. Sergio might as well have drawn a bull's-eye on his back. The battle would be over in minutes. No defensive tactic could work against such an onslaught.

"What's that?" Elora jumped to her feet and leaned forward, supporting herself on the desk with clenched hands. "That's another BattleMech!"

"Where did it come from? I do say, that Jerome Parsons might be sneakier than I credited him with being. He must have hidden it until this moment," Tortorelli said.

"No, he didn't. That's Sergio Ortega's old Battle-Mech."

"The one with the hideous paint job rusting away in the museum?" Tortorelli frowned as he studied the screen in front of Elora. Angrily, she switched the feed so the entire wall, where Cingulum's skyline had been a few seconds earlier, came alive with the details of the BattleMech.

"Captain Mugabe," Elora said, her voice barely controlled, "attack the BattleMech. Don't let it reach a point where it can defend the Palace!"

"That's my job, Elora. I should be the one giving orders," Tortorelli said, almost pouting.

"I gave the orders in your name, Calvy. Sit down; watch what *your* forces can do against a BattleMech," she soothed.

She saw the *Centurion* taking huge strides toward the Palace, intent on safeguarding Sergio Ortega. But the field commander was the head of Tortorelli's elite force and had practiced in simulators in the event of such a tank-versus-'Mech battle. Captain Mugabe sent her Condors out on either flank and then attacked fiercely with both infantry and Hauberk-battle-armored fighters. When the individual soldiers were driven away, the tanks opened up to good effect.

"That's the way," Elora muttered, seeing a particularly devastating Gauss rifle attack rip away part of the *Centurion*'s chest armor. After sustained attack focusing on the right leg, the BattleMech staggered and fell backward, crashing to the ground so hard it caused her camera to wobble from the shock wave.

"Get him, get him," she said. Her vengeance would be even sweeter now. "That has to be Austin Ortega in the *Centurion*. Who else could it be?"

The tanks drove in to deliver the coup de grâce. She silently cheered them on. Austin Ortega brought his autocannon to bear—the cannon jammed. This time she did cheer.

The cheer turned to strangled rage when she saw the new combatants.

37

Austin Ortega struggled to save himself and saw nothing but death staring him in the face. His laser refused to fire. The autocannon had jammed, leaving deadly rounds in the breach where they might explode at any instant. From his position on the ground, he couldn't get back to his feet and use what power remained in the ancient *Centurion* to fight back.

The alarms in his cockpit went crazy as the Condor lowered its main autocannon and pointed it directly at him. Austin could not scramble away. *Sergeant Death* was going to become a metal coffin in seconds.

Austin refused to give up. Working frantically, he got the *Centurion* flopped over and rising on hands and knees. A myomer bundle snapped, dropping him to one side. In this position he stared directly down the tank barrel.

Then he flinched and tried to shield his eyes from the sudden fountain of sparks that exploded into the air. In disbelief he watched as a diamond-edged cutting wheel rose again and came back down on the tank. The first pass had severed the barrel of the heavy gun. The diamond cutting wheel spun so fast it was only a blur until it hit the top of the tank and cut away half the turret.

"Who's there?" Austin asked, trying to find a frequency where he could contact his savior. He got no answer and gave up. His comm was faulty. Austin heard the heavy rattle of an autocannon firing, and then an explosion lifted him and rolled him a few meters.

His reactions were superb. Austin used the impetus from the blast to get the *Centurion* to its knees and then erect. His eyes flashed about the controls. Most were dead but what he saw showed him he had enough power to continue. In spite of the damage to his right leg, he could still move. The Palace would not fall, not while Austin Ortega had trusty old *Sergeant Death* for a ride.

From his loftier view ten meters above the ground he saw a modified IndustrialMech making short work of another medium tank. The cutting wheel on its left arm that had carved up the tank hung at a crazy angle. Teeth had broken off and the drive unit gushed heavy black, oily smoke. Another cutting wheel mounted on the upper left shoulder still spun in a deadly arc, but the real damage was wrought by the hammering autocannon in its right arm.

Austin started stamping to keep the light infantry away. The heavier battle-armor-clad soldiers worked toward him, only to find themselves at the mercy of the IndustrialMech's autocannon. The pilot of that 'Mech was a maestro with his weapons. Austin doubted it was true, but it looked as if every single 50-mm round found a target and dispatched one of the attacking soldiers.

A grating sound was quickly followed by a small explosion on Austin's right shoulder. To his surprise, he found that his autocannon had cleared and he could fire again. He hobbled over and stood with his back to the refitted 'Mech, firing at any target he saw. Austin lifted his autocannon to fire at movement showing on the edge of his radar screen, only to have the weapon jam again.

For a change, he let out a heavy sigh of relief at the weapon's failure. Austin would have fired reflexively on another of the MBA 'Mechs, this one a modified MiningMech firing salvos of SRMs at infantry and light-armored vehicles as it came. The autocannon mounted on its other side was silent, having jammed like Austin's.

Austin checked his console again, but he was weaponless. His rear-facing laser had been removed before the *Centurion* had gone on display and the one on the right side of his torso struggled to recharge. Given its wildly fluctuating voltage, the laser might never work again. And the autocannon? Jammed beyond repair.

A heavy blow knocked him forward a few steps. He swung the *Centurion* around as quickly as he could and faced his rescuer. Through the forward view screen Austin saw the other pilot gesturing to the radio.

Austin shook his head to indicate he had lost all communication capability. The other pilot signaled that Austin should eject, but Austin wasn't going to abandon *Sergeant Death*. That would be like leaving a fallen comrade for the enemy. It had shown itself to be as deadly a resource now as when his father had driven it.

He coughed, then blinked as smoke burned his eyes. Austin saw the trouble now. Red lights had replaced all the green on his control console. The recycling pump for his coolant had died. Stealthy fires worked their way along most of the wiring, spelling death for the magnificent BattleMech. Austin hit the emergency shutdown, then scrambled to unstrap and pull off hoses going to the coolant vest. Twisting until he thought he would tear himself into pieces, he got free of the pilot's couch and scrambled up and out of the hatch.

Standing on the *Centurion*'s shoulder, he waved to the IndustrialMech. The deadly spinning blade on the 'Mech's shoulder slowed and finally grated to a stop. Only then did the 'Mech move closer. With a powerful jump Austin shot through the air and grabbed frantically for a handhold. He slid a few centimeters, then found both footing and a secure grip.

From the hatchway of the *Centurion* erupted flame so intense his pants legs began to smolder, though he was five meters away. The 'Mech driver was already turning away to protect him with the bulk of the fighting machine. With practiced ease, he bent to let Austin jump to the ground.

The hatch on the 'Mech popped, and Austin got another surprise.

"Manfred!" he called, staring at his rescuer. "You're alive!"

"Be grateful you can't get rid of me so easily!" Manfred laughed and then dropped to the ground to clutch Austin in a powerful bear hug.

"How? I saw you blown up!"

Manfred laughed and shook his head. "Your father called me as I was leaving the limo and warned me about some missing explosives. Borodin had found out and told the Baron in time for him to tell me. The Kuton station is such a threat to Elora that it didn't take long to figure out that a DropShip filled with supplies headed to the moon might not be the safest place for me to be." Manfred turned somber. "I never entered the 'Ship."

"I saw you. Marta saw you!" Austin protested.

"The bulk of the 'Ship blocked your view. I made a serious mistake then. I didn't go into the 'Ship, but I tried to contact the pilot. All I had was one of the Span-net phones. No one in the DropShip could pick up that frequency, so I couldn't warn them."

"You should have told Marta. She could have contacted them through the control bunker," said Austin.

"The engine ignition sequence started, and I ran like a fool to keep from getting fried. I found a ditch to protect me from the backwash. Then it was too late. The 'Ship blew up as it lifted off. There was nothing I could do, so I thought it would be better to let Tortorelli and Elora think they had actually killed me."

"But where did you get the 'Mech? You must have told Marta you were alive."

"Sure, but by the time I got in touch, you'd disappeared. Your father and Marta knew I was alive. Maybe even Borodin, though I doubt it. I bet if you asked him, he'd say he knew."

"You saved me," Austin said, looking around. Governor's Park was silent now. Craters had been blown in the ground and smoldering tree limbs littered once immaculate lawns. But Austin ignored that. The dam-

age to the Palace of Facets seemed minor, although a
fire chewed fitfully at the south wing and immense
chunks had been blown out of the eastern section.

"My father?" Austin asked.

"He's alive. Borodin's watching him."

"What do we do now?" asked Austin. "It looks
peaceful here."

"There's still a war to be won. We took out the
medium tanks and set the infantry here to running,
but the Behemoth withdrew and there's an entire city
full of Home Guard going after an *Atlas*."

Austin looked at the *Centurion* and knew its fighting
days were at an end.

"Get me a ride and let's go mop up the Legate's
troops in town," Austin said.

"Nothing for you to maneuver. I've radioed for the
other MBA 'Mechs to converge on the *Atlas*. Fighting's got to be stopped there, but your place is here,"
Manfred said. He turned to get back into his 'Mech.

"You can't do this. I want to fight. I *deserve* to
be there."

"Sorry," Manfred said, vanishing into the 'Mech.
The hatch clanged shut like a peal of doom for Austin.
He stood staring as Manfred got the modified 'Mech
moving toward Cingulum.

Austin refused to be left behind. He ran to the
south entrance of the Palace and was met by Dmitri
Borodin and a half dozen soldiers he recognized as
FCL.

"Master Sergeant," Austin said. "Is everything
under control?"

"Lieutenant, we got things all quieted down. We
lost a fair number, but it's no surprise we gained a
fair number as the Home Guard runnin' the tanks
bailed out and surrendered. Came to us, not wanting
to fight the Governor." Borodin smiled and added,

"The Governor might have had a part in it, too. He used our short-range radio and asked for all loyal to The Republic to come to our side."

Austin grinned. *Maybe there's some fight left in the old man after all.*

"Two tankers and a fair number of infantry," Borodin confirmed. "I'm not too sure about the captain in charge of the mission—the one in the Behemoth. I think she might be fixin' to quit, too."

"Excellent work, Master Sergeant," Austin said. "You are in command."

"You're rankin' officer, Baronet," he said. "I think the Baron wants to see you."

"How fast are the tanks, the ones that surrendered?" Austin asked.

"You don't want to get in those metal coffins," Borodin said, his eyes fixed on Austin. "That wouldn't be a fittin' way for the Baronet to travel. What you want is something that'd go in style."

"I won't mention it to the Baron if you don't," Austin said, his heart racing. He looked at *Sergeant Death* and knew his ride wouldn't be a BattleMech. Even if Manfred had a spare modified 'Mech for him, it would take too long to program the neurohelmet so he could get into the thick of battle.

Borodin took out his radio and spoke in it, then looked skyward.

For a moment, Austin didn't see anything. Then a small dark dot appeared at the far north end of Governor's Park.

"An FCL sergeant talked the crew into letting her give you a look at the battle," Borodin said. "FCL's got our fingers stuck about everywhere. You might keep that in mind, Lieutenant. They're all loyal troopers, no matter what uniform they're wearing."

"I understand, Master Sergeant. Thank you." Austin threw up his arm to protect his face as a Lamprey Transport VTOL—it looked like a modified model—kicked up dirt and debris all around him. Austin turned, saluted Borodin, knowing he would keep the Palace and the Baron safe, then put his head down and sprinted for the open door.

The battle at Governor's Park was over. The war had yet to be won.

=== 38 ===

"Welcome aboard, Lieutenant," shouted the pilot over the rotor noise. Austin recognized her as an FCL technician in spite of the Home Guard insignia she now wore.

"I didn't know you could fly a Lamprey, Sergeant Posner." Austin swung into the rear infantry bay next to the machine gun mounted in a side door and started to strap himself into a drop seat.

"I learn fast, sir. I've always liked choppers and spent a lot of time in simulators, so the Legate stuck me in one. You thinking on using that gun, Lieutenant?" Posner called back. "Put on the door gunner harness. Don't want you getting sucked out."

"See how fast you can get us to the fighting, Sergeant," Austin said, taking her advice, getting out of the drop seat and climbing into the web harness. He had barely finished cinching up the broad straps when the helicopter surged, shooting upward like a rocket as Posner applied full lifting power to the rotors.

Austin found a helmet and put it on, checked to be sure he could speak to the pilot, then dropped the face guard to keep the whipping wind from making his eyes water. He wanted to see everything. And from five hundred meters, he did. Austin turned grim as he stared down at the destruction Governor's Park had sustained that he had been unable to see from ground level. The Behemoth had left deep ruts and the lighter Condors had chewed up a considerable amount of landscaping, but the real demolition had come from the fight between the BattleMech, the IndustrialMech, and the invading force.

A catch came to Austin's throat when he saw the damaged bulk of *Sergeant Death* sprawled on the ground. As the VTOL gained forward speed, he spotted Manfred dutifully striding toward Cingulum in his modified 'Mech just beyond the park perimeter. The Lamprey flashed overhead at its top 150-kilometer-per-hour speed, leaving Manfred to plod along. Austin started to wave, then heard an explosion that brought him around.

He cycled on his helmet faceplate magnification and studied the city. Ahead he saw amber lasers licking across the *Atlas*. The BattleMech struggled to avoid the punishment as it replied with its own lasers. The explosion had come from a tank being hit by return fire. Austin couldn't tell what type of tank had been destroyed—he was still too far away to look down into the urban canyon formed by the buildings. But the secondary, internal magazine explosion told him it was unlikely any of the crew escaped.

"Where to, Lieutenant? The middle of the action?" Sergeant Posner spoke to him now over the radio in his helmet.

"Circle the fight. I need to see what we can do to help out most." He clung to a handhold welded on the side of the Lamprey as Posner banked sharply. Austin saw the battle centered in Havoc. Many buildings had been destroyed, leaving mountains of debris. Sharp, shining steel beams poked out of the rubble like bones of a skeleton. Worst of all were the immense craters that had been blown in the ground. Some were deep enough to swallow the *Atlas* whole.

"The BattleMech's taken some serious damage, Lieutenant," the pilot said. "It's not putting up much of a fight. Not shooting unless it's shot at. But it doesn't look to be in immediate trouble."

"When the 'Mech does respond, it's pinpointing its target. No collateral damage, if it can avoid it." Austin knew the orders had to go beyond that. Keep loss of life to a minimum. The *Atlas* had been given the unfortunate task of restoring order while faced with armored units of the Home Guard and not just unarmed, unarmored rioters.

"Whoa!" Posner exclaimed, the helicopter sideslipping suddenly. Austin was glad he had fastened the harness. He was thrown outward and might have tumbled from the Lamprey otherwise. "We're taking fire from below. What do you want to do, Lieutenant?"

"You've got missiles. Respond," Austin ordered. The VTOL shuddered as Posner launched a salvo of four SRMs. The smoke trails snaked off toward the ground, but Austin couldn't tell if the pilot hit her target. The Lamprey banked sharply to avoid return fire. Austin saw LRMs shrieking past, almost close enough for him to reach out and touch them. The helicopter was too lightly armored to withstand a full salvo, but Posner showed great skill avoiding potential disaster.

"Their battle armor is moving in on the *Atlas*," Austin radioed to Posner. "Get us down where I can do some work keeping the mites off the giant's leg."

"I'm trying to contact the *Atlas*, sir. Radio signal's jammed."

"Elora," Austin grumbled. Louder, he said, "Keep trying to signal the BattleMech to clear out. There's no reason for it to stand and take a beating."

"It's built to take punishment," Posner said. As if to prove her claim, the BattleMech took a full barrage of missiles. It lost a small amount of armor on the left torso, possibly damaging its own SRM launcher, but otherwise shrugged off the assault.

Austin knew the *Atlas* could withstand repeated attacks, but that wasn't why it had been built. It had been constructed to dish out destruction.

The chopper swung around and then dropped like a rock between tall buildings. Posner flew at ten meters above the street, flashing over a battle-armored squad moving quickly toward the BattleMech. She pulled back sharply, spun about 180 degrees, and put Austin in position to fire.

He gripped the machine gun and drew back the loading lever. He hesitated for a moment, then opened up. The machine gun chattered noisily as it spat out leaden death. The stream of bullets stitched across concrete and asphalt and caught the leading battle-armored soldier squarely. The heavy bullets sang off the armor and knocked the trooper back.

Then the VTOL suddenly rose. Austin lost his balance and swung out, looking straight down. The squad he had fired on had scattered, taking cover. They wore Hauberk armor and all trained their lasers on the Lamprey. Austin saw the laser fire miss, splashing against nearby buildings, blowing off hunks of steel, vaporizing glass and filling the air with concrete dust.

Posner swung back and Austin got into position. The machine gun sights swept across the battle-armored squad again, and Austin squeezed off a long burst. He saw the squad leader jerk about, then smash into the ground facedown. A muffled explosion lifted the ton of battle armor up and dropped it down. Austin had struck the missile launcher and the soldier's own armament had destroyed the armor.

And the soldier.

Then the helicopter flashed past and Posner climbed fast.

"Tank," she said needlessly as a football-sized hunk of nickel fired from a Gauss rifle seared past.

"Behemoth," he agreed. "Moving in on the Battle-Mech. Any luck getting in touch with the *Atlas*?"

"None, but I've picked up comm on a different frequency. One used by the AWC."

The VTOL shuddered as autocannon fire struck and rebounded from its armored belly. As it struggled to gain altitude, Austin got a quick glimpse of new troop movement below. Tortorelli's forces were making an all-out assault on the BattleMech. A company of battle armor moved up slowly under the covering fire from a Condor tank. In the distance Behemoth tanks systematically leveled the buildings with Gauss rifle and heavy laser fire to further expose the BattleMech.

"The MechWarrior is pretty clever," Posner radioed. "He's using the rubble well to keep away the attackers, but he's running out of time. They have it circled and are tightening the noose."

"Patch me through on the AWC frequency," Austin

said. He scanned the battle-torn terrain and saw how the *Atlas* was being inexorably pushed forward by the lighter tanks to a point where a trio of Behemoths could concentrate their fire.

"You got it, Lieutenant."

"AWC force, come in," Austin said. He shifted his focus for a moment to send a long burst from the machine gun raining down against a Condor tank. The tank's armor was more than up to the task of deflecting his rounds, but he got the tank driver's attention and halted its advance. For a few seconds.

"Who is this?" came the suspicious reply.

"Lieutenant Ortega, FCL," he identified himself without thinking. "Are you bringing up modified IndustrialMechs?"

"We need more ID, Lieutenant."

"There's no time. Manfred Leclerc is on his way in his 'Mech from Governor's Park. The Palace is secure and Governor Ortega is safe. I'm in a VTOL above the city and the *Atlas* is being boxed in."

"Can't contact the BattleMech," came the reply. "Frequency is jammed."

"How far away are you? Can you clear a retreat path for the *Atlas*?"

"We're under heavy fire from a tank, a Behemoth," came the reply.

Static drowned out contact, but a distant voice came through that set Austin's heart racing. He shouted, as if this could make Manfred hear him better.

"Manfred! How long before you can engage?"

"The other MBA 'Mechs are under attack," Manfred reported. "I'm using a frequency to them that Elora's not jamming."

"I need to break that jamming. Can you send a 'Mech to the Ministry of Information and destroy the broadcast towers on top of the building?"

"Done," Manfred reported a few seconds later. "The 'Mech will reach the Ministry in a few minutes."

Austin came to a quick conclusion. There wasn't time to wait. The *Atlas* was advancing into the shooting gallery formed by three Behemoth tanks. If they all opened up on the BattleMech, it would be seriously damaged and the battle-armored troops on the ground could disable it.

"Engage immediately. We have to let the Battle-Mech get free."

"I'm not going to worry about collateral damage," Manfred said.

"Tortorelli's troops are still citizens of Mirach," warned Austin. He now saw firsthand how terrible a civil war could be. Anyone dying wasn't "one of them." It was a neighbor or friend, a brother or sister.

"Understood. Now attack!" cried Manfred.

The Lamprey swung around above the *Atlas* so Austin could take in the situation. Directly ahead, not a klick down the main thoroughfare, waited a Behemoth tank. Along streets branching at right angles were two more, ready to fire as the Condor and battle-armored soldiers behind the *Atlas* herded it into the Behemoths' sights.

"There's no chance for us to take out a Behemoth," Austin radioed the pilot. "We go after the forces behind the BattleMech."

He saw an IndustrialMech making its way down a broad street, heading for one of the Behemoths. Austin started to warn the 'Mech away. It was a converted MiningMech, armed with an autocannon and LRMs. As it neared the tank, the 'Mech opened fire, letting fly salvo after salvo of missiles. The Behemoth returned fire with its lasers, and then Austin lost sight of that deadly contest in a hurricane of smoke, dust, and flying debris.

"Here we go, Lieutenant," Posner said. Austin felt his stomach try to leave his body through his throat as they plunged downward. Grimly gripping the machine gun, he started firing. The slugs bounced off battle armor and, he thought, brought down one soldier. More important, he had forced the squad to take cover.

Then the battle changed drastically. Manfred lumbered into view, his modified 'Mech firing its autocannon into a Condor tank. Bright ricochets off the armor filled the air like crazy fireflies. A few of the deflected rounds hammered into the underside of the Lamprey as they flashed past. Austin cut loose with the machine gun and added a few extra kilos of slugs to the fray.

But it was Manfred's attack that stopped the tank. The tank responded with laser fire, then vanished in a cloud as Manfred cut loose with his autocannon.

"Go get 'em!" Austin cheered. Manfred lurched forward, the damaged cutting wheel on his left arm spinning wildly. The 'Mech was swallowed by the dust cloud, and sparks began flying.

"Got him," came Manfred's excited report. "Tank is down."

Austin lurched as the chopper swung about. He fired a few rounds in the direction of another tank— a Demon—but missed.

"Battle armor moving on the *Atlas*. They're getting frantic now," reported Sergeant Posner. "The other mod 'Mech disabled the Behemoth before going down. Gauss rifle round fired almost point-blank got it."

"We can sweep the street clear for the BattleMech," Austin said to Sergeant Posner. "Keep us down low."

He used the cocking lever to load in a new ammo belt, then concentrated on hitting every battle-armor-clad soldier he could find in the street. As the Lamprey flew back and forth, Austin saw Manfred going after another tank. A laser bolt slashed at Manfred's right side and bathed him in deadly energy that boiled off much of his armor. From the way the 'Mech limped, more than armor had been damaged.

"What's the status on bringing the Ministry of Information towers down?" he asked.

" 'Mech is almost there, sir," reported Posner.

"Manfred's tangled with another tank and this one's stripping him naked. Fly closer so we can lend support." Austin wished he had more than a single machine gun in the infantry bay door. They swooped down so Austin could concentrate on the tank, but the Condor launched a volley that crashed into the Lamprey, sending it reeling.

The shock of missile impact dazed Austin for a moment. He sat up, not sure how he had ended up away from the machine gun.

"Got it," came Manfred's cry of triumph. "But I'm losing power. The internal combustion engine's not up to sustained fighting."

"What about the 'Mech going to the Ministry?"

He got his answer when a cacophony of voices filled his head. A dozen soldiers all shouted in his ears at the same time, the jamming lifted so they could again communicate.

"Attention, Home Guard," Austin broadcast as Posner patched him through on the Legate's command frequency. "Cease fire. I repeat, cease fire. This is Baronet Austin Ortega ordering you to hold your fire."

"Not much happening, sir," said Posner.

Austin wasn't going to give up if there was a chance the carnage could be halted here and now. He searched for the words that could make a difference.

"Home Guard of Mirach," he began slowly, "anyone who can hear me: for the last three months, you've been bombarded with messages about the tyrant Sergio Ortega, and now Legate Tortorelli and Lady Elora Rimonova have ordered you to take up arms against him." He paused and wondered, *How can I reach them?* He could hear Elora's voice over other comm channels, egging the soldiers on . . . and then he knew the answer to his question.

"But these orders aren't Legate Tortorelli's, are they?" he asked. "Listen to the voice giving orders: it's Lady Elora. The Minister of Information has ordered you into the streets to defend Mirach against Governor Ortega, whom many of you have met and have served under for years, a hero of The Republic—a man who has been a prisoner in the Palace of Facets for the last week, unable to contact anyone, unable to help his own people.

"This fight isn't about defending Mirach from its Governor. It's about defending ourselves against the propaganda war being waged by the Ministry of Information. The Republic sent that *Atlas* to Mirach to help restore the order and reason its Governor believes in. And look—the *Atlas* has not attacked. It has only defended itself and the city." Now Austin's voice grew passionate.

"I appeal to all FCL soldiers, cease fire. You know what I'm saying is true. For the sake of peace in Cingulum and a united Mirach, lay down your weapons. We can't let fear and misinformation tear our world apart. I urge all those following Lady Elora's orders, cease fire!"

There was a buzz of static from the radio, then a cacophony of chatter.

"Some units are breaking off, sir," said Posner.

"What's the nearest that isn't?" he asked.

"Almost directly below us."

"Manfred, can you still fight?"

"I'm with you!"

The Lamprey swung about and spotted a squad of battle-armored troopers trying to double-time advance on the *Atlas*.

"Battle armor, break off your advance on the *Atlas*!" Austin yelled into the radio. He fired the machine gun, careful not to hit the combatants, but aimed close enough to scare them. The troops scattered as Manfred's 'Mech roared up, diamond-edged cutting wheel on his left shoulder looking like fire as it spun. None of the soldiers was in danger, but the sight of the 'Mech broke their attack.

"The *Atlas* is backing off. It's not going into the cross fire trap laid by the Behemoths," said Posner.

Austin was too busy firing to respond. Then the machine gun belt ran out. No more ammo. But he had a clear comm channel and used it.

"Cease fire! Don't put any more citizens of Cingulum in danger."

"You really the Baronet?" came a faint question on Tortorelli's command frequency.

"I am. Surrender, and no action will be taken against you for following orders."

"I see one of those refitted 'Mechs coming toward me."

"All AWC units, stand down," Austin ordered. He hoped they would listen to him. If not, he had to waste valuable time and relay orders through Manfred—or Marta Kinsolving.

"Standing down," came the replies, one by one. Austin was surprised that he received five acknowledgments. Some of the mod 'Mechs were still on their way to Cingulum but reported in to show how much firepower was being mustered.

He heard other chatter, mostly FCL urging others with them to stop fighting. If they were persuasive enough and confirmed that he was not the sort to lie about amnesty, units all over the middle of Cingulum should be stopping. They were.

The *Atlas* strode past. Austin looked down on the mighty fighting machine and saw the damage was extensive but not irreparable.

Austin played on the BattleMech's still functional armament, repeated the threat of the approaching MBA 'Mechs, and then let the First Cossack Lancers, wherever they might be scattered among the battle-armored troops, complete the surrender.

"We got a problem, Lieutenant. A big one."

Austin swung out the side bay and saw the Behemoth rumbling down the middle of the street, heading directly for Manfred's damaged 'Mech. The Gauss rifle was loaded and aimed.

"Captain Mugabe, I am placing you in command of Legate Tortorelli's troops. See to the orderly surrender immediately," Austin radioed.

"That's Mugabe in the Behemoth? Tortorelli's top tanker?" asked Posner. "Will she—"

That was as far as the pilot got. A crisp message came through from the Behemoth commander.

"Captain Mugabe in receipt of your orders, Baronet."

The Gauss rifle elevated off target.

"All Home Guard units, stand down. Do not fire; I repeat, do not fire. This is Captain Mugabe. Do not fire."

Austin let out a breath he hadn't known he was holding, made sure he was on an open frequency, then radioed, "Governor Ortega, the city is secure. I am ordering Captain Mugabe to establish patrols to maintain order."

"Well done, Austin," Manfred radioed him on a closed frequency. "That lets everyone know where they stand, especially Mugabe."

Austin stared down from the Lamprey at the *Atlas*, carefully picking its way through the city streets, hunting for the route to take it out of Cingulum while causing the least damage.

"Yes," Austin said. "Well done. Well done, all around!"

39

Palace of Facets, Cingulum
Mirach
12 May 3133

"The last tank commander has surrendered out by the Blood Hills Barracks," Sergio Ortega announced, looking pleased with himself. "Without a shot being fired. Captain Mugabe was instrumental in negotiating the capitulation. I think she'll prove herself even more useful as we rebuild and reconstitute the Legate's forces." His colorless eyes fixed on Austin, who stood to one side of the vast office. "Good sense has prevailed over force of arms."

Austin didn't flinch. "If I hadn't powered up the *Centurion—your* BattleMech—Tortorelli would have overrun the Palace and you'd be dead. Mugabe had her *Behemoth's* Gauss rifle pointed straight at your head."

"But she refused to obey Tortorelli's—Elora's—order to destroy the Palace. It was too powerful a symbol of The Republic for her to blow up."

"The *Centurion* held her at bay and gave her time to consider how wrong her orders were," Austin shot back.

"You've forgotten what really happened? I contacted Manfred," Sergio said. "The show of force was enough to compel Mugabe to surrender."

"After more than a hundred soldiers died." Austin swallowed and tasted bile at this terrible statistic.

How could I have done it differently? he wondered. *Was there a way to keep my father safe without killing any of the Legate's troops?* If there had been a way, he couldn't see it—neither in the heat of the fight nor in its aftermath. The threat of force was meaningless without the use of force if the bluff was called.

"Are you forgetting my role in all this?" asked Manfred Leclerc. "You were dog meat until I saved you."

"My point is made, Father," Austin said. "Without that cutting wheel and autocannon of Manfred's, I'd have been dead."

"You should never have gotten involved in the battle. Your presence is what put you at risk."

"If I hadn't engaged Tortorelli's forces from the helicopter until Manfred and the other MBA 'Mechs arrived, we'd have lost everything."

"Your plea to the soldiers caused many to reconsider the legality of the orders Tortorelli—and Elora—had given," said Sergio. "Words, not bullets, turned the fight."

"If I hadn't fought to clear that channel, I'd never have been able to contact any of them."

"Please, you two," cut in Manfred. "Stop arguing.

You'll never get the other to agree. Governor Ortega
has a point, Austin. The combination of Parsons' political muscle and Marta Kinsolving's loyalty to Mirach
made victory over Elora and Tortorelli inevitable
sooner or later. And," Manfred hastily said, turning
on the Baron, "you needed force to bring about your
goals. Without the MBA's 'Mechs you would have
been killed."

"As Manfred said so colorfully before, 'dog meat.' "
Austin grinned.

"The use of force means failure of diplomacy," Sergio said. "Diplomacy and a certain element of stealth
served me far better than brute violence. That's how
I contacted Manfred and warned him about taking off
in the cargo DropShip."

"Baron," said Manfred, inclining his head slightly
in the direction of the open office door.

Marta Kinsolving came into the office, Envoy Parsons at her side. She looked a little flushed, but her
brief glance in Manfred's direction might have explained that.

"Envoy Parsons, Ms. Kinsolving, so good of you to
come." Sergio stood and graciously indicated that they
take comfortable leather chairs in front of his desk.

"This meeting must be short," Jerome Parsons said
brusquely. Austin compared this with the man's earlier
visit and the way he had seemed diffident then. Now
he was all business. "I am pleased with the outcome of
my mission to your fine planet and commend you all."

Austin looked at his father. Something sounded
wrong in Jerome Parsons' compliment.

"Why did you choose to bring an *Atlas* here at all,
Your Excellency?" asked Austin. He left the rest of
the question unstated, but his father did not.

"Why did you put the *Atlas* under the command of
the MBA?" Sergio asked.

Parsons took a deep breath, looked around the room, then glanced over his shoulder to be certain the office doors were closed.

"You have proved your loyalty. All of you."

"Loyalty to The Republic," Austin said.

"Quite so," Parsons said. "Quite so. I allowed Ms. Kinsolving and her trade organization control of the BattleMech because I wanted to reinforce their loyalty. I had not realized how closely she would adhere to your recommendation to refrain from using the BattleMech's power, Baron."

"You were afraid we would forge an alliance with Bannson?" Marta asked. "The BattleMech was an indirect way of showing the advantage of remaining loyal to The Republic and giving us the support we needed against the government?"

"There was that," Parsons admitted, "but there was another element to my plan. I was certain Governor Ortega remained loyal to The Republic but would not deploy the *Atlas* because of his philosophical leanings."

"You shouldn't have brought it," Sergio said. Austin heard something more in the Envoy's words.

"I had to be certain that you weren't loyal first and foremost to Aaron Sandoval, and only *then* to The Republic," Parsons went on.

"It's not the same thing, is it?" Austin said, his mind racing. "What haven't we been told because the HPG net is down?"

"Austin," Sergio said sharply.

"It's all right, Governor. It's time to share our secret," Parsons said. "I am loyal to The Republic, but no longer can I say the same with regard to Aaron Sandoval."

Silence fell in the room.

"Who are you working for, if not the Lord Governor?" asked Austin.

"Let us say a Paladin of The Republic and leave it at that. Sandoval, however, thinks I am still his faithful Envoy."

"A double agent," Manfred said in a whispered voice.

Austin looked at his father, whose enigmatic smile suddenly spoke volumes. Sergio had insisted he had a plan; for two months he'd kept silent. Austin looked to Parsons again.

"Yes, a double agent." Parsons looked at each of them in turn. "This information could be my demise. My life is now in your hands.

"Though he continues to act as Lord Governor of the Prefecture, the truth is that Aaron Sandoval is no longer loyal to The Republic. With the destruction of the HPG net, he has tasted new power, as has Kal Radick. You may have heard rumors about their defections. These rumors are true. Given the chaos that has descended upon us, there's been little time and too few resources to address the question of putting new leaders into place." Parsons' look turned grave.

"Know this. I willingly risk my life for The Republic. I am trying to shore up support amongst the worlds, and am not loyal to any single individual. The ideals of Devlin Stone are bigger than that. Come what may, I will fight and die for the unity of The Republic of the Sphere."

"Mirach may not be a large, rich planet, but you can count on our fealty," Sergio said.

"Your differences are few," Parsons said, "and your patriotism is great. Thank you. Now," he said, looking at his watch, "time is short. I must leave." Parsons did not move a muscle.

"The secret of your mission will never leave this room," Austin said. "Thank you, Excellency." He shook Parsons' hand. The Envoy's eyes told of iron resolve and utter loyalty.

Parsons nodded, then shook hands with each in turn until he came to Sergio. He smiled at the Baron and said, "If all worlds were ruled by such steadfast, capable leaders, there would be no cause to worry about The Republic's future." With that, Jerome Parsons hurried from the room.

"We must prepare for any contingency, if Sandoval and Radick aren't to be trusted," Austin said. He turned to Marta and said, "We'll need your refitted 'Mechs placed under the direct authority of the Governor."

"No!" blurted Sergio. "Their modified 'Mechs should be turned back to industrial uses."

"You heard the Envoy. Mirach might become a pawn in a battle between—" Austin started.

"Austin, be sensible," cut in Sergio. "Mirach will remain loyal through strength of will. Who can forge patriotism from steel?"

"What patriot can stand against the steel of a BattleMech?" shot back Austin. "That was Parsons' message to us. The *Atlas* and other 'Mechs are a sword against our enemies."

"His message was that we can triumph over them. The FCL remained loyal and I purposely allowed them to be scattered throughout Tortorelli's units. More companies in the Home Guard surrendered because the FCL undermined their feeble allegiance to Tortorelli. Force of arms had little to do with it."

"Without the refitted 'Mechs, moral suasion would have meant nothing," Austin said. He saw how clever his father had been, though. Tortorelli had accepted the FCL as a gift and had never thought it might remain a weapon for the Governor. Manfred had been given the freedom to work with the modified IndustrialMechs and build a bridge to Marta Kinsolving and the MBA. His father had used the FCL not as soldiers but as spies. Austin acknowledged this, but knew that force had been necessary for Borodin to protect the Palace and its occupant. Austin started to point this out.

Marta and Manfred stood close to one another, listening to the argument that threatened to go on endlessly until Sergio held up his hand.

"We have other pressing matters to discuss." He fixed his colorless eyes on his son. Austin settled down, realizing his father was right. This was a disagreement that could go on for a long, long time.

"There will be some small realignment of authority on Mirach," Sergio said. "Envoy Parsons has agreed in principle with me on this."

"What realignment, Baron?" Marta asked.

"You will not find the changes too onerous, Ms. Kinsolving," said Sergio. "Rest assured, the government will do nothing to compromise the assets of any MBA member or other privately held company. We are most appreciative of the aid you have provided. The loan of your 'Mechs was especially timely."

"Do we retain the 'Mechs?" she asked.

"We need the 'Mechs," Austin said. "We might never use them to defend Mirach, but if what the Envoy said is true about shifting loyalties in the Prefecture, we just might. Our first priority should be to repair the *Centurion*."

Sergio thought for a moment. He looked from Austin to Manfred to Marta, and Austin got the impression he was considering each of their positions.

"Perhaps you are right, Austin, but only about the modified IndustrialMechs. They can be placed in the

FCL, which is returned to my personal control." Austin almost laughed when his father added, "If the FCL is in my control, I can choose whether or not to use the 'Mechs. But," he said, hurrying on, "the *Centurion* goes back into the museum. It's too powerful a weapon, and I don't want us to be tempted to resort to that level of violence."

Austin thought wryly, *I got it out of the museum once; I can do it again if matters ever go that far.* With such a compromise, he'd be content.

Sergio continued. "The real changes will be in governmental sectors. Lady Elora has been removed as Minister."

"That's as much to your advantage as ours, Baron," Marta pointed out. "What are you going to do about her?"

Sergio rocked back in his chair, tented his fingers, and rested his chin on the top. He looked thoughtfully from Manfred to Austin and then to Marta before speaking.

"A public trial would only open old wounds. She is to continue in her position as a reporter for the Ministry of Information."

"You can't do that, Father! She—"

"She can perform her minimal duties from a different location. Say, on Kuton? You have a comfortable repair station on our largest moon, do you not?" he asked Marta.

"It's not comfortable. Hardly. But what could she transmit from there? It's only a relay station."

"Perhaps she is on extended assignment without need to actually transmit her stories," Sergio said, as if thinking aloud. "Let her stay in the airtight shelter some distance from the actual equipment AWC has positioned on the moon."

"Without a pressure suit?" Manfred suggested.

Sergio shrugged. "Rebuilding Cingulum will require a considerable investment. Since we won't be taking Mr. Bannson's grant, not every project can be fully funded."

Austin felt no sense of triumph. Lady Elora would be exiled to Kuton, unable to do anything but wait anxiously for the next supply DropShip and its crew to give her any direct human contact. In his gut he knew she had been responsible for the deaths of Dale and Hanna, but she would never be tried for those crimes. The proof was hidden away too well, but he would continue looking—for his own peace of mind. Exile to Kuton was as severe a punishment as she could receive, especially if it was for life.

Then his father dropped a bombshell.

"As to Legate Tortorelli, he is to continue in his post."

"You can't do that," protested Austin. He saw that Marta was equally outraged but Manfred grinned slyly. "What do you have in mind for him?"

"I suspect Tortorelli would object strenuously to his own removal, since appointment of a Legate is the jealously guarded prerogative of the Prefect. Considering all that Envoy Parsons has told us, it would be unwise to draw unwanted attention to Mirach. Legate Tortorelli will remain at his post, but the past few months have shown what a difficult, demanding job it is for a single man."

"A liaison would help him, wouldn't it, Father?" Austin asked, understanding now. "Do you think Captain Leclerc would be suitable?"

"Captain?" Sergio nodded approval at his son.

"Accepted," spoke up Manfred.

"Do what you can to make poor, overworked Calvilena's work as simple as possible. Keep me informed of all matters relating to recruitment and procurement, Captain Leclerc. And day-to-day oversight of the armed forces. And anything else that might occur. That should lighten the Legate's burden considerably and give him time for his hobbies, whatever they are."

"You'll need new comm equipment, won't you, Captain?" asked Marta. Her smile was as large as Manfred's.

"The two of you can negotiate that matter later," Sergio said.

Marta, Manfred, and Austin's father delved into discussion of other matters ranging from rebuilding Cingulum to the need for Span-net to be finished as quickly as possible. Austin's new position as his father's chief of staff would be a full-time, hectic job. So much to do, not the least of which was the restoration of a certain *Centurion* before its return to a place of honor in the Museum of Modern Mirach.

ROC

MechWarrior: **Dark Age**
A Call To Arms
A BattleTech Novel
by
Loren L. Coleman

MechWarrior-aspirant Raul Ortega finds himself called to battle when warring factions—who have seceded from the Republic—wage war on his home world to obtain one of the few working interstellar communication nets.

0-451-45912-1

To order call: 1-800-788-6262

R342/Coleman

▨ *Don't miss out on any of the deep-space adventure*
of the Bestselling **BATTLETECH**® *Series.*

To order call: 1-800-788-6262